THE SAVAGE NIGHT

THE VAMPIRE WORLD BOOK 2

PT HYLTON
JONATHAN BENECKE

JOIN THE NEW HAVEN CREW

To be the first to find out about PT and Jonathan's new releases and get updates on future Vampire World Saga books, visit:

http://www.pthylton.com/newhaven/

WHAT CAME BEFORE

ALEX GODDARD is a member of the Ground Mission Team, an elite task force that supplies the ship *New Haven* with resources recovered from the vampire-infested Earth's surface. *New Haven* believes it is the last human city, and they've remained alive for one hundred fifty years by staying in the sky, circumnavigating the Earth to remain in sunlight.

But some aboard *New Haven* believe it's time for a change. They are convinced that humans should resettle the surface. They are led by DANIEL FLEMING, a charismatic young city councilman from the wrong part of town. He and his followers force a public vote on the matter of Resettlement. When Resettlement passes, the City Council steps in, voiding the results of the vote. They believe Resettlement is too dangerous, even if it is the will of the people.

Meanwhile, a malfunction in the control unit of *New Haven*'s nuclear reactor sends Alex and the GMT scrambling on a search for parts. After a few failed missions, including one that cost them the life of recon expert Simmons, the team learns the parts they need are in NORAD, an ancient facility in the Rocky Mountains.

Alex and her crew race down to NORAD, leaving their injured field commander Captain Brickman behind, but their ship is shot down near their destination. Continuing on foot, they desperately race to reach the facility before sundown. While they're ultimately successful, Drew is killed by vampires hiding in the snow and Wesley is badly injured.

Meanwhile, on *New Haven*, Fleming makes his move. He blows up the City Council chambers, leaving himself as the sole remaining member of the Council. He then takes control of the city, arresting General Craig, the leader of the GMT and the police force. He also arrests Captain Brickman, but offers him a deal: he will allow CB to rescue Alex and the GMT if the captain agrees to help with the Resettlement efforts. CB has no choice but to take the offer.

In the Rocky Mountains, Alex and the GMT are shocked to find NORAD occupied. There's a whole city in the mountain, a place the residents call Agartha. They have the parts the GMT needs to repair *New Haven*, and Jaden, Agartha's apparent leader, gladly offers to let Alex take the parts with no strings attached.

Jaden then reveals the truth about Agartha. There are one hundred vampires among its population. And he's one of them.

HOPE BRIAR HURRIED through the door of the Ground Mission Team headquarters, cursing with each step. She'd waited five years for this meeting, and now she was going to be late.

In her defense, she hadn't expected Captain Brickman to call her in the middle of the night while she was working a double in Sparrow's Ridge. Now, here she was, still in her badge's uniform, headed to her first meeting with the GMT.

Her footsteps echoed loudly as she hurried across the hangar to the briefing room. When she reached it, she was unsurprised to see all three of her fellow GMT recruits already seated and waiting.

They were badges, just like her. And while they currently spent their days enforcing the law in the last human city, they all dreamed of getting the call to join the GMT.

Was it possible the time had finally come? And if it had, what did that mean for the current GMT? Where were Alex, Drew, Wesley, Owl, and Firefly?

Hope found a seat and sank into it, nodding a greeting to

the other three. There were usually five backup GMT members at any given time, but Wesley had recently been called up to replace Simmons. That left the four of them.

The Barton brothers, Ed and Patrick, had been Sparrows Ridge legends since childhood for their eagerness to pick fights with anyone at any time. Then there was Chuck Williams, a thoughtful badge, who worked in the Hub.

"Okay, I've had it with this oppressive silence," Patrick Barton said. "Who's got a guess as to why they called us down here in the middle of the damn night?"

"There's no need to guess," Hope pointed out. "Calling all four of us at once? Something happened to the team."

Patrick and Ed nodded, as if that confirmed their suspicions, but Chuck shifted uncomfortably in his seat at Hope's words.

It had been a crazy few days in *New Haven*. First there had been the vote for Resettlement, a vote that had passed, only to be vetoed by the City Council. Then, there had been the freak explosion that had killed every member of the Council except Fleming, the one Council member who happened to be pro-Resettlement.

It didn't take a genius to figure out that the explosion hadn't been an accident.

"So, what happened to the team?" Ed asked. "I'll bet they made a move against Fleming. They're probably sitting in jail down at the Hub right now."

Patrick shook his head. "No way. You think the soft desk jockeys they have stationed at the Hub could take down the GMT? Not a chance." He glanced at Chuck. "No offense."

"None taken," Chuck answered. "And you're right. If the GMT made a move against Fleming, we'd be talking about civil war."

Hope grimaced. Not that long ago, the GMT had been

above politics. It didn't matter who you supported for City Council or what your political leanings were. The GMT was about gathering the resources people needed to survive, end of story.

That had all changed when Fleming took control of *New Haven*. There was no such thing as politically neutral anymore. Add to that the fact that Fleming's central issue was resettling the Earth, and that put the GMT in the dead center of the political discussion.

"My guess is they're just trying to get everyone in line with the new chain of command," Patrick said. "Things are changing fast, and they have to make sure we're on board."

Ed raised an eyebrow. "In the middle of the night?"

Chuck rubbed his chin thoughtfully. "When Captain Brickman radioed me, he asked if I was comfortable flying the backup ship. On the way in, I noticed the main GMT ship isn't in the hangar."

That comment sobered the group, and they waited in silence for another two minutes until the briefing room door swung open. Captain Brickman and another man marched through the door. It took Hope a moment to identify the second man as Brian McElroy, the head of research and development for the GMT.

The recruits leapt to their feet and stood at attention. Brian shut the door behind him as CB moved to the front of the room.

CB motioned for them to sit. "Take it easy. We have a lot to discuss."

A twinge of worry tingled the base of Hope's spine at the sight of these two clearly weary men. Brian looked pretty rough, but CB looked twice as bad. His usually crisp uniform was a wrinkled mess, and he had heavy bags under his eyes. His right arm was in a cast. CB usually maintained the image of military excellence and discipline, but that day, he was falling far short of the ideal.

When he spoke, Hope heard the edge in his voice.

"All right, let's get to it. In seven hours, the four of you will be deployed on your first mission as members of the Ground Mission Team."

He let that hang in the air a moment before continuing.

The energy in the room changed at CB's words. Before, the recruits had suspected they were about to join the team, but now they *knew*. A strange combination of fear, excitement, and trepidation hung in the air.

CB continued, "And it's going to be one hell of a first mission." He tapped the screen in front of him, and the wall behind him came to life, displaying an aerial photograph. "This is an area formerly known as El Paso County, Colorado, in the United States. It was the home of NORAD, a military mountain facility our team believed could have the nuclear reactor components necessary to repair *New Haven* and keep her in the sky. The GMT was deployed to retrieve these parts yesterday morning. Their ship was shot down as they were landing."

The recruits glanced at each other as they realized the implication of these words.

Hope raised a tentative hand. "Shot down, sir? By whom?"

CB met her gaze. "I'll be honest with you. We don't know. We also don't know their current status. We believe..." CB paused, then corrected himself. "We think there's a chance the team could have made it to the NORAD facility, and it's possible they survived the night. Your mission will be to locate the downed ship and track the team from the crash site. We're going to find them and bring them home."

He gestured to Brian. "This is Brian McElroy. If you don't

know him, you're going to want to rectify that situation. He and his team create the gear that keeps us alive down there. He'll be outfitting all of you prior to departure. Questions?"

After a long moment, Chuck raised a hand. "Sir, I don't know a polite way to ask this, so I'm just going to spit it out. With the City Council gone and General Craig locked up, who does the team report to? Above you, I mean."

CB's answer was almost a growl. "Councilman Fleming is currently heading up all government functions. That means he's our commander of operations." He turned away from Chuck and looked at the rest of the group, clearly wanting to move on from the question. "What else?"

"Chances of hostile encounters down there?" Hope asked.

"It'll be daylight. That said, a vampire broke my arm in the middle of the day. I've seen plenty worse than that happen too. We'll have to be ready for anything." He scanned their faces before continuing. "Look, I can tell you're a little freaked out, and I don't blame you. Things on *New Haven* haven't exactly been normal lately. Now we're asking you to go save a team shot down by an unknown enemy." He paused a moment. "I can't promise you things will go smoothly down there, but I can tell you this. You are the right people for this mission. Otherwise, you wouldn't be here. You've never been to the surface before, but you've trained your asses off to get this far. If you're committed to the GMT, I promise I will be committed to you, too. The Ground Mission Team has been through this before. I lost a team, the whole damn lot of them. We rebuilt from scratch and built that group into the best fighting unit *New Haven* had ever seen."

He motioned to the aerial map.

"I believe our GMT brothers and sisters are alive down

there. But even if they're not, the GMT is alive and well in this room. Now, gear up. We leave in seven hours."

———

"HAVEN'T you figured it out yet?" Jaden asked. "We're vampires. The defenders of Agartha are the last one hundred true vampires, and we're going to save humanity."

For a long moment, Alex couldn't move. She could barely think, aware only of Jaden's words echoing around in her skull like a bullet.

Two words in particular: *We're vampires*.

With each reverberation of the statement, another image flashed in her mind. Ancient humans, running in fear as vampires—vampires like Jaden!—hunted them down and slaughtered them. The people of *New Haven*, confined to a prison in the sky because of the bloodthirsty bastards. Drew, being dragged up a wall of ice, and the gut-wrenching *crack* as a vampire snapped his neck.

And Simmons. This last memory came back so strong, it was almost like she was experiencing that horrific moment again. The man she loved trying to fly up to her, then vampires swarming all over him, dragging him down into the darkness.

"I can see you need a moment," Jaden said, a bemused smile on his face.

The control room they were standing in seemed different suddenly. Everything around her took on a new and ominous aura. The monitors showed areas around the city. Why? So that the vampires could watch them? And what about the man sitting in front of the monitors? What about all the humans in the city? Where they just livestock? Sacks of blood waiting for the vampires to feed on them?

Owl must have sensed the tension rising in Alex, because she looked pointedly at her and gave her head the slightest of shakes.

"Listen to your friend," Jaden said. "Look, I get it. You've been training for years to kill vampires."

"Yes," Alex said. Her voice sounded distant in her own ears.

"And how's that going for you?" He took a step forward. "Maybe it's time you consider—"

Alex's pistol was in her hand before she even realized she'd drawn it. "That's close enough."

"Alex, don't," Owl said.

"It's okay," Jaden said, his smile even wider than before. "This is...interesting."

"Interesting?" Alex asked, not hiding the annoyance in her voice. "Is that what you call it?"

"Yes. I sometimes forget that humans have such a limited capacity to deal with the unexpected."

Alex wasn't sure what to make of that. Something about the way this vampire talked made her feel like she was a child being addressed by an elderly relative. It wasn't condescending, exactly. More like he found her entertaining.

Owl's gaze flickered past Alex, and Alex realized someone must have entered the control room through the door behind her.

Then something *slammed* into her, and she was knocked to the ground. She lay sprawled on the floor for only a moment.

In an instant, she was back on her feet, spinning toward her attacker. It was one of the other vampires she'd seen with Jaden at the doors of the city.

She raised her pistol, but the vampire was already in motion. He moved so fast, her eyes had trouble tracking him. One moment he was standing across the room from her, and the next he stood directly in front of her. The gun twisted in her hand, and suddenly he was holding it.

She blinked hard, trying to process what had just happened. Struggling to control her temper, she considered the situation. She and Owl were trapped in a room with two vampires, one of whom had just attacked her.

She didn't know if she could take out these vampires, but she was definitely losing the fight with her temper.

"It's okay, Robert," Jaden said with a chuckle. "We were just talking."

The other vampire frowned. "She was pointing a gun at you. I wasn't about to let her shoot you. You get cranky when you get shot, and none of us want to deal with that tonight."

The conversation was the only opening Alex needed. Taking half a step forward, she drove her knee into Robert's groin. As he doubled over in pain, she stepped back, giving herself enough space to draw her sword.

This was over, Alex knew. A millisecond from now there would be one less vampire in the world.

She swung her sword, bringing it down on Robert's neck. Only, instead of the steel sinking into flesh, it *whooshed* through empty air. Before she processed the fact that she had somehow missed a target two feet in front of her, something powerful slammed into the blade near the hilt, and her sword went clattering to the floor.

Robert grabbed her wrist with a firm hand and snarled.

"Alex, calm down," Jaden said. "You're not in any danger here."

She struggled to control her breathing. If she was going to have any chance of taking Robert down, she needed to adjust her strategy.

"Not that this isn't entertaining," Jaden said, "but you have to realize you can't win a fight against a vampire."

"I can't?" Alex asked. "I've left a pretty big pile of vampire corpses that would disagree with you."

"That may be, but those were not—"

Alex spun, twisting and pulling away from Robert until he was left holding her coat. She almost smiled. He'd fallen for the same trick twice. Robert might have been fast as all hell, but if she got Jaden talking, she could catch him off guard. She knew this nugget of information was important. Against enemies like these, any advantage was a precious commodity.

Jaden crossed his arms and leaned against the wall, clearly enjoying this.

Owl drew her weapon and held it in a two-handed grip, as if not sure where to point it.

Robert paused for just a moment, looking at Alex dumbly with the jacket in hand. Then he reached out and grabbed her by the wrist once again. This time, his eyes widened as his hand began to smoke, and he drew in a quick breath before pulling it way.

Jaden stared in surprise at her silver chain mail suit. Clearly, he hadn't been expecting that. "Fascinating."

She lunged at Robert, throwing a flurry of punches, aiming for his face. The punches wouldn't be enough to take him down, she knew, but maybe she could keep him off balance long enough to get her sword back.

Each blow met only air. The vampire moved so quickly, she barely knew where to aim her jabs. Still, she kept attacking. As long as he was on defense, he couldn't be on offense. If she just kept going at him maybe she could—

"Enough," Robert said firmly.

Alex didn't see the punch, but she certainly felt its

impact. His fist slammed into her stomach, and the air rushed out of her. She fell to her knees, gasping for breath.

She watched through watery eyes as Jaden turned to Owl. "Would you please lower your weapon?" He nodded toward the man at the control desk, who was watching all this with wide eyes. "Anthony is very much human, and a bullet will kill him. If your friend wants to throw a temper tantrum, fine, but if you shoot Anthony, I may get cranky."

Temper tantrum? That made Alex even angrier than before.

She struggled to her feet, regaining her breath a little more with each gasp.

Owl wavered, looking back and forth between Robert, Jaden, and Alex. After a moment, she lowered her weapon.

"Thank you, Owl," Jaden said. "Nice to see cooler heads can prevail. Now that we're through with that nonsense, we can talk like civilized people."

Owl sighed. "You clearly don't know Alex very well."

Alex lashed out with her leg, knocking Robert's feet from under him.

He barely touched the ground before he popped back up. Grabbing her by the throat, he lifted her two feet off the ground. A few tendrils of smoke drifted from where the bottom of his hand touched the chain mail, but he ignored it.

Alex beat at his arms and hands, squirming to get out of his grip, but to no avail.

Robert's eyes glowed red as he glared up at Alex.

Jaden turned to Owl. "She's not going to stop, is she?"

"Alex, calm down. I don't think he is our enemy!" Owl yelled.

Alex didn't pay any attention to Owl's advice. Instead,

she pressed the chain mail covering her arms against Robert's hand, causing it to smoke even more.

Jaden shook his head sadly. "All right, then. Sorry about this in advance, Alex. Robert, put her out."

With the flick of a wrist, Robert sent her flying across the room. She slammed against the wall, sank to the floor, and the world went dark.

2

AFTER THE BRIEFING with the GMT recruits, Brian followed CB to the hangar. Neither man spoke as they walked, both wanting to make sure they were out of earshot of the recruits before they had their conversation.

When they reached the hangar, CB led him aboard the backup ship. It was of a similar design to the away ship the GMT usually used, but not as well maintained. For years, this ship had gotten the second-best parts and the second-most attention. It also hadn't had Owl obsessing over every inch of it the way, like the main away ship had.

"You know what Owl's going to say when she sees us pull up in this pathetic thing?" CB had his hands on his hips, and he cast a disdainful eye at the cargo hold as they stepped aboard. "She's going to laugh her ass off. And that's before she sees a team of green recruits pile off and start mucking around in the snow."

Most of the gear for the mission had already been loaded aboard by Brian's team, and once the crew received their personal gear, there would be nothing left to do but wait for the ship to be in the correct position for the flight to the surface.

Brian felt a twinge of envy as he thought of the recruits heading down to search for the team. Not that he had any desire to set foot on the surface. He'd lived his entire life in the sky, and he had no intention of changing that now. Nor did he have any desire to fight the vampires who lived there. Whatever it was inside the members of the GMT that caused them to get excited at the thought of deadly combat and life-threatening adventures, Brian didn't have it. He preferred the intellectual thrill of a clean, new design and the knowledge that his work was saving lives.

He sighed as he looked around the ship. "It may not be as sleek as the main ship, but it'll get them to their destination and back. I have no doubt about that."

CB just nodded absently. It was clear that his mind was on other things.

Brian waited a moment, and then he asked the question he'd been waiting to ask since they walked out the briefing room door. "Captain, what's the real plan?"

CB turned and looked at him, a confused expression on his face. "What do you mean?"

For a moment, Brian wasn't sure how to respond. "The plan. I heard what you told the recruits, but what are we actually going to do, here?"

"I still don't understand. The plan is the plan. The recruits are going dirtside to bring our team home."

"Okay, yeah, I get that. But what are we going to do about Fleming?"

CB just looked away.

Brian didn't know the details of CB's conversation with Fleming, or why exactly they'd been released from their jail cell in the Hub. All he knew was that CB had been taken away by some guards to have a discussion with Fleming, and thirty minutes later Brian had been released from his cell. He hadn't asked CB for the details. He hadn't needed to, because he trusted the captain. He trusted that whatever trick he'd pulled to get them out of there had been rooted in the knowledge that they would move against Fleming

But for the first time, it occurred to Brian that that might not be the case. A sickening realization came to him, and shocked anger quickly followed. "CB, tell me you didn't make a deal with Fleming."

"I did what I had to do," the captain replied, his voice void of emotion. "My only objective was giving us a shot at saving our team. We'll figure out everything else later."

Brian couldn't believe what he was hearing. "Fleming blew up the Council. He's got General Craig locked up in the Hub! We have the best weapons in *New Haven* and a team of recruits trained to use them. They might be green, but they'd follow you into hell. You know they would. So, what are you thinking?"

CB took a step toward Brian, and his voice was almost a snarl when he answered. "You want to know what I'm thinking? I'm thinking, Alex. I'm thinking, Drew. And Owl. And Wesley. And Jessica. I'm thinking about the nuclear reactor down there, and the parts that can keep this ship afloat. I'm thinking about my team—my friends—down on the surface, in the darkness. Best-case scenario, they're huddled inside NORAD, desperately hoping they'll make it through until morning. That's what I'm thinking about, McElroy. The rest of the world can go straight to hell."

Brian drew a deep breath before continuing. "Look, I'm not saying we don't go after the team. I'm just saying—"

"I know perfectly well what you're saying. You've got a fantasy of us storming the Hub, guns blazing, and throwing

Fleming into a cell. Reclaiming *New Haven* for the good guys. Only it wouldn't go like that. We take up arms against the Hub, we better be strapped in for a long fight. How many badges will side with us? How many with them? How long before the civilians start taking sides and picking up weapons?"

"I don't have all the answers."

"You damn well better. If you're going to start a civil war on this ship, you better have counted the cost." CB turned away and stared into the depths of the ship for a long moment before continuing. "Look, I get it. I'm just as pissed off about what that bastard did as you are. But our first priority has to be getting our team back. That's our responsibility. You know damn well that if you and I were trapped on the surface, Alex would be doing anything she possibly could to get down there to search for us."

Brian had to admit the captain had a point there.

CB continued, "Besides, look at the practical side of it. If we want to have any chance of taking back this ship, we need our best people. And right now, our best people are down there, waiting for us to come grab them. That's our first priority. We'll figure out everything else when we get back."

Brian nodded slowly. What CB was saying made sense. He didn't like it, but he couldn't argue with the logic.

"So, are you onboard?" CB asked. "I need your head in this thing one hundred percent. We're running a dangerous mission to the surface with a bunch of recruits who've never set foot off *New Haven*. It's going to be tough enough without having to worry about whether you're second-guessing me. Can I count on you?"

Brian paused for only a moment before he answered, "You can count on me, Captain."

He didn't like the fact that CB seemed to be ignoring the harsh realities of the GMT's situation, and he definitely didn't like that they were taking orders from the man who'd killed the rest of the City Council. But he'd go along with it. He'd trust CB. For now.

———

THE FIRST THING Alex saw when she opened her eyes was Wesley. He was lying on a bed across the room from her, and he was out cold.

For a long moment, she had absolutely no idea where she was. Everything looked unfamiliar. She had the sudden, nonsensical idea that she'd made a terrible mistake and slept with Wesley. But then, why was he in another bed?

It all came rushing back in an instant. The crash. The vampires in the snow. The hidden city in the mountain. Jaden...

She sat up with a start. Jaden! The city of vampires.

A hand touched her shoulder, and she almost lashed out. A familiar voice spoke before she could.

"Relax, Alex. You're safe."

It was Owl. Alex turned and saw the rest of her team gathered around her. Not just Owl, but also Firefly and Jessica.

As her head began to clear, she turned back to Owl. "I'm safe, huh? That's exactly what Jaden said, before his buddy threw me against the wall."

"You think you had it bad?" Firefly asked with a grin. "I'm going to have to live with the knowledge that I missed watching you get your ass kicked. Anyone ever tell you that you suck at making new friends?"

"It's been brought up." She put a hand to the back of her throbbing head.

"You got a nasty lump," Owl explained, "but no permanent damage. Luckily, it was just your brain, and you weren't using that anyway."

Alex flopped back onto her pillow, and the room seemed to spin. She squeezed her eyes shut until it passed. "So, you guys are good with being trapped in a city with a hundred vampires?"

"Not good at all," Firefly said. "But what's the alternative? Besides, if they wanted us dead, they could have just left us outside in the snow. Or they could have killed us in that hallway the moment we walked in. Instead, they patched up our boy." He nodded toward Wesley. "They saved his leg, not to mention his life."

"I'm not ready to trust them just yet." Alex sat up and swung her feet over the side of the bed. "I am done lying here, though."

"Good," Jessica said with a smile. "I have someone you need to meet."

Jessica led them out of the hospital and to Engineering. They crossed paths with a few citizens of Agartha on their walk. Most of them nodded a friendly greeting as they passed, but none exchanged any words with the *New Haven* team. If they knew these people were strangers to Agartha, they gave no indication.

They walked through a set of double doors and into a large, open room with a dozen or so people bustling around. A balding man in his fifties gave Jessica a friendly wave when he saw them and hurried over.

"This is George," Jessica told Alex. "He's the head of Engineering. Speaking of which, how are we coming, George?"

"Ahead of schedule for once," he answered. "The console is just about packed up and ready."

Alex raised an eyebrow and looked at Jessica. "We got the parts we need?"

"Without a doubt." Jessica was practically beaming with pride. "George, fill Alex in on what you were telling me about life in Agartha."

George's head bobbed up and down. "Of course. Where to begin? I've lived here all my life, so it's difficult to know what's unique about this place. But based on what I've read, it does have some advantages over most societies of the past."

"Like the vampires?" Alex asked dryly.

George nodded. If the comment offended him, he didn't show it. "People in Agartha are free to pursue life basically as they see fit, as long as they don't hurt others and they contribute to society in some way. Humans and vampires work side by side to keep things running smoothly."

"What if you want to leave?" Alex asked.

George thought a moment. "I suppose you could. Though it might not be a good idea, with all the Ferals out there."

"'Ferals' is what they call the less friendly vampires outside the city," Jessica explained.

Alex nodded, still trying to wrap her head around a society that distinguished between good and bad vampires.

George continued. "We're pretty self-sufficient, but when we need supplies, the vampires go out and get them. The Ferals leave them alone, for the most part. No human blood. I guess they smell different than we do."

"Of course," Alex said, as if it were the most natural thing in the world.

"What else? We have schools for the young ones, and

every family has their own bunk unit. Space is tight here, but we make do."

As he continued talking, Alex noticed a woman who couldn't have been more than five feet tall and maybe ninety pounds walk up to a massive crate, lift it up like it was nothing, and approach them.

"Where do you want this, George?" the woman asked.

He gestured toward the other end of the room. "Oh, on one of the Jeeps, if you don't mind." As the woman walked away, George laughed and shook his head. "I hear you don't have vampires where you come from. How do you survive without them? How do you get supplies?"

Owl started to answer, but Alex cut her off.

"We make do." She wasn't ready to start revealing the details of *New Haven* to these strangers. There wasn't a protocol for this kind of thing, but she knew she needed to be careful.

Yesterday she'd thought *New Haven* was the last human city. Now she knew not only that there was another city, but that they had vampires fighting on their side. If some conflict did arise, the only advantage *New Haven* would have was that their location would be a mystery. She didn't know if Agartha had any planes, but she wasn't about to risk it.

"Ah, glad to see you're up and about!" Jaden walked toward them, his gaze fixed on Alex, an easy smile on his face. "Ready for round two?" He held up his fists and screwed up his face in the goofy imitation of a snarl.

Alex felt herself blush. She'd hoped to have a little more time to compose herself before having to talk to this vampire again. "Jaden, I need to apologize. To you and Robert, both. You invited us into your city, and I shouldn't—"

He waved the thought away. "Don't worry about it.

Honestly, that was the most fun I've had in months. Things have gotten stale around here."

"For the record, I'm not usually like that. It's been a tough week."

He turned to Jessica and George. "So, did we get the parts squared away?"

"That, we did," George said.

"Good. Now we can attempt to contact your people and have them come pick you up."

Alex hesitated before answering. "Look, we really appreciate all you've done for us, but I think it would be best for all of us if we rendezvoused with our team somewhere away from Agartha."

The smile slipped from Jaden's face, and he nodded slowly. "That's understandable. We'll do whatever makes you comfortable. I guess trust has to be earned." He paused for a moment. "Speaking of which, Alex, could I talk to you alone for a moment?"

Concern leapt into Firefly's eyes, but Alex gave him a reassuring look.

"Of course," she said to Jaden.

The vampire led her away from the group and into a long, empty hallway. He stopped and turned toward her.

"Alex, I thought it was time we had a conversation. We need to talk about *New Haven*."

For a moment, she couldn't breathe. "How do you even know that name?"

Jaden chuckled softly. "Oh, Alex. I know about *New Haven* because I helped build it."

3

"You helped build *New Haven*?" Alex asked, the skepticism clear in her voice. "Was this before or after you became a vampire?"

He drew a deep breath. "Look, you have to understand, things were crazy then."

"That's not an answer."

"No," he said with a smile. "It's not. Like I said earlier, trust has to be earned."

She stifled a laugh. "Fair enough. When you say you helped build it, are you saying you were one of the guys holding a wrench or a blowtorch or whatever, actually putting the thing together?"

"In a manner of speaking."

"Okay, now I know you're screwing with me."

"I got involved fairly late," he explained. "It was already clear humanity was on the way out. We'd been ravaged by the first two waves of the infestation, and we had two desperate plans left, both of them crazy. Build a city in a mountain or build a city in the clouds. The teams were kept separate for fear of both becoming compromised. I was one of the few who knew about both."

"So, you were a bigwig then?"

Jaden shrugged. "My point is I'm glad to see *New Haven* is still flying. There were plenty of people who said it couldn't be done, just like there were plenty of people who said we couldn't turn this small NORAD facility into a functioning city. We proved them wrong on both counts."

Alex thought for a moment. "Do the people here know about *New Haven*?"

"Just the vampires. And I think it's best if we keep it that way, for now." He stifled a yawn. "I'll have George take your team to the communication room. It's fairly limited, but once *New Haven* flies within a few hundred miles of here, they should be able to pick up your signal. In the meantime, it's nearly morning. That means it's bedtime for me and mine."

Alex chuckled. "What, you can't stay up past your bedtime? You're underground. No sunlight."

"It's not that I *can't* stay up. More like, it would be a terrible idea. Vampires feel sick during the day, even if there's no sunlight. It's painful, and our minds don't work as well. Best to just sleep through it."

Alex nodded, filing that information away. Of course, she knew that vampires were weaker and slower during the day. At least, she knew that was the case with the types of vampires Jaden and his friends called "Ferals." But it was fascinating to hear it from the perspective of a vampire. To know how it actually felt.

As strong as vampires were, it was good to know humans would always have one advantage over them: humans could sleep whenever they damn well pleased.

"There's a spot in a valley about five miles from here

that would work as a rendezvous point," Jaden continued. "We'll help you and your team out there. Then we can pull back before your friends arrive, if it makes you more comfortable. Like I said, I'm just happy to help *New Haven* keep flying."

He turned and started to walk away, but Alex called to him.

"Jaden." She waited until he turned back to continue. "Thank you. For everything."

He nodded, then walked away.

Twenty minutes later, Alex was in the communication room with Jessica, Owl, and Firefly. George had given them a quick demo of how to use the equipment before he left them alone, and they'd been attempting to contact *New Haven* ever since.

"You don't think this is one of those things where they say we can use their equipment, but it doesn't actually work, do you?" Firefly asked. "Call me crazy, but I'm not ready to trust a bunch of vampires just yet."

"Not likely," Owl replied. "They said this comm only has a range of a couple hundred miles. *New Haven* won't be overhead for another hour or so. Assuming they are even passing close to this longitude."

"They will," Alex said. "No way would CB let them give up on us this quickly. Keep trying to signal them."

Owl kept speaking into the comm unit, and she was getting the same lack of results for her effort.

During one of the lulls between Owl's attempts, Jessica spoke up. "Guys, we need to talk about what this place means for the future of *New Haven*."

Firefly frowned. "What? That we're not the last human city?"

"That's only part of it," Jessica said. "The technology

here is incredible. There's so much we can learn if we work with them."

"You really think the Council's going to agree to work with vampires?" Firefly asked. He paused for a moment. "The new Council, I mean. Assuming one gets set up soon."

"Maybe not at first. But they did save Wesley's leg. And they gave us the parts we need to save *New Haven*."

"Let's worry about getting home," Alex said. "We can figure out what to tell the Council after we've ensured *New Haven* can keep flying."

———

CB PACED the length of the ship, casting a critical eye on everything from the equipment in the hold to the controls in the cockpit. Not that he was going to find anything new. He'd already walked the entire ship three times. While it wasn't the beautifully maintained, immaculately clean ship the old one had been, he couldn't find much to complain about. At least, not much that could be fixed in the hour before they were scheduled to depart for the surface.

When he reached the cargo hold for the fourth time, he stopped and forced himself to take a deep breath. He hated this part. The waiting. The moments when his mind ran through all the ways that the mission could play out over and over again, each iteration slightly different from the last.

He always disliked this part, but today was worse than usual. Because he knew that going on this mission was a very bad idea, and if he stopped moving too long, or let himself really contemplate what they were about to do, he just might talk himself out of it.

He couldn't let that happen. Granted, the odds that any of his team members had survived a night on the surface were very long indeed, but he had to know for sure. If there was even a sliver of possibility, he had to work on the assumption that they were alive.

The fact that he'd managed to get this mission approved at all practically qualified as a miracle. If it hadn't been for Fleming's desperation to get CB on his side, and for the leadership void left when the general was locked up, there was no way they'd be heading to the surface.

Hell, if CB thought about it too hard, he'd start to have doubts himself.

So, he kept pacing.

The newly minted members of the GMT began to arrive twenty minutes before departure. A few of them made jokes, but it was clear that every one of them was terrified.

A heavy ball of worry formed in CB's stomach as he considered what it would be like to encounter vampires with these green recruits at his side. He was still sporting the cast that had been his souvenir from Wesley's first mission. He knew from experience that a single newbie could throw things into chaos. A whole team of them could do a hell of a lot worse.

As he'd told the team, he'd done this before, back when he was the sole survivor of the attack on his first team. The difference was they'd been able to build up slowly, taking short, safe missions to the surface, with little chance of vampire encounters.

This new team would not have that luxury.

After exchanging a few words with each of the team members, making sure they were ready for this thing and weren't freaking out too much, he checked his watch and was surprised to see how much time had passed.

He touched the radio on his chest and spoke into his headset mic, addressing both his team and the crew outside the ship. "All right, people, it's time." He paused, wishing there was something more eloquent to say, but he shrugged and made his way through the passenger hold.

The familiar whir of the engines starting sent vibrations through the ship and up into CB's feet. The team was dead silent, every one of them staring into the void. Tension hung thick in the air, and CB could have sworn it was a few degrees hotter in that hold than in other parts of the ship.

He didn't say anything more to them. He'd already given his pep talk. Now was the time for them to get their heads right. They'd either cut it or they wouldn't. Nothing he said would make a difference now. He made his way to the cockpit for takeoff.

Chuck sat hunched over the controls, staring intently at the opening hangar door.

CB sank into the copilot's chair. "How many times you been off *New Haven*?"

Chuck kept his eyes focused on the door. He leaned on the controls and the ship rolled smoothly forward toward the blue sky beyond the hangar. "I don't know. A few dozen times. I had to log a hundred hours to get certified to fly, and I have to do ten a year to recertify. Never more than fifty miles from the city, though. And never anywhere near the surface."

CB chuckled and slapped him on the arm. "Time to expand your horizons, son. Take us out."

As they shot through the hangar door and into the void beyond it, CB flipped a switch on his radio, setting it to transmit to the team. Unlike Chuck, the rest of this crew had never been off *New Haven*. "Welcome to the wider world. You're part of an elite fraternity now. It won't be long now before you have real Earth dirt stuck to the bottom of your boots."

The team didn't respond, but that was all right; CB hadn't expected them to.

He spent the next twenty minutes studying the terrain map of the area where his team's ship had disappeared.

Chuck shifted in his seat. He'd been gripping the controls hard ever since they left *New Haven*. "So, Captain... the other ship was shot down, right?"

CB grunted in the affirmative.

He cleared his throat softly. "And, um, are we concerned about those guns?"

"Very," CB said. "They must have been automated. An old defensive system meant to protect the NORAD facility, maybe." He set down his map and turned toward Chuck. "Look, the team was caught off guard. That won't happen to us. We're going to approach with extreme caution. We'll start circling the area so high, they'd need to fire a missile to—"

The radio crackled, and a distant, unintelligible voice spoke. Then it was gone.

Chuck glanced at CB, beads of sweat standing on his forehead. "Is that *New Haven*?"

CB didn't answer, but he knew it wasn't. *New Haven* wouldn't have any trouble reaching the ship. This was a weaker signal. And that voice... He hadn't been able to make out much, but it had almost sounded like—

"*New Haven*, do you copy?" The voice was clearer this time, and there was no mistaking the speaker.

Alex.

The blood drained from CB's face as he snatched the radio from its cradle and held it close to his lips. "Goddard? Is it really you?"

A long silence answered him, and for a terrible moment, he thought the signal had faded.

Then the radio crackled again. "Holy hell, CB, it's good to hear your voice."

CB couldn't have wiped the grin off his face even if he'd wanted to. "Are you safe?"

"Safe enough. I'll explain when we see each other. Think you can give a girl a ride home?"

"Goddard, don't you know me better than that? I'm already on my way."

———

ALEX SHIELDED her eyes with a hand as the ship appeared in the sky and sped toward their location. It was a bright, sunny morning, but she was still ready for anything. She knew from painful experience that vampires could be hiding under the snowbanks. Granted, they couldn't come out in the sunlight, but that didn't mean they couldn't reach out and pull her in.

Wesley lay on a cot next to Alex. He was awake but groggy. The doctors of Agartha had given him the best treatment possible, but it would be at least a week before he was walking again.

Owl had her eyes fixed on the ship as she leaned against the stack of parts the vampires of Agartha had helped them bring to this location. "The backup ship. I hate the backup ship."

"It's the only one we've got now," Alex pointed out.

The ship settled gently down into the snow and the cargo door almost immediately groaned open.

Alex took a step toward it, but a hand on her arm stopped her.

"Hey," Firefly said. "Before we go back, I just wanted to say thanks. For everything. You're a great leader, and... Well, just remember I appreciate all you've done for me and the team."

Alex stared at him a moment, caught off guard by the comment. Before she could respond, CB stepped off the ship.

She waited twenty feet away, conflicting emotions swirling inside her. She was delighted to see CB and anxious to get the parts back to *New Haven*, but that also meant she'd have to tell him she'd lost Drew. Saying the words out loud would cement it as reality, and not just part of this bizarre fever dream of a trip to the surface.

CB marched toward her at a fast clip, his face screwed up with emotion. For an awkward moment, she thought he was going to hug her, and she kind of wanted to hug him back. But he was her commanding officer, so he just grabbed her by the shoulder.

"Goddard, thank God you're alive." He looked at the others. "Thank God you all are alive." He paused. "Wesley, are you...?"

"I'm ready for my next mission," he said with a weak smile.

"Glad to hear it. Wait. Where's Drew?"

Alex hesitated. "I'm sorry, CB. The vampires got him."

CB's eyes snapped shut as he mouthed a curse.

Alex continued. "We've got a lot to tell you, Captain."

CB nodded grimly. "Same here. But let's get those parts on the ship first. It's time to go home."

4

THEY'D ONLY BEEN BACK an hour when Alex got the call that Fleming wanted to see her.

Learning what had happened in *New Haven*—that the Council had been murdered and Fleming had seized power —had been a terrible shock. She'd only been gone a day, but somehow the whole city had changed during that time. And CB had promised to help Fleming with Resettlement in exchange for the opportunity to save her and the rest of the team.

After everything that had happened in the last twenty-four hours, this final blow felt like too much to bear. Not only was reality on Earth different than what she'd always assumed, but life on *New Haven* had changed too.

Brian walked with her to the Hub. CB was already with Fleming, briefing him on the Agartha situation and the status of the ship repairs.

As they walked, Brian caught her up on what she'd missed. "Fleming made an announcement to the whole city this morning. He told them an accident had killed the Council."

"Convenient accident for him," Alex muttered.

Brian nodded. "Based on the limited number of people I've talked to since the speech, many are actually buying it."

"You're kidding me," she growled. "He's already rewriting history."

"I have to admit, it was a good speech. Trying times ahead. We must pull together. He's taking control until elections can be arranged. Blah blah blah."

"I won't be holding my breath for those elections," Alex said.

Brian nodded. "CB says we have to play nice, for now."

"I'll do my best, but no promises."

When they reached Fleming's office in the Hub, he greeted them warmly and ushered them inside, where CB was already waiting.

He turned to Alex, his eyes wide with compassion. If the emotion wasn't genuine, the man was one hell of an actor.

"Lieutenant Goddard, I want to personally thank you for your service and express my deepest sympathy for your loss."

She nodded quickly. "Thank you, sir."

When they were seated, Fleming smiled at Alex. "I hope you realize what an amazing opportunity we have here. Your mission proved that Resettlement is possible. If Agartha can do it, so can we."

Alex glanced at CB. His face was unreadable. "Due respect sir, that city is protected by vampires."

Fleming waved her objection away. "We'll be protected by guns and soldiers. Have a little faith, Goddard."

"I gotta side with Alex on this one," CB interjected. "It's hard to imagine what things are like down there, if you haven't set foot on the surface yourself. Maybe we could set up a camera down there and—"

Fleming didn't let him finish. "You made me a promise, Captain Brickman. I allow you to rescue your team, and you commit yourself to making Resettlement a reality. I held up my end."

CB grimaced. "I'm not saying I won't help, but doing this right will take years. Hell, it'll take more resources than it took to build this ship."

"I highly doubt that," Fleming replied.

"That's because you haven't seen it," Alex snapped. "We can't just throw some guns and soldiers down on the planet and call it a settlement. They'd be dead ten minutes after sunset. Besides, shouldn't we be electing a new Council? Do you even have the authority to do any of this?"

"We are all fighting for the same thing: the future of our people. Even now Jessica is restoring the reactor. Soon, every citizen will feel safe again."

"That proves Alex's point," Brian said. "We're safe. No need to rush Resettlement."

"You saw the vote," Fleming pointed out. "The people believe in Resettlement as strongly as I do. In fact, some are fanatical about it. One gentleman told me he was willing to kill all the anti-Resettlement people in the agricultural sector to ensure loyal citizens would control the food supply. Of course, that's barbaric, and I would never allow it. I'm only telling you this so that you'll know how passionate the people are. Going against the will of the people would cause a revolt."

There was a long silence, then CB spoke. "If the people are so loyal to you and your ideals, wouldn't it be best if you told them to take it down a few levels?"

"Of course. I always discourage violence. For example, several badges in the prison wanted to kill General Craig. I put an end to that and got them under control, but if something were to happen to me, I can't say what they'd do."

Alex looked at CB for a long moment as those words hung in the air. Fleming had just told them that he was willing to kill half the people in agriculture and hijack the food supply to keep power. He'd also let them know that if anything happened to him, General Craig would die. Alex could only hope that CB knew a way to get the upper hand, because she didn't see a way to beat Fleming, right now.

Fleming ended the silence "Let's not focus on all of the negative possibilities. This is a time of great opportunity for the human race, and for you, personally. I know that the task ahead is difficult, as you have pointed out again and again. That's why I need the best people to carry it out. First, we need to fill a few open positions. CB, General Craig won't be returning to active duty, and I'd like you to fill the role as executive commander of the GMT. That means a serious promotion is in order. Congratulations on making colonel."

CB's mouth fell open in surprise, but Fleming continued before he could respond.

"Alex, you're going to oversee the day-to-day operations of the GMT. You'll receive the rank of captain, and you'll be tasked with getting the team in shape and ready for action as quickly as possible."

The news was so unexpected that for a moment, she thought he was joking. Fleming hated her. Now he was giving her command of the GMT?

She'd never considered doing CB's job. She didn't even know if she wanted it, yet she found herself saying, "Thank you, sir."

Damn military training kicked in before her brain did.

Fleming turned to Brian. "I want you to focus all your efforts on Resettlement. We're currently putting together a group of three hundred settlers, and we're going to need a lot of innovation from your team to make this happen."

"Of course, sir," Brian said. "There are some projects I've been working on. For example, a have a proto-type echolocation system. It needs significant testing, but—"

"Forget all that. Everything gets bumped except Resettlement. We're going to move fast here. I'm talking months, not years."

CB's mouth fell open for the second time in two minutes. Alex started to speak, but CB caught her eye and gave her a barely perceptible head shake. She got the message. They needed to regroup before questioning Fleming too much on this madness.

Still, she did have one question that couldn't wait. "What about Agartha?"

"What about them?" Fleming asked. "I don't trust Agartha, no matter how helpful the vampires pretend to be."

"We're in agreement there," CB growled.

Alex wasn't sure how she felt about Jaden and his people yet. They'd been nothing but helpful, but they were vampires. That was a tough detail to look past. "I don't disagree, but if we're going to do this Resettlement thing, maybe we need to learn from them. They've survived on the surface since the infestation."

Fleming scratched at his chin. "What are you proposing?"

"Jessica seemed to have good rapport with Agatha's head of engineering. What do you say we send her down there for a while once the reactor's fixed? Call it an exchange of information."

CB nodded along. "In the meantime, she can investigate Agartha and find out what's really going on down there."

Fleming thought a moment. "I like it. If they're willing to allow us to insert a spy into their city, we should take advantage of that." A smile crept onto his face. "This is what I'm talking about. I know we've had our differences in the past, but we need to put that behind us. We're the team that's going to bring humanity back to Earth. It's time to trust each other."

———

"I DON'T TRUST HIM," Alex said.

She was sitting with Brian and CB at their usual table at Tankards, their favorite watering hole. They'd come there directly after their meeting with Fleming, to let off some steam and say the things they weren't able to say to his face.

CB nodded his agreement. "The guy thinks Resettlement is his holy mission. He was willing to blow up the whole Council to clear his path to leadership, and he's somehow already winning the people over to his side. There's no telling what else he'll do to get his way."

"It's downright diabolical," Brian said. "In accepting his promotions, you two are basically acknowledging him as the rightful leader of *New Haven*. If you turn them down, you lose the GMT, access to weapons, and all your authority."

Alex sighed. She hadn't thought of it that way, but Brian was right.

"And now we have to focus on filling two slots on the GMT," she said. "With Drew gone and Wesley out of commission..."

"Actually, it's three slots," CB said. "Fleming told me this morning. Firefly won't be returning to the team. He's being assigned to the Resettlement project. And promoted, apparently. He'll be leading the first wave of Resettlers who take up permanent residence down there."

"You're kidding me," Alex said. She spoke softly, bringing up the possibility as gently as she could. "Seems an odd coincidence. Firefly being promoted right after what happened to the Council."

Firefly had been the demolitions man for the GMT. He was also a big fan of Fleming's politics. They'd only been back a few hours, and Firefly gets a sudden promotion?

Neither of the two men answered, and the silence hung thick in the air.

"I'm sorry, but we have to at least consider it," Alex pointed out. "I know you don't want to think anything bad about a member of the team, CB. I don't, either. But the City Council room blew up, and Firefly had access to more explosives than anyone else in this city. He's not exactly the name that would leap to mind to head up a major project. Not unless you owed the guy a favor."

"She has a point," Brian allowed.

After a long moment, CB sighed. "I'm not going to jump to any conclusions, but I will admit it looks bad for Firefly. We'll look into it, but nobody will assume the worst until we have proof. We owe him that much."

"Unless he's guilty," Alex said. "Then we owe him the beatdown of a lifetime."

For a moment, neither of the men objected. Then CB spoke again. "No. We have to handle this differently."

"How so?"

The new colonel leaned forward. "Right now, the people of *New Haven* are on Fleming's side. That's bad enough. But soon, he'll have an army. He wants them trained and ready to deploy to the surface as quickly as possible."

"And again...Firefly's leading them? Our Firefly?"

CB nodded. "We have to put a stop to this before Resettlement."

"Why wait?" Brian asked. His eyes were alive with anger. "You meet with Fleming all the time. A bullet to the head would solve a lot of problems."

Alex raised an eyebrow. "Damn, Brian. I never knew you were so cold."

CB ignored the comment. "Then what? We kill Fleming, it's civil war."

"Who gives a shit?" Brian responded. "It's no worse than what Fleming did to the Council."

"A lot of innocent people would pay the price. Besides, you heard what he said about his loyal badges killing General Craig, if anything happened to him. We have to be smart about this."

"We need to win over Firefly," Alex said.

CB nodded. "Exactly. Firefly is leading the military phase of Resettlement. If we have him, we have an army."

"And how are we supposed to do that?" Alex asked. "This morning, he was my buddy. Now I find out he was probably working with Fleming all along. We have no idea where he stands."

"Then we find out. We can't afford to write him off. We need all the allies we can get."

"Good," Brian said. Alex could see that he was feeling better about things now that they had a clear goal. "What else?"

"I need to work on Kurtz," CB said.

That made sense to Alex. Kurtz was the head of the badges. If they could get him and his badges on their side, they would have the power to arrest Fleming and hold him accountable.

"Kurtz can help us with evidence," CB continued. "This

is going to be a battle for the hearts of the public, and right now Fleming has their hearts. If we want to convince the people, we need hard evidence."

"What about me?" Brian asked.

"Two things. First, go along with what Fleming's asking you to do. We don't want him suspicious of your motives. Second, you and Jessica need to figure out who in your departments is loyal to Fleming and who is willing to hear the truth."

"You got it," Brian said. "I'll talk to Jessica."

"Good." CB raised his glass. "But that can wait until tomorrow. We've earned a night of R&R."

They clinked glasses and drank.

Alex grinned slyly at CB. "So, do we have to call you Colonel now?"

CB grimaced. "Officially? Yes. Unofficially? I've kinda gotten used to people calling me CB."

"You know," Brian said, "as much as I hate Fleming, he is right about one thing. We can't stay up on this ship forever. It will take years of preparation, but at some point, we're going to have to take back the Earth."

CB took a long drink from the mug in front of him, then he said, "You may be right. But if we're going to do it, I wish we'd do it right."

"You'll get no argument from me," Brian said.

Alex raised her glass. "Brian. Colonel Brickman. Here's to Resettlement."

5

"You're serious about this?" CB asked.

"I am."

CB looked around at the trappings of Fleming's office. In the short time he'd been in command, he'd erased any hint of the former City Council leader's existence. Fleming had assured the people that this was a temporary arrangement, but CB knew better.

Now that he had this much power, Fleming would never let it go.

Fleming continued, "The people want a leader who can move quickly, and I'm that man."

CB struggled to keep his face even. The plan that Fleming had laid out was beyond aggressive. He'd identified a site, a former supermax prison in Colorado. Fleming believed they could utilize much of the existing infrastructure for lights and electricity. The place was extremely fortified, and it was in a great position in relation to NORAD. Whatever the relationship with Agartha ended up being, the prison was in an advantageous location to either provide them assistance or to attack them if necessary.

The prison was also rural, so there had been no major cities too close by during the infestation. Theoretically, that should mean less vampires in the area.

"I don't have any problem with the location," CB clarified. "It's the speed I'm worried about."

Fleming pushed his chair back from the desk and stood up. "I don't know what else to tell you, Colonel Brickman. The decision has been made. It's time for you and your team to get on board."

After the meeting, CB walked the to the GMT training facility. He moved briskly, taking out his frustration on the concrete beneath his feet. He knew there was no way for him to change Fleming's mind, yet still he wondered if there was something he could've said, some point he could've made, that would've caused Fleming see things in a new way.

He'd lost enough team members recently. He wasn't keen on losing anyone else.

As expected, he found Alex and the team hard at work, training. Most of the team stood around watching the two people struggling on the mat. He cast a cool eye over his new team, appraising them one more time. There was Hope, who would take Firefly's place as the demolitions expert. Now that Owl was back as pilot, Chuck was replacing Simmons as the recon man.

Finally, there were the Barton brothers. Ed was currently crying out in pain as Alex pinned him to the mat. She had him on his stomach, a knee pressed into the small of his back. His right arm was locked behind his back, and she was pushing on it with such force that CB was a little concerned that it might break.

Ed frantically tapped his hand on the mat, yelling, "You win!"

Alex immediately let him go and stood up, brushing herself off. She reached out a hand and pulled him to his feet.

"Not bad. But you have to learn to use your size. If you'd have—"

A burst of laughter cut her off mid-sentence. All eyes turned to Ed's brother, Patrick, who was laughing uproariously on the side of the mat.

Alex scowled at him. "Something funny, Patrick?"

The man dabbed at his eyes as he tried to get his laughter under control. "No, ma'am. It's just... Ed, I've never seen you lose to a girl."

CB stepped forward, taking a place at the edge of the mat. "I'm sorry, but were you laughing at your commanding officer?"

Patrick straightened up, the laughter finally fading. "No, sir."

"Really?" CB crossed his arms. "Because that's what it seemed like to me. It seemed like you were laughing at Captain Goddard."

"No, sir." Patrick shook his head frantically. "I apologize, sir."

CB sighed. "Well, I'm glad to hear that. Because if you were laughing at your commanding officer, I would have to get involved. But seeing as you weren't, we can get back to training. Is that all right with you, Patrick?"

Patrick nodded, clearly relieved. "Yes sir."

"Good." CB nodded towards Alex. "Let's get to it. Get on the mat, and knock Captain Goddard out."

Patrick tilted his head, as if not sure he'd understood correctly.

Alex took a step toward him. "Did you hear that order from the colonel? Get your ass over here and knock me out!"

Patrick hesitated, looking to his teammates. None of them spoke, clearly not wanting to get involved. After another moment, Patrick hesitantly stepped towards Alex.

An easy smile came onto CB's face. Patrick had four inches and fifty pounds on Alex, but CB never doubted the outcome of the fight he was about to watch.

Patrick raised his fists in a boxing stance, then glanced nervously at CB one more time.

"What are you waiting for?" Alex asked. "You have your orders."

The new GMT man sighed, then stepped forward, moving lightly on the balls of his feet. He threw a quick jab, but Alex was ready. She dodged to the left, and his fist whizzed through the air next to her head.

She brought up her right knee, driving it into his stomach, and the wind rushed out of him. As he doubled over, she stepped back, giving him a moment to recover.

"Captain Goddard is still conscious, Lieutenant!" CB yelled. "Were my orders unclear?"

Patrick stood up straight, his eyes fixed on Alex. This time there was no finesse to his attack. He charged, his arms outstretched, trying to use his size to take her to the mat.

As he grabbed her arm, she sidestepped, using his momentum to flip him forward. He landed on his back with an *ompf*.

Alex still had hold of Patrick's arm, and she threw her leg over it, getting him in an armlock that, from the look on Patrick's face, was anything but pleasant. It was clear to everyone around the mat that Alex could snap Patrick's arm, if she chose to do so.

CB chuckled. Even with everything that was going on

with Fleming, Resettlement, and Agartha, watching Alex work still brought a smile to his face.

Patrick tapped the mat, and Alex let him up. CB kept one eye on Ed, but somehow, the man managed to suppress any laughter.

As Patrick brushed himself off and returned to his place at the edge of the mat, CB stepped to Alex's side.

"Captain Goddard, have you ever seen a vampire during the day?"

"Yes, sir."

"And what chance would you have in a fight against a vampire during the day?"

She answered immediately. "None."

CB nodded and turned to the rest of the team. "Every one of you was chosen for this team for a reason. You're all skilled. You're all dedicated. You are among the best *New Haven* has to offer. You've proven yourself aboard this ship. But tomorrow, you have to prove yourself somewhere else. On the surface. And let me be very clear. That is something entirely different."

"We have a mission, sir?" Owl asked.

"Tomorrow morning. Captain Goddard will brief you." He paused for a moment. "Make me proud, team."

———

ALEX ATE the last bite of her casserole, set down her fork, and sighed contentedly. "Damn, CB, how come you never told me you can cook?"

"What are you talking about? You've been here plenty of times."

Alex gestured to the empty plate in front of her. "Maybe so. But I've never cleaned my plate."

"Okay, fine. Maybe I did break out a special recipe tonight, but tomorrow is a big day."

That was exactly what Alex had been trying not to think about. Still, if she'd really wanted to get away from thoughts of work, maybe she shouldn't come to her boss's quarters for dinner.

"So, you got any words of advice for me, Colonel?"

CB frowned. "Cut out that shit. We're after hours. Let's stick with CB." He paused a moment, thinking. "You really want my advice?"

"Of course. Otherwise I wouldn't have asked."

CB folded his hands on the table, his eyes suddenly serious. "They're a good group. You know they are."

"That's not the issue. My concern is, they aren't a team. At least, not yet. They don't have... I don't know. An identity."

The newly minted colonel shifted in his seat uncomfortably. "This isn't going to be what you want to hear, but I'm afraid there's nothing you can do about that. It's going to take time. More than a few missions."

Alex sighed. "I was afraid you'd say that. Not one of them has ever faced a vampire. And here they are, stuck with a commanding officer just tasked with her first squad."

That was the crux of the issue, Alex knew. If CB had been leading the team of new recruits, she wouldn't have been worried. But they didn't have CB. They had her.

And she wasn't sure if she'd be enough.

CB looked her in the eye. "Listen, Alex, there was a reason we picked you to lead the squad."

"Was it because I was the last person standing?" she asked with a chuckle.

"Well, there is that. But no. We picked you because things are about to get very difficult."

"Geez, CB, this isn't exactly the inspirational speech I was expecting."

CB chuckled, but there was no joy in his laughter. "Maybe not, but it's the one you need right now. Even if Fleming is right, even if Resettlement is the way to go, there are hard times coming. This will have a cost, and Fleming sure as hell hasn't counted it."

Alex leaned forward and lowered her voice a little. "You don't have to convince me, CB. You say the word, and we'll storm the Hub right now. We can't let him get away with this. He killed the Council."

"Agreed. But we have to be patient. I'm meeting with Kurtz tomorrow. For now, you have one job, and one job only: keeping your team alive. We'll carry out Fleming's mission, but if it comes down to the mission or the team, pick the team. Every time."

With that, CB stood up and cleared the dishes from the table. He carried them off into the nearby kitchen and set them down with a clack.

"Remember the good old days, when Firefly used to cook for us?" He didn't wait for a reply before continuing. "Want a beer?"

"You're the boss."

They talked for another twenty minutes, drinking their beers and enjoying each other's company. Every time she tried to work the conversation around to the mission, the team, or Fleming, he shut her down fast. Apparently, he'd had enough shop talk for the evening. He just wanted to enjoy a couple of beers with his good buddy Alex.

She went to bed soon after returning to her own quarters, but she lay awake long into the night, thinking of her teammates, old and new, and what the next day might bring.

6

ALEX CLOSED HER EYES, not to sleep, but to block out the rest of the world for a moment.

They were ten minutes out from their destination, and Alex had spent the whole of the flight so far focused on her team. She'd given Hope a pep talk, discussed the layout of their target with Chuck, and told dirty jokes with Ed and Patrick. Whatever each person needed, she'd given them. Whatever she'd sensed would help them get in the right headspace.

Now she needed just a moment to get her own head right.

The communicator in her ear hissed to life, and Owl's voice came through. "Ladies and gentlemen, we will soon be landing at the former site of the United States Penitentiary, Administrative Maximum Facility, also known as ADX Florence, Supermax, and the Alcatraz of the Rockies. If you don't know what Alcatraz was, see me after. I'd be happy to explain the reference."

"Captain," Patrick called, "can you tell Owl to shut up?"

"No," Alex snapped, her eyes still closed. "This is a GMT tradition."

Owl continued in her chipper voice. "The facility is located in an area that was called Fremont County, Colorado, approximately one hundred miles south of Denver. Fremont County was the home of fifteen prisons, and about twenty percent of the population of the county was incarcerated. ADX Florence was the only supermax prison. Meaning that the guys they kept there were the worst of the worst."

"And now we get to fight their undead vampiric corpses," Ed pointed out. "Cool first mission, Captain."

Alex cracked a smile. "Nothing but the best for you, my beloved team."

"In lighter news," Owl continued, "Fremont County is a great place for you bicyclists. A five-thousand-mile trail called the American Discovery Trail passes through here."

"What the hell's a bicyclist?" Hope asked.

"Please enjoy the rest of your flight, and prepare to kick some ass. See you on the ground."

Alex opened her eyes as Owl finished, and she looked out the window. They were descending now, and she could see the prison below them. From up here, it looked like two big triangles. One of those, she knew, was the lobby and administrative facility. They wouldn't be worrying about that section, at least not today. It was cut off from the cell blocks, connected only by an underground tunnel. They would have to block up that tunnel for now and deal with it later.

As much as she hated Fleming, she had to admit this place was a perfect choice for Resettlement. She'd studied the blueprints, which had been among the treasure-trove of data they'd liberated from NSA on an earlier mission, and what she saw was a set of buildings with an amazing defensive setup. There were guard towers and lights that stood one hundred and fifty feet high. The facility had eight small buildings that had been used as cellblocks, as well as one main building, all of them surrounded by a thirty-foot wall.

The only thing that concerned her from a defensive perspective was the wall. Thirty feet might *sound* impressive, but Alex knew that a vampire at the height of its powers would leap that wall like it was a puddle on the concrete. Fleming intended to combat that with heavy use of daylights. Alex wasn't convinced it would be enough.

Still, she had her orders, and she was going to follow them. At least for now.

Owl set them down in the yard near the center of the cluster of buildings, and Alex was the first off of the ship. She scanned their surroundings, trying to decide on an approach.

"It's a nice day for it."

Alex looked up and saw Hope standing next to her, a wry smile on her face. It was strange seeing this young woman with short, black hair carrying the demolitions equipment, instead of Firefly.

"Yeah, it's not bad," Alex agreed. The sun shone brightly overhead, and though there was nearly a foot of snow under their feet, the yard was clear of most vegetation even after a century and a half of zero upkeep. She remembered Owl saying something about the arid climate in this part of the world.

"Where do we start, Captain?" Patrick asked.

Alex nodded toward the nearest building. Then she turned back to the team. "Slow and steady. That's how we get this done. We stay close together, and you listen for my orders, got it?"

They responded that they did.

Alex led them to the first building. There were no windows, but the door stood wide open. She hoped that was a good sign. Maybe they'd simply let all the prisoners out near the end. If so, it was possible that this place was still empty. She wasn't counting on it, though.

She donned her headlamp and ordered the team to do the same. Then they stepped into the cell block.

Alex scanned their surroundings and immediately felt a little better about their mission. The space was open and there were clear sight lines. She imagined this was so that the guards could see the prisoners from any angle. There were two levels of cells and a narrow walkway running along in front of them. The walkways were covered with the bars and plexiglass.

All the cell doors stood open, adding a little more credence to Alex's hopeful theory that maybe this place was already empty.

Chuck, the recon expert, nodded toward the floor. "This is solid concrete, and it looks tacked down. At least we know vampires won't be popping up through the ground."

"That's something," Patrick muttered. "I'm probably not supposed to say this on my first mission, but this place is creepy as hell."

Alex couldn't disagree. The strangest thing was how well preserved it was. A thick layer of dust covered everything, but that aside, this place could have been in use yesterday.

They crept through an open gate, staying in tight formation, and reached the first of the cells.

Hope scanned it with her eyes. "Holy hell. I can't believe this place. I've spent a few nights in jail back in *New Haven*, but it wasn't anything like this. What are these cells? Like six feet by ten feet?"

"Something like that," Alex confirmed.

Each cell contained only a bed, a sink, a toilet, and a tiny slit that served as a window. Alex reminded herself that the worst criminals of the pre-infestation era had been held here.

And now Fleming wanted to make it home to the people of *New Haven*.

The team cleared the first building without incident, and one hour later, they were ready to move on.

Aside from the creepy factor of the still-made beds and the well-ordered cells, Alex felt better about this mission. The team was focused and responding to her orders well.

But she wouldn't let her guard down. Not now; not ever again.

As they stepped back out into the sunlight, she turned to her team. "Well done, people. Moving on to building two."

———

THE TEAM SEARCHED the next two buildings without incident, moving carefully through the darkened, eerie structures.

While Alex never let her guard down, she did allow herself to relax ever so slightly. The layouts of the buildings were identical, and once they'd cleared the first, it was simply a matter of repeating the procedure. First, they checked the cells. Then, on to the cafeteria. Then, the guard areas. Finally, the small basement, which contained four even more private cells, in what Alex assumed was an isolation wing.

It also gave her the chance to assess her team. Overall, she was impressed. They stayed focused, and they followed orders well. Just as importantly, they remained alert throughout the long, boring search.

Midway through the third building, Alex nudged Chuck. "You take the lead for the rest of this building."

His eyes widened in surprise, but he quickly recovered, nodding and taking Alex's place at the front.

Alex fell back to the rear to observe him in action. She'd known from day one that she was going to need a right-hand man, someone to whom she could delegate leadership responsibilities from time to time, the same way CB had to her and Simmons.

Even though Owl had been on the team the longest, she was the first to admit that she wasn't a leader and didn't want to be. She preferred to stay with the ship, when possible.

That left the new recruits. From among them, Chuck was the obvious pick. He was clear-headed and insightful. He was respectful, but also unafraid to speak his mind. Even though it was their first real mission to the surface as a team, Alex wanted to get him started on the path to leadership immediately, even in a small way.

He performed admirably as he led them through the third building, and Alex clapped him on the back as they headed for the fourth cellblock.

"Well done. You kept a good eye on your teammates, and I like how you barked at Ed when he tried to hurry. Next time—"

A noise like a high-pitched whine came from the depths of the fourth building, cutting Alex off.

"What the hell was that?" Hope asked.

Alex clutched her pistol in a two-handed grip as she edged toward the door. "That was a vampire howl."

"You gotta be kidding me," Patrick muttered, his voice thick with concern.

"Afraid not."

Alex glanced back at her team, spending a moment studying each of their drawn faces. The fear was evident in every one of them, but none of them were freaking out. That was a good sign. She pushed her own apprehension aside. "Looks like this mission just got a little more exciting. Have your weapons ready, but don't fire at anything unless you know what you're shooting at. I'll take the lead." She gave them a moment, then turned back toward the door. "Let's earn our pay."

They moved slowly through cell block four, searching even more methodically for the vampire they knew was hidden somewhere in the structure. While the work was the same as in the other buildings, the knowledge that an undead creature was not only possible, but was a reality, cast a heavy cloud of tension over them as they searched.

When they were halfway through the upper row of cells, they heard the howl again.

Chuck exchanged a glance with Alex. "That's definitely coming from below us."

Alex nodded. She'd been thinking the same thing, but wanted to let one of them say it. "Well, let's not keep our friend waiting."

She led them down the stairs to the small basement. As they reached the bottom, she instructed Owl to guard the stairs, to make sure nothing came at them from behind.

Just like in the other buildings, the basements were divided into two sections: one that housed the mechanical systems, and one that housed four cells. The two sections were separated and walled off from each other. Alex led the way into the area with the cells, and they found three of the doors were open. The fourth was dented from the inside.

"Looks like we found our howler," Ed whispered.

Alex took a small step toward the closed door. "Looks that way."

"That thing's solid steel," Hope said. "What the hell could have dented it like that?"

"Something that's been pounding on it for one hundred and fifty years." Alex took another step forward.

Each of the doors had a slot, to allow in a little light, Alex surmised. As soon as the beam from her headlamp fell across the slot, something slammed against the inside of the door, and the steel boomed like thunder with the force of the impact.

The thing inside the cell crashed against the door again, and this time the boom was accompanied by a cracking sound. The vampire was hitting the door with such force that it was breaking its own bones, Alex realized.

She glanced back at her team. Chuck was visibly shaken, and beads of sweat stood on his forehead. Hope didn't look to be doing much better.

But everyone was holding fast, waiting for orders.

A sallow, thin finger poked through the slot in the door. Then another. Then a third. The vampire was clearly trying to push its hand through. The hand caught on the one-inch slot, but still the vampire kept pushing. The flesh of its hand tore and peeled back, until the muscles beneath were clearly visible.

The team watched in shocked horror.

After another moment, the vampire pulled back its ruined hand and put its face to the slot.

Alex fired, and the vampire squealed and fell backward.

"Oh, hell yeah, Captain!" Patrick shouted.

A whimpering sound from inside the cell confirmed Alex's suspicions: the thing wasn't dead yet.

Alex turned to Hope. "We need a one-foot-by-one-foot hole in this door."

Hope nodded, then pulled the cutting tool out of her pack and went to work.

Alex couldn't help but think about the last time she'd seen this tool used. Firefly had cut a hole in the floor, allowing them to escape to a vacant level of the nuclear power plant. A short while later, they'd escaped. All of them except Simmons.

Hope finished, and the piece of steel crashed to the floor, exposing the inside of the cell. The team stared in awe, most of them seeing a vampire for the first time.

Alex's bullet had torn away part of the creature's face, but as they watched, the wound was already healing. It stumbled forward, letting out a weak moan as it clambered toward the door. Alex considered whether this might be the most wretched creature in existence. The damn thing had spent one hundred fifty years alone in the dark, waiting for her to show up and kill it.

"This is the enemy," she told the team. "You'll see plenty more of them in your time with the GMT, but you'll never forget your first. Take a good hard look."

She fired two rounds into the creature's heart, ending its miserable existence.

———

ALEX STOOD in the doorway of the final building of ADX Florence. They'd successfully cleared the cell blocks, and this was the last building. Unfortunately, they only had an hour and a half of daylight left, and this building was significantly larger than the other eight.

"All right, folks, this is the time to focus up. We've had good luck so far, but the end of the day doesn't mean things are automatically going to be easy."

With that, Alex stepped through the door. She immediately tensed at what she saw.

"So much for that good luck, Captain," Ed said as he sidled up beside her.

"You can say that again." Alex looked around, taking in the destruction around them. This building had clearly been the site of a firefight. It reminded her of the nuclear facility in Texas. That place had clearly been torn apart by a major battle, and this building was no different. They passed through a series of open gates and made their way to a large open common area, surrounded by two levels of cells.

Chuck stepped beside Alex. "Captain, do you think we should —?"

She held up a hand, silencing him.

A rustling noise on the second level caught her attention, and she stood stone-still, waiting to see if it would come again.

She didn't have to wait long before a vampire stumbled out of one of the cells.

Alex remained frozen, her gaze fixed on the vampire as she silently willed her team not to move.

It didn't matter. As the vampire reached the waist-high rail, it breathed deeply through its strange, ruined nose, sniffing. Then it glared down at them, and its eyes locked on them.

Alex raised her pistol just as the creature vaulted the rail. It dove down at them, howling as it came. It stretched out its arms, revealing the web-like wings between its arms and torso.

Alex squeezed off three quick shots, killing the vampire before it hit the ground.

"Circle up!" she called to the team. "Eyes on those cells. We don't know how many more of those things are in here."

A heavy silence filled the air as the team waited, gazing at the open cells a vampire could leap from at any moment.

"There!" Patrick called. He and Ed fired in unison, peppering the vampire with bullets as it came out of the lower-level cell to their right. The vampire fell backwards with the bullet holes all along its neck and shoulders, but it quickly got up again and lunged towards them.

Patrick and Ed let loose another heavy barrage of fire, and this time they removed the vampire's head completely from its neck.

Another vampire leapt from a cell on the other side of the room, and Chuck raised his rifle, training it along with the vampire's movements. The vampire moved around the group, putting Hope's head directly between Chuck's gun and the creature.

"No!" Alex called. She swung her arm upward, slamming it against the bottom of the barrel just before Chuck fired. Thankfully, the shot went high.

Hope was ready to fire, but she recoiled and put a hand to her ear as Chuck's gun went off so close to her head.

Alex sprang into action. The vampire was heading straight for Hope now, and there was no way Hope would get her gun up in time to stop him.

Alex put three rounds in the vampire's chest. It dropped to the ground, but continued to squirm. Alex was almost glad. She drew her sword, then brought it down hard on the vampire's neck. The decapitated head rolled two feet away.

The team formed back into a circle and waited a tense two minutes, trying to steady their breathing as the adrenaline coursed through them. No more vampires appeared.

When she was sure no more were coming, Alex turned to the team. "Let's keep moving."

There would be time for accolades and reprimands later. For now, they had work to do.

———

THE FLIGHT back to *New Haven* was very different than the one to the prison had been. On the way to the mission, the ship had been filled with tension, a strange mix of fear and excitement. Now it was like the air had been released from a balloon. The tension was gone, but what remained was different from person to person.

Chuck sat in silence, his head down. Alex had yet to address his nearly shooting his teammate. She would do so when they got back, but she wasn't looking forward to the task. Killing vampires, she could do; having a difficult conversation with a subordinate was a whole other matter.

Hope was keeping to herself as well, but her demeanor seemed less upset and more reflective, as if she was going over the events of the mission second by second in her mind. Her hand occasionally went to the side of her head.

Alex touched her arm. "You okay?"

Hope nodded slowly. "I've got some ringing in my right ear, but shipshape, other than that." She nodded towards Chuck and lowered her voice when she spoke again. "Don't be too hard on him. It's my fault, as much as his. I should've gotten out of the way. Or taken on the vampire myself."

For a moment, Alex wasn't sure what to say. She had assumed Hope would be angry at Chuck. Alex certainly would've been. "It wasn't your fault. You stayed in formation."

"Yeah, but the vampire was in my quadrant. He was my responsibility. I should've taken him out before Chuck even had the chance to fire."

Technically, she was correct. The vampire was in her area of responsibility. Still, that was all the more reason for Chuck to not take a shot.

"You did fine," Alex assured her. "You kept your composure. You faced off against your first vamp, and you didn't freak out. That's a pretty good start."

Ed and Patrick sat across the aisle, excitedly recapping the events of the mission.

"You did pretty well, Ed," Patrick said with a sly smile. "It's a shame I had to take out that vampire for you."

Ed's eyes grew large. "What are you talking about? I blew its head off while you were shooting its shoulders."

Patrick shook his head. "No, I don't think so. Did you see the angle of the head, when it fell? The kill shot definitely came from my direction."

Alex glared at them. "You're pretty proud of yourselves, are you?"

Patrick shrugged. "First time facing vampires. We walked away and they didn't. Seems like a win to me."

Alex fought the conflicting urges to smile and to walk over and smack the man. On the one hand, she completely understood where he was coming from. Hell, it hadn't been that long ago since she'd been saying very similar things to CB. On the other hand, she couldn't afford that kind of naïveté on the team.

"We walked away because there were only three of them. I've never seen vampires so groggy. You guys acted as individuals, not as a team. If there'd been more than three of them, or if it'd been night time, they'd be licking our blood off their lips right now."

"Captain Goddard." It was Owl speaking through Alex's earpiece. "It's time to check in with CB. You want to give him the mission report, or should I?"

Alex touched the radio on her chest. "Nah, I got it." It was as good an excuse as any to get away from her team for a bit.

She made her way to the cockpit, and plopped down on the seat next to Owl.

Owl glanced at her and grinned. "Newbies, huh?"

"You said it." Then, remembering she was the captain now, she quickly added, "They'll be okay. They just need to get into the swing of things a little."

She hailed CB and gave him the full report, including the number of vamps they'd killed. She considered leaving out the part where Chuck had almost shot Hope, but she decided she better not start her new position with a lie of omission.

"You want me to talk to him?" CB asked.

"No. Training and discipline both fall under my jurisdiction. I'm on it."

"Good." He paused for a moment. "I hope you liked the prison."

Alex raised an eyebrow. "Yeah? Why's that?"

"Because Fleming's pushing hard. You're going to be spending a lot of time down there in the next few weeks."

7

JADEN ARRIVED in the conference room before the others, and he took his seat near the head of the table. Over the past few hundred years, he'd gotten pretty good at time management.

He'd purposely scheduled this meeting for shortly before sunrise, as he did most meetings with the human leaders. It allowed him a hard out, so the conversations couldn't go on for too long.

The vampires and humans in Agartha mostly stayed apart, mainly because the vampires slept all day. Many humans in the city had absolutely no contact with Jaden and his team. Jaden liked it that way. It kept things clean. The vampires did their job of keeping the humans alive, and the humans did...whatever it was humans do. It had been so long since Jaden had been one himself that he barely remembered.

The others trickled in over the next few minutes. Robert—Jaden's fellow vampire and right-hand man—sat across from Jaden. The other two, George, from Engineering, and Cynthia, the human leader of Agartha, entered together. As always, Cynthia took the seat at the head of the table. Positions of power were important to humans, and it didn't much matter to Jaden what chair he sat on. They were all short-sighted, silly human concerns to him.

Along with time management, the years had brought a bit of perspective and the ability to find amusement in the fleeting things too many humans stressed over.

After they'd exchanged greetings, Cynthia got right to the purpose for their meeting. "Our communications department let me know they're getting low on copper. If their project is going to stay on track, they need more."

"No problem. We'll make that a priority on our next supply run." Jaden waited for her to continue. That information could have easily been conveyed in a quick radio communication. She clearly wanted to talk about more than that. He suspected he knew what was coming next; he'd been waiting for it since the *New Haven* crew had shown up on their doorstep in desperate need of help.

She looked Jaden in the eye. "How long have you known about the existence of *New Haven*?"

There it was.

He didn't hesitate before responding. "Ever since it was built. A hair under two hundred years, give or take a decade."

Cynthia gritted her teeth, as she always did when unsuccessfully trying to hide her anger. "So, why'd you keep it to yourself? Didn't you think the fact that we were not the last humans on Earth might have been important for us to know?"

"No, actually."

George and Cynthia exchanged a glance, and George cleared his throat nervously. "Could you elaborate?"

Jaden smiled patiently. Sometimes, he felt like he spent

half his time trying to get humans to think rationally. It was a battle that he only occasionally won, but it was always an interesting challenge. "There are only two slivers of humanity left. Agartha and *New Haven*. We decided early on that it would be safer to keep them apart."

"Why?" George asked. "From a practical perspective, wouldn't it be easier to survive if we worked together? If we shared ideas? Resources? *New Haven* travels to places that we can't. It's much easier for them to get supplies from anywhere on Earth."

Good old George, always thinking like an engineer.

"From a practical perspective, sure," Jaden agreed. "But we had to think more broadly than that."

Cynthia's eyes narrowed. "Explain."

"At the end of the infestation, things got bad." Jaden briefly considered how deeply to delve into this topic. Some of the things he'd seen—things done by vampires to humans, and things done by humans to themselves—he still didn't like to think about. It was the stuff of nightmares, even for a vampire as old as he was. Those were dark times; times when the light of humanity very nearly went out.

After a few moments, he decided not to elaborate. It was difficult for the humans of Agartha to comprehend the scope of the pre-infestation world. Which meant they couldn't very well understand what its destruction had been like.

"Let's say a leader with evil intentions takes control of one city or the other," Jaden explained. "Or maybe worse, a foolish leader. It's not inconceivable that a city could be wiped out because of a few foolish decisions. Not with all the Ferals roaming the Earth. Now, imagine that leader controlling both cities."

"So *New Haven* is the backup plan, in case we blow it?" George asked.

Robert smiled. "Depends on your perspective. Maybe we're the backup plan."

"The point is," Jaden interjected, "we've kept the cities apart for a reason. If our people, who have spent their lives inside a mountain, find out there's a city on an airship traveling the globe, don't you think they'll want to take a ride?"

"I know I do," George said.

"Exactly. And the same goes for the people of *New Haven*. If they find out about a safe city on the surface, I'll bet a bunch of them will want to declare their endless voyage at an end. I say we keep the existence of *New Haven* secret for now."

Cynthia frowned. "I see your logic, but we'll have to do a better job keeping any visitors from *New Haven* contained. Too many people know already for us to keep this secret forever."

"Speaking of visitors," George said, "it looks like we're getting another one. Jessica would like to spend some time here. She wants to work with me and exchange information. Even if the general populations of our two cities can't work together, maybe our engineers can."

Jaden nodded slowly. "That's smart. And it will give us the chance to extract more information about *New Haven*."

A sly smile crept across Cynthia's face. "So, you're not above all our conniving human ways after all."

"It's not conniving, it's just caution. There's so much we don't know about *New Haven*. Their political structure, the quality of their living conditions, their general outlook on life. For all we know, they've started a religious cult that worships the moon."

"Now *that* would be information we could use," Robert

joked. "We can say the moon told us they're supposed to give us all their food."

Jaden ignored the comment. "Caution is the name of the game here. Ideally, we want a healthy, productive relationship with *New Haven*, but we have to be ready for things to go the other way. I'm going to have my team prepare the surface-to-air missiles in case of an attack."

"Agreed," Cynthia confirmed. "If they want to be friends, we can make that happen, but we're not going to sit here like suckers if they try to take advantage of us. Their city is a flying fortress, for all we know."

Jaden raised a finger. "The thing about flying fortresses is that they can be shot down. I much prefer my fortresses on solid ground. If it comes to a fight, we won't be the ones tumbling out of the sky."

———

CB's MORNING was not going well. He'd already had to stomach a meeting with Fleming, who'd told him he wanted more frequent reports. Never mind that CB was already up to his eyeballs in administrative work.

Work that he should be doing now. Instead, he was heading to Sparrow's Ridge, looking for an old friend.

The GMT was off serving as the world's most highly-trained transportation service and delivering Jessica down to Agartha. CB hoped he'd have good news to share with Alex when she got back.

He found the man he was looking for in badge head-quarters in Sparrow's Ridge.

Kurtz's eyes lit up when he saw his old friend. "Ah, my fellow colonel!"

CB grinned. "Who ever thought the two of us would be running the GMT and the badges, huh?"

"Certainly not our mothers. They thought we'd wind up on the other side of the jail bars."

CB chuckled. "Ain't that the truth. Listen, is there somewhere private we can talk?"

Kurtz led him to an office in the back of the building. When the door was shut and they were both seated, Kurtz folded his hands on the desk. "So, what's up?"

CB hesitated, not sure where to begin.

A slow smile crept across Kurtz's face. "Let me save you the trouble. You want to know how I feel about Fleming."

Now it was CB's turn to smile. "Talk about cutting right to it."

"Hell, Brickman, you don't have to be coy with me. I know he had you locked up after he blew up the Council. I imagine you're not a big fan of the guy."

"That's an accurate statement," CB allowed. "Where do you stand on the matter?"

Even though they were alone and the door was shut, Kurtz leaned forward and spoke softly. "Fleming killed his political rivals, took control of the city, and is hiding the crime. I'm the top badge in *New Haven*. How the hell do you think I feel about him?"

"Good," CB said. "I figured as much. If he thought he could buy us off with promotions, he's got another thing coming." He paused. "When you say you're against him, how far are you willing to go?"

Kurtz thought about that a moment. "As far as I need to. But it won't be easy."

"I know. The public loves him."

"It's not just that," Kurtz said. "He called me in yesterday and gave me a list of badges who are being reassigned to the Resettlement project under your old pal, Firefly. Nearly half my people. And it just so happens, they're the ones who aren't big fans of Fleming and his plans."

CB's face went pale. "You're kidding me."

"Afraid not. It's sort of genius, really. He sends his political rivals to the surface. If they survive, great. His plan for Resettlement worked and he's a hero. If something happens... Well, that's very sad, but at least it wasn't his people that got it."

CB put a hand to his mouth. "This is insane."

"And it's not just us," Kurtz continued. "The way I hear it, Fleming supporters just happen to be getting promotions in nearly every department in *New Haven*. You ask me, we need to take him down."

"My thoughts exactly," CB agreed. "I'm working on Firefly. But we need hard evidence, if we're going to convince the people a military coup is the answer." He paused a moment, studying the other man's face. "Why are you smiling, Kurtz?"

"Because I know something Fleming doesn't. There's a hidden security camera in the Council chambers."

CB's eyes widened as he took in the implications of his friend's words. "We'd be able to see who planted the explosives."

"Exactly. The tape holds months' worth of video. We just have to get it from the camera without anyone noticing."

"That, I can handle," CB said.

———

JESSICA LOOKED at the broken fifty-caliber automated gun with amazement. The team had destroyed it when trying to gain access to NORAD. She had assumed it was a normal weapon. Now she saw how incorrect she'd been.

It turned out to be a railgun.

The engineering behind it was amazing. It used an electromagnetic catapult design to hurl its ammunition at an incredible speed. It used only a minimal amount of energy and took away the need for gunpowder, something that was always difficult to acquire.

And this was just one small example of the technology she'd seen in this place. And she'd only been here for a few hours.

Coming to Agartha had been so much better than she expected. She'd spent most of her time with George so far, and they'd instantly connected. She could talk to him in a way that would have gone over the head of anyone on *New Haven*. It was amazing how liberating it felt to talk with someone on her mental level.

Beyond that, she genuinely liked the man, and he seemed to enjoy their conversations just as much as she did.

George spoke, interrupting her thoughts. "What do you think? Would you like to help me rebuild it?"

She was so surprised at the offer, it took her a moment to answer. Letting her help rebuild the weapon would give her an intimate knowledge of the technology, knowledge she could take back to *New Haven* and theoretically use to advance their weapons arsenal.

"Yes," she said as soon as she recovered from the surprise.

"Excellent," George said, genuine excitement in his voice.

Agartha had a much stronger focus on technology than *New Haven*, and it was taking Jessica a while to adjust to their reality. Everything in *New Haven* was focused on the perpetual movement of the ship and efficient use of resources. But here, the priorities were defense and comfort. The best part was that the Agarthans seemed happy to share. Jessica couldn't wait to take all of the knowledge that she had gained back to *New Haven*.

She'd seen some amazing things. A classroom filled with young children learning pre-infestation history. An automated vertical farm filled with rows and rows of plants being nourished by grow lights; a place that George said fed everyone in the city, despite its surprisingly small size. Even an auditorium that George said was used for performances of ancient plays.

For her own part, Jessica had gone back and forth about how much to reveal about *New Haven*. In the end, she'd told him that her city was in a confined space, where they needed to maximize usage of every square foot, just like Agartha. If he was annoyed by her lack of candor, he didn't let on.

"Can I ask you something?" she asked as they stood over the damaged railgun.

"Of course."

"What do the vampires here eat?" She paused a moment, then quickly added, "I'm sorry if that's a rude question. I'm not sure the of the etiquette. The only vampires I'd seen before coming here were more the rip-your-face-off type rather than the have-a-conversation type."

"Not rude at all. Perfectly logical." He started walking toward the door. "Come on. I'll show you."

She followed him through a twisting corridor to a door with a large red cross on it. He swiped his keycard, then he ushered her into the room.

"Since the sun's still up, we'll have the place to ourselves," he said.

The room was refrigerated, and the cold prickled at her skin. Or maybe it was the sight of shelves lined with hundreds of bags of blood.

"What is this?" she asked over the hum of the cooling system. "Where's it come from?"

"It's donated. The people volunteer to give a little blood every month or so."

"You're kidding." She turned slowly, doing mental calculations. There had to be hundreds of gallons of human blood in this room.

"You mentioned our focus on efficiency. This is just another example. We need vampires to help us survive, and we help them survive. All without the loss of life."

Jessica turned toward George. "Maybe not now, but there were eleven billion people on the planet before the first wave of the infestation. How many did the vampires kill?"

"Those weren't our vampires. Jaden and his friends had nothing to do with that."

"You know that for sure?"

"I do."

His voice carried the conviction of a true believer, so she decided not to press him further.

"Let me ask you one more thing," she said. "You have a team of vampires and the most impressive weapons arsenal I've ever seen. Why are you still living under a mountain? Why not expand?"

"We've talked about it. Jaden assures us that we will eventually. But the time isn't right."

"Huh." Jessica thought about that. If Agartha didn't think Resettlement was a possibility, what chance did *New Haven* have?

George gestured to the door. "Let's get back to the lab. We've got a gun to repair."

8

"FREMONT COUNTY IS a great place for you bicyclists. A five-thousand-mile trail called the American Discovery Trail passes through here." Owl paused, then said, "Déjà vu, huh? Anyway, enjoy your trip back to Florence ADX."

Alex shifted in her seat, mentally preparing for what lay ahead of them. The passenger hold was a little more crowded than usual, today. Along with the members of the GMT, they had two engineers along with them, Ron Oralee and Yoko Darby. Now that the prison was cleared of vampires, Fleming had tasked these two with figuring out a way to tie in generators to the old electrical system. The GMT was there to make sure that the engineers were able do their work without getting their throats ripped out.

"It's a classic," Hope said, picking up a conversation she'd been having before Owl's speech. "You really gonna rag on a classic?"

"A classic for people who can't shoot properly," Ed responded. "Point a shotgun in the general direction and pull the trigger. Where's the finesse in that? Where's the art?"

"The art's splattered all over the wall when you blow your enemy's head off with the thing," Hope replied.

"I'll take precision any day." Ed paused. "Tell you what. How about we keep a tally? I'll bet I take out more vamps than you today. Loser buys drinks tonight."

Alex couldn't help but chuckle at their conversation. She'd made plenty of similar wagers with Drew back in the day. In happier times.

"You're on," Hope immediately answered.

Patrick shook his head. "We're not going to encounter anything today, dumbasses. We already cleared this place out. This mission is just a babysitting job." He paused a moment. "That said, you're going to let me in on the contest, right?"

Hope grinned. "Maybe you two want to combine your scores? We all know it takes both of you to kill one vampire."

The ship set down in the yard, and the team gathered outside the ship.

A light snow was falling, and large snowflakes drifted down, landing on their helmets and gear. With the ship shut down, the place was eerily silent.

Alex gave them a moment, letting them take in the beauty of the falling snow, letting them feel the crisp air on their faces for a moment longer before they had to go back into the dark, musty cell blocks. Then she took a good look at the ground in the yard, and the tranquility of the moment slipped away. The familiar crackle of adrenaline rushed into her muscles.

"What the hell?" Owl said. "There weren't any tracks here last time."

The snow around them was full of marks that it had taken Alex a few moments to identify. With the thin layer of freshly fallen snow covering them, it was difficult to see the divots for what they really were: footprints.

Alex turned to Ron and Yoko. "You two need to go back in the ship. Wait for me to give you the all-clear."

The engineers exchanged a glance, but they didn't argue. They hauled their heavy backpacks filled with gear and electrical testers back onto the ship.

Ed nudged Patrick, an excited grin on his face. "Babysitting mission, huh?"

"Looks like we're back in the vampire-hunting business." Alex gestured toward the nearest building, cell block four. "I'll lead the way. Ed, Hope, take my flanks. Patrick and Chuck, I want you two in the doorway. Stay in the light and get ready to cover us if we need to make a quick exit."

"Hell, yeah," Ed said. "Let's put these animals down."

Alex, Ed, and Hope passed through the entry to the building and made their way slowly down the long corridor that led to the old security checkpoint and the cellblock beyond, their headlamps lighting the way. The air carried a musty scent like rotting leather. Though the smell conjured images of old things, it hadn't been here a few days ago when they'd cleared this building.

As they passed through the checkpoint, they saw the vampire. It was slumped in the corner, huddled up and apparently asleep.

Ed raised his weapon.

"Hold your fire," Alex ordered in a soft voice. She glanced back down the long hallway, mentally running through what to do next. "Come with me."

She led them back down the corridor, moving just far enough that they were still able to see the vampire.

"Get ready to run," she said. Then she raised her weapon and fired.

Her round caught the vampire in the upper leg, and it let out a howl of pain.

"Go!" Alex shouted. The three of them dashed to the entrance.

The vampire followed, running awkwardly on its injured leg, but still closing the gap at an alarming rate.

Ed, Hope, and Alex reached the entrance and hurried through.

The vampire made it to the door a moment later and stopped just short of the sunlight. It glared at them with furious, wild eyes and howled.

"What the hell was that, Captain?" Ed asked, his voice short as he tried to catch his breath. "You're always bitching at us about aiming for the head and the heart. You didn't even hit a vital."

"Patience, Ed," Alex replied. She held her weapon at the ready, but she didn't fire at the vampire. Not yet.

The vamp let out another howl as it stared at them hungrily from the doorway. But this time, it wasn't alone. A dozen more howls answered, some from cell block four, and some from the other buildings.

"Holy shit. Holy shit. Holy shit." Chuck muttered the litany softly, his weapon trained on the vampire in front of them.

"Sounds like its friends woke up," Patrick observed.

Hope gripped her shotgun tightly. "Brilliant deduction, Patrick."

A sound like a thousand rats scurrying over a concrete floor filled the air. A second later, fifteen more vampires appeared, cramming themselves into the corridor behind their injured friend.

Alex said, "Now you can aim for the vitals."

The team opened fire, immediately obeying the

command.

Hope's shotgun roared as she fired again and again. Ed, Patrick, Owl, and Chuck mowed through the vampires with their automatic weapons. Alex stuck to her pistol.

The vampires fell as bullets tore through their heads and hearts.

After a moment it was over, and a pile of dead vampires filled the corridor.

Angry howls came from the other buildings and echoed through the prison grounds.

"Looks like this is going to be a long day," Chuck said.

———

"CAN WE RESET?" Hope asked. "I have no idea who killed which vampire."

"You wish," Ed said, a smile on his face. "I took out at least half of those undead bastards."

"Um, no. I will admit you took out more than Patrick, though. I swear, half his shots went over the vampires' heads."

A pained expression appeared on Patrick's face. "What battle were you guys watching? I was like a surgeon."

"A drunk surgeon, maybe," Hope joked.

Owl scratched her head as she surveyed the pile of vampire corpses piled near the door. "I don't understand. These guys weren't here two days ago."

Hope looked at Alex. "Any idea what changed, Captain?"

Alex thought a moment before responding. She had a theory, but it was little more than that. "The only thing that changed was us being here. They must have picked up on our scent and come here to find us."

"Huh," Hope said. She sounded skeptical.

"There's no way they can smell that far, is there?" Chuck asked. "I mean, none of us even shed any blood. We were here in the middle of the day. Are you telling me they could smell us so strongly hours later that they came running from God knows where and just hung out here in the hopes we'd come back?"

"Don't know," Alex said. It felt odd to admit her lack of knowledge. After all, she was supposed to be in charge here. But she knew that the only thing more dangerous than an inexperienced leader was one who pretended she knew more than she did. "Their senses are heightened at night. So, it's possible."

Chuck nodded slowly. "Okay, so what do we do next, Captain?"

Alex gestured to cellblock five. "We get back to work. We still have a mission to finish. We'll clear out the other buildings the same way we did this one. Then, once we've swept them all, we'll bring Yoko and Ron in to do their engineering thing."

They started at cellblock five, Alex again leading two of them inside, injuring one of the vampires to wake it up, then getting the hell out of there as quickly as possible. Then the team stood in the safety of the sunlight and took out the vampires that gathered at the door.

After the third building, Patrick said, "Man, Captain, I thought the GMT was going to be tough. This is almost too easy."

"No kidding," Ed agreed. "Why haven't we tried Resettlement before?"

Alex grimaced. "Go up against a vampire at night, then tell me Resettlement is a good idea. And that's the last I want to hear about this being easy. *Easy* means we all go home alive. That's not always the case on the GMT."

That shut them up.

Alex tried to push away the anger she felt at their words. She couldn't blame them; she'd made similar comments not long ago. Maybe humans were doomed to keep making the same mistakes, generation after generation. She'd underestimated the vampires until she'd learned through painful experience how formidable they were. CB had underestimated them, too, in his youth, and his first team had paid the ultimate price.

Alex vowed to herself she wouldn't let that happen to her team. She might not be able to protect her people from danger one hundred percent of the time, but if one of them died, it wouldn't be because their captain had underestimated the enemy.

They moved on, and Alex let Chuck take the lead on cellblock eight. She'd hoped he'd develop into a leader, but after the mission the other day, she wasn't so sure about him. Or her judgment. Still, the guy needed confidence, and sometimes trial by fire was the best way to gain it. He managed to shoot a vampire, and they got to the safety of the sunlight in time. However, this time, only five vampires gathered in the doorway.

Alex assumed that cellblock eight just happened to be more lightly populated then the first few buildings. But when they moved on to cellblock nine, they found it even more sparse. They moved down the long corridor and stopped at the edge of the open room where they'd shot the vampires in the other cellblocks. This time, there wasn't a vampire in sight.

Alex raised her pistol and squeezed the trigger, firing into the open room. As the echo from the gunshot faded, she heard shuffling sounds from deeper in the cellblock, but no vampires showed themselves.

"We need to get out of here," she ordered. "Move."

Chuck immediately turned toward the door, but Hope hesitated.

"I heard them in there. Shouldn't we flush them out?"

"You have your order," Alex growled. "We'll talk in the safety of the sunlight."

Hope hesitated a moment longer, then headed for the door.

Alex stifled a chuckle as she followed. Hope was too much like Alex for her own good. Alex would have to ask CB for some tips on dealing with recruits who questioned orders during the mission.

When they were back outside, she gathered the team around her. "The vampires are learning."

Patrick laughed. "You're kidding, right? Those things are animals. They can't learn."

"Animals learn all the time," Owl pointed out.

"Fine," Patrick allowed. "But we've killed every vampire we've encountered. How would the ones in this building know what we were doing?"

"I don't know," Alex answered. "But I've seen them make decisions as a group before."

"As have I," Owl added.

"We're not taking any chances. There's no reason we need to clear out every building today. The electrical system should be the same in each of them. Owl, get Ron and Yoko."

A few minutes later, the team entered cell block four once again. They'd just passed over the threshold, stepping past the bullet-ridden corpses of the first few vampires, when Ron spoke in a shaky voice.

"I'm sorry, Captain Goddard, I can't do this."

Alex frowned, but one look at the engineer's face

confirmed he was barely holding it together. He was nearly as pale as a corpse, and he rested one hand on the wall to steady himself.

She nodded. "Understood. Owl, take him back to the ship." She turned to Yoko. "How about you?"

The female engineer didn't look much better, but she met Alex's gaze. "I'm fine. Let's keep moving."

"That's what I like to hear."

Alex shot Patrick a look, intending to convey for him to keep a close eye on the engineer. To her relief, he responded with a quick nod.

It was impressive how quickly this team was learning to communicate effectively in the field.

She looked at her team. "We can't assume the vampires all ran to the doorway and followed their friend to the slaughter. Some of the deep sleepers might still be snoozing in the shadows. Stay frosty."

The team made a quick but thorough sweep of the cells and found nothing. As time inside the cell block passed, Yoko seemed more on edge, but she was managing to keep it under control so far.

Before they headed to the utility area in the basement, Alex put a hand on Yoko's shoulder. "This is your time to shine. You ready?"

"I'm ready." Her voice was even, though the wild look in her eyes betrayed her fear.

"Good. If something does happen, if one of those undead freaks shows up, I want you to freeze. Don't move. We *will* protect you, but if you start running around, you're likely to get shot or bit. Understand?"

Yoko laughed softly. "Freeze? That I can do."

They moved down the stairwell, the team in formation.

"Solitary cells first," Alex told her team.

They crept toward the part of the basement with the cells, weapons at the ready, Yoko wedged between Chuck and Patrick.

They reached the four cells, and Hope stepped forward, shining the light from her headlamp into the first cell.

As her beam hit the cell, a howl came from inside so loudly, Alex could feel it rattling in her chest. The moment the sound stopped, four vampires leapt through the doors, one from each cell.

The team was ready, and Hope, Patrick, Ed, and Chuck all sprang into action.

Hope fired a moment before the rest of the team, and her shot was true. Her shotgun removed everything from above the nose of the vampire. Ed and Patrick acted almost as one, putting three rounds each into the chests of their respective vamps with their automatic weapons.

Alex walked the line of cells, checking each one and putting an extra bullet in the heart of each vampire.

"That was damn nice work, team," she told them. She looked at Yoko. "Time to do your thing, girl."

They headed for the utility area, and Yoko went to work.

After only a few minutes, Yoko stood up and smiled. "This is better than I'd expected. They had a backup generator hooked up. It's one of the old-fashioned ones that uses gasoline, so we'll have to replace it with one that uses biodiesel. But once we do that, we'll have power."

Alex clapped her on the back and forced a smile onto her face. Once they had power, Fleming would be one step closer to making Resettlement a reality. "That's excellent. What do you say we head back to *New Haven* and give them the good news?"

Yoko's smile widened. "Now, that's an idea I can get behind."

9

FIREFLY STOOD in front of the gathered recruits, watching as they ran through hand-to-hand combat drills. There were one hundred and fifty of them lined in front of him, all former badges. They'd taken nearly half the badges to make this happen. Colonel Kurtz hadn't been pleased, but Fleming had insisted. Getting a group that already had some training was the only way that they were going to have any chance of meeting Fleming's insane timeline.

This would only be half the Resettlers. The rest of them would come from other departments and would each bring specialized skills needed for survival. They'd have engineers, farmers, electricians, and more. Firefly had a lot of work left ahead of him before they'd be ready.

Still, he was pleased that they had forward momentum. And apparently, that was what the people of *New Haven* wanted to see. Sure, there were some who hated Fleming for what he'd done to the Council. But, to Firefly's surprise, many believed that the explosion had been an accident. And plenty who didn't seemed willing to look past that as long as Fleming continued to deliver results. Never mind how he'd gotten power, at least he was getting them one step closer to the surface.

A wave of nausea rolled through Firefly at the thought of what had happened to the Council and his own role in it. Not that he'd known what would happen. Granted, he'd have been a fool to believe Fleming had a happy plan for the explosives Firefly had provided. But he'd never imagined they'd be used to orchestrate an actual coup.

But what was he going to do about it now? He couldn't change the past; he could only do his best to make sure it was all worth it.

Most of the time, he believed that, but sometimes, he had the sneaking suspicion that nothing he could do would make up for helping to kill twelve people.

As if conjured by his thoughts, a familiar voice came from behind him.

"They look good," Fleming said.

Firefly nodded. "They've got a long way to go, sir, but they're an impressive group already."

Fleming clapped him on the shoulder. "Did you ever think you'd been leading so many?"

Firefly considered that a moment. The week or so since his return to *New Haven* had been a whirlwind, one in which his life had changed in countless ways. Ten days ago, he'd been a member of the GMT, and that team had been his world. True, he'd believed in Fleming and in Resettlement, but there had been something academic about the whole politics thing. It had been a hobby; the GMT was his life.

Then he'd returned from Agartha and found Fleming in charge of the whole damn city. The politician had been quick to show Firefly his appreciation for providing the explosives that had finished off the Council. He'd offered

Firefly his choice of a number of positions in his administration, and Firefly had selected this one.

Firefly had always known that CB didn't respect his leadership abilities. And now look at him. He was on the vanguard of humanity's future.

"I always knew I'd lead someday," Firefly answered. "I just didn't know it would be so many. Or so soon."

Fleming grinned at him. "I appreciate you stepping up." He nodded toward the recruits. "They doing all right?"

Firefly nodded. "As well as can be expected. Honestly, sir, it's not the people I'm worried about. It's the supplies."

"I understand. But I'm going to need a little trust on that one. Brian McElroy and his team are working around the clock on the daylights. They're a little behind schedule, but we'll make sure they are ready when we are."

"It's not just the lights."

"Engineering is stripping everything they can from the ship to make generators. People are going to have to do without some things for a while."

Firefly cast a nervous glance at Fleming. "Are they going to be okay with that?"

"They won't be thrilled about it. But as long as we keep our forward momentum, they'll accept it." He turned and looked at Firefly, his eyes alive with passion. "That's the key to this whole thing. It's dangerous, it's costly, and it requires every person on this ship to make sacrifices. If we keep running at our goal, the people will go along with us. But if we blink, even for a second, so will they."

Firefly nodded slowly. "I'll leave the politics stuff to you, and I'll stick to the guns. By the way, what's going on with General Craig?"

"The trial's been set for next month. It'll be nice to finally have all that behind us."

"Yeah." Firefly hoped his voice conveyed more confidence than he felt. In truth, he still didn't understand what grounds they even had to put Craig on trial. He'd tried to stop a coup. Yes, someone had gotten hurt, but hadn't Fleming hurt people, as well?

And if Craig were found guilty, how would CB and his team react? Firefly had to believe they wouldn't watch their leader's execution without reacting. Any vehemence they felt toward Fleming would only be increased once their general was gone for good.

Fleming clapped Firefly on the shoulder again. "You need to trust me, Firefly. Focus on getting these folks ready to defend our new home. I'll take care of everything else."

"Of course, sir." He hesitated. There was something else he'd been wanting to discuss with Fleming, but the moment hadn't felt right yet.

Fleming tilted his head. "What is it? Something you want to say?"

Firefly cleared his throat. "Yes, sir. It's just...I'm a captain now. Firefly was a lieutenant for the GMT. I'm not that man anymore."

It took Fleming a moment to get it. Then realization dawned. "You want to go by your real name."

"Yes, sir, I do. It's Gar—"

"I know your name." He smiled and nodded toward the recruits. "All right then. Captain Garrett Eldred, I'll be back to check on your progress later in the week."

Garrett smiled. "Thank you, sir. I'll have them ready when you need them."

"Good. Because we are heading down to the surface at the end of the month."

———

ALEX SCANNED the basement with her eyes as Yoko loaded her equipment into her pack. "You're sure we got what we need?"

The engineer shrugged. "As sure as I can be without checking the other buildings. Everything in this one seems in order." She paused a moment, shooting Alex a look. "That was not a suggestion that we clear out the other buildings, by the way. This was more than enough excitement for one day."

As Yoko finished packing, Alex turned to the rest of the team. "Form up around our engineer friend, same as on the way down here. Chuck, you still good to take point?"

He nodded briskly.

"Good. Who wants the anchor position?"

"I got it," Hope said.

"Fine," Alex said. "The rest of you form up around Yoko. Don't assume there aren't any more of our Feral friends in here."

"Feral?" Ed asked.

Alex hadn't realized she'd used the term. "Yeah. It's, uh, something the people of Agartha call the wild vampires."

"Heh," Ed laughed. "Wild vampires. Are there any other kind?"

Alex didn't have time for this discussion now. She'd explained Agartha to the team at a high level: that another city existed in the Colorado mountains, and that the GMT had been saved by the people of the city. She'd left out the part about their saviors being of the non-breathing variety.

Patrick frowned as Hope took up her position at the rear of the team. "You just wanted anchor so you could get a shot at another vampire if one comes up behind us."

Hope didn't bother denying it. "If we're not counting the

ones we shot in the doorway, the score's tied up. One kill each."

"Yeah, yeah," Patrick grumbled.

Yoko slipped her arms through the straps of the pack and hoisted it to her back.

"Let's move out," Alex said.

They made their way through the basement and reached the staircase. Chuck led them up the stairs, Alex close behind.

She was about six stairs up when she heard a growl from below. She turned just in time to see a vampire leap from the darkness beneath the stairs.

Hope stood at the bottom of the stairs. She pointed her shotgun at the creature, but it was on her in the blink of an eye, grabbing the barrel, ripping the weapon from her grasp before she could fire.

The vampire lunged, crashing into Hope. The momentum sent both of them careening to the floor.

"Holy shit!" Ed yelled.

The entire team had their weapons pointed at the vampire, but the way it was tangled up with Hope, there was no way to get a clear shot.

Light from a headlamp flashed off of fangs a moment before they sank into the upper, unprotected part of Hope's neck. She shouted in pain, thrashing, trying to get out of the creature's grasp.

Alex tried to push her way down the stairs to help her friend, but the narrow staircase was too crowded. She couldn't get past her teammates and the engineer.

The vampire stood, holding Hope in its arms. Its teeth were still buried in her neck, and the slurping sounds made it clear that it was still feasting on her blood. Smoke rose from its lower jaw, the part in contact with the silver mail that Hope wore, but it didn't seem to notice.

As it drank, it began to change. The color of its skin shifted, changing from dead gray to white, then to tan. Its ears shrank and grew round, appearing more human by the moment. The wing-like flaps of skin between its arms and body shriveled and fell away.

Alex barely noticed. The only thing she was focused on was that she had a clear shot. She squeezed off two quick rounds, and the back of the vampire's head disappeared in a cloud of mist.

Hope fell from the vampire's limp arms, and the creature collapsed.

Alex fired again, putting a round through the creature's chest. Though she was silent, inside she was screaming. Her worst nightmare was coming true.

She should have seen that vampire under the stairs. Had it been there all along? Had they even checked when they first came down? Or had it snuck down the steps while they worked on the electrical equipment?

It didn't matter now. All that mattered was Hope. Maybe it wasn't too late for her.

"Chuck, Ed, you two get Yoko to safety. Patrick, help me get Hope. Everyone stay alert."

She squeezed her way to the foot of the stairs and shone her headlamp at Hope. The woman was unconscious, and her neck was torn up pretty good. But there wasn't as much blood as Alex would have expected coming from the wound. Maybe it wasn't as bad as she'd thought.

With Patrick's help, she managed to drag Hope up the stairs and through the building. They made it to the exit and burst into the sunlight.

A wave of relief washed through Alex. They'd made it out.

Owl ran to meet them, medical kit in her hand. She didn't ask what had happened; one look at Hope and she didn't have to.

Alex and Patrick laid Hope down, then Alex looked around, checking her teammates. "Everyone else okay?"

They let her know that they were.

Owl crouched next to Hope and began checking her over. She looked up at Alex. "No pulse."

Ed's eyes grew wide as he stared down at his injured teammate. "What the hell is that?"

Alex followed his gaze. The exposed skin on Hope's face and neck were changing color before their eyes. It turned an angry red, then blisters formed. Thin tendrils of smoke rose from her face.

No, Alex silently pleaded. *Not this. Anything but this.*

Hope's eyes shot open, and she gasped. Springing to her feet, she stumbled forward, her hands clawing at her face as she let out a guttural scream.

Owl stumbled backward, quickly getting away from her teammate.

"Hope!" Alex shouted. "It's okay. You're hurt, but we're going to—"

Hope screamed again, cutting Alex off.

Her wild eyes settled on the entrance to cellblock four, and she dashed toward it, moving with uncanny speed.

When she reached the protective shadows of the entrance, she began frantically tearing at her clothes. Smoke was pouring from her entire body now.

"The silver mail," Chuck whispered, his voice heavy with shock. "If she's...one of them now—"

"I know," Alex said. Time seemed to slow as she strode toward the entrance of the building, pistol in hand.

Hope fell to her knees, and flames burst from her body. The silver mail had set her aflame. Still, her screaming continued.

Alex raised her pistol and fired three rounds.

Thankfully, the screaming finally stopped.

The team stood in shocked silence, and Alex was silent with them. Out of the corner of her eye, she saw Yoko fall to her knees and vomit. The rest of them remained still.

For Alex's part, she kept her eyes on Hope. Her body was still wrapped in silver mail, so it continued to burn even after the vampiric life had gone out of it.

Alex briefly considered saying something. After all, this was the closest thing to a real funeral Hope was ever going to get. No way could they bring that body back to *New Haven*.

But what was there to say? Hope's captain had failed her. She'd been attacked, turned, and died a horrific death.

There were no words. So, Alex just watched. She watched for a long time until the flames finally went out.

10

THE NEXT TWENTY-FOUR hours went by in a strange blur for Alex. Later, she'd remember snippets of events, things that she could vaguely recall saying or doing, but somehow, she felt detached from it all.

She managed to keep it together during the flight back to *New Haven*, staying strong for the team. To her surprise, Patrick was the most distraught. She sat next to him on the flight, talking to him, making sure he was able to hold it together, too.

The next thing she remembered was sitting in CB's office across from CB and Fleming, recounting the events of the mission. She heard her own voice as she told the tale. She sounded detached, objective. She relayed the events as best as she recalled them, doing her best to paint herself neither as the hero nor the villain of the story. It was just a mission that had gone wrong.

When she finished, they all sat in silence for a moment.

CB looked her in the eye. "You did the right thing by putting Hope out of her misery. Even if she hadn't been on fire. We couldn't have doomed her to live like that."

Fleming looked oddly thoughtful. "How long was it from when Hope was bitten to when she changed?"

"Two minutes," Alex guessed. "Maybe two and a half."

Fleming shook his head in amazement.

CB turned to the councilman. "Do you see how dangerous this game is, now? If something like this can happen to the GMT, and *after* they've already cleared out the prison, what chance does Resettlement have?"

"I'm aware of the danger, Colonel." Fleming spoke softly, respectfully, but there was steely resolve in his voice. "We knew there'd be a human cost. Hope knew that, too. This is how we bring humanity home."

As Fleming spoke, Alex felt the control she'd been fighting so desperately to maintain beginning to slip away.

"Are you kidding me, Fleming?" she asked, fury in her voice.

Fleming turned to her, unfazed at the outburst. "Alex, I promise you Hope's death was not in vain. Her blood will help pave the way for our future."

"Are you really this dumb?"

CB started to rise. "Alex, please—"

Fleming held up a hand. "No, it's okay. Have your say, Alex. We've been polite for too long. I want to know what you really think."

That caught Alex off guard, and it gave her pause. But if he wanted to hear what she really thought, she was happy to tell him. "Hope was selected for the GMT because she was one of the most qualified to survive on the surface. That sleepy vampire took her out in twenty seconds. What do you think it could have done to someone without training?"

"I see your point. If the average citizen of *New Haven* went down to that unprotected prison, they'd be torn to shreds."

"Exactly!"

A gentle smile crept across Fleming's face. "But we're not sending them down to an unprotected prison. By the time they Resettle, the place will have power. And daylights. And armed guards manning the walls. They'll be protected."

"Says the man who's never set foot on the surface. Why don't you come down there with us next time? The way I see it, a vampire's fangs are the only things sharp enough to get through your thick skull."

CB's eyes flickered with concern, but he said nothing.

Fleming leaned forward and looked Alex in the eyes. "Thank you. I appreciate your honesty."

"I don't want your damn appreciation. I want your common sense."

He sighed. "Resettlement is moving forward. I'll give the GMT two days off, but then you need to get back to work. You trusted me once before, Alex. I need you to trust me again."

Alex squeezed her eyes shut. She didn't want to think about that now. About how she'd once been a true believer in Fleming. About how she'd smuggled the daylights aboard the away ship for him. She'd been a fool.

Would things be different today if she hadn't done that? Would Hope still be alive? Would Drew? Would Simmons?

Fleming stayed a few more minutes, offering vague platitudes and promises of the glories of Resettlement that would soon be coming. It was all Alex could do not to punch him.

After he left, CB waited a full thirty seconds before speaking. "Take the day. Tomorrow we have to get back to work. First thing, you'll go to Fleming and apologize. Tell him you're on board with the mission. That you've slept on it, and Hope's death has filled you with a burning desire to

Resettle the Earth and destroy every vampire in the world."

"CB—"

"Don't CB me," he said through gritted teeth. "We have a plan. Win over Firefly. Find evidence. Take the power from Fleming. We have to follow it."

She knew he was right. Angry outbursts wouldn't bring Hope back. But if they could stop this premature Resettlement, it could save thousands of others. "Okay. You're right. I'll apologize."

"Good. Then we have to start looking for Hope's replacement."

That stung just as badly, but she'd been through it before, when Wesley had replaced Simmons.

She started to stand, but CB stopped her.

"Alex, I'm so sorry this happened. If you want to talk about—"

"I'm fine."

"I know what it's like to lose someone under your command. I doubt you're fine. But I know you'll learn from it, and I know you'll use the pain to drive you. I'm here if you ever want to talk."

She left CB's and wandered, no destination in mind. As she walked, she let her mind go blank, not thinking about anything.

She wasn't exactly surprised when she found herself at Tankards, the bar in Sparrow's Ridge.

A few of the regulars greeted her when she walked in, a few of whom she knew, and a few she didn't. She was used to that; being on the GMT afforded her a minor celebrity status. She ignored all of them and headed straight to the bar.

The bartender's eyes lit up when he saw her. "Alex, how's the exciting life of the GMT treating you?"

"Two shots, please, and make it quick. How's that for an answer?"

The bartender whistled softly. "That bad, huh? All right. Chaser?"

"Yeah. A third shot."

She knocked back the three shots in quick succession, and the burning sensation brought the image of Hope to mind, and the way she'd screamed as the fire consumed her. For the first time in a while, the desire to see Simmons again hit her hard. It was like a hunger. She would have done anything to hold him, to feel his arms around her.

"Two more shots," she told the bartender. "Same chaser."

The bartender gave her a long look, but he poured what she'd ordered, and that was all that mattered.

The next morning, Alex woke to the sensation of coarse sheets against her bare skin. She opened her eyes and saw a strange ceiling above her. The man beside her snored softly.

Naked, lying next to a man whose name I don't know, and sporting the hangover of a lifetime, she thought. *Cool stress-management techniques, Goddard.*

She wanted to get up, but she knew the nausea would hit her full force once she stood, and she'd most likely vomit. So, she lay where she was, hoping the world would simply disappear.

Maybe CB was right; maybe she wasn't okay.

———

AS THE SUN set outside Agartha, Jaden opened his eyes. It was night, which meant it was time to go to work.

Although he was the commander of the vampires of Agartha and the head of the Agartha defense team, his quarters were no different than those of the other vampires. He had a single twelve-foot-by-twelve-foot room with a closet. Space was at a premium in Agartha. He knew first-hand how difficult it had been to carve the city out of the mountain.

To Jaden, the most important parts of his quarters were the reinforced steel door and the locking system that rivaled a pre-infestation bank vault. Killing a vampire at night—especially one as old as Jaden—was incredibly difficult, but during the day, it was significantly easier. If someone could get into his room while he was sleeping, they could theoreti-cally drive a steel spike through his heart before he even woke up.

He'd been thinking more about this lately, especially since the encounter with Alex Goddard. He was sure that any one of his vampires could take any human one on one even in the day, but the gusto and lack of fear she'd shown in attacking Robert had made his confidence waver.

It helped to know that the security of the room kept everyone out during the daylight hours.

As he always did, he sat up and meditated for a few minutes after he woke. These moments of listening to the world around him were part of his daily routine. Then he got dressed and headed out to his city.

He made his way to his team's command center, and he was surprised to find someone waiting for him.

"George, how are you, man?"

The engineer stood up as Jaden approached, a friendly smile on his face. "I'm doing well. Good sleep?"

"Always. How's our guest?"

"Good." George's eyes drifted to the ceiling. "Very good,

actually. Being around someone from the outside has sort of, I don't know, made me appreciate what we have, you know? And she's been a great help. She's brilliant, and I think she genuinely has the good of her city at heart."

Jaden raised an eyebrow. "And you want to nail her."

George blushed. "No, of course not."

Jaden knew otherwise, but he just shrugged. If George didn't want to talk about it, that was his business.

"Anyway," George continued, "there's something I wanted to discuss with you."

Jaden glanced past George. Through the doorway, he saw Robert and a few other vampires gearing up. "Okay, but we'll have to make it quick. We've got a supply run tonight."

"Yeah, I figured. It won't take long. Jessica's going back to *New Haven* soon. I was thinking it might be a good idea for me to go with her. Might be nice to get a feel for their city. Only seems fair, since we let Jessica visit us."

"And you want to nail her," Jaden said.

George scowled, but didn't deny it this time.

"Tell you what," Jaden said. "I'll reach out to the head of *New Haven*. This Fleming guy. Maybe if I talk to him, he'll listen to reason."

"Do you want me to talk to Jessica about this?"

"In time."

George chuckled and shook his head. "In time. You say that so much, I'm starting to hate that phrase."

Jaden clapped him on the shoulder. "That's the benefit of immortality, my friend. When you've been around as long as I have, rushing from one task to another doesn't seem so important."

After he'd said goodbye to George, Jaden went into the mission center, where Robert was prepping the gear.

The vampires didn't take much along with them on

these runs. They preferred blades to guns, so each was armed with a sword and a good knife. They dressed lightly, even in winter, since the weather didn't affect them. They only other items they carried were large-frame backpacks and Kevlar ropes. The packs were empty now, but if all went well, they'd be loaded with supplies on the return trip.

"How we doing, Robert?" he asked.

Robert grinned as his friend approached. "Not as good as we're going to be in about twenty minutes. Nothing like a supply run on a cold winter night to make you feel alive. Relatively speaking."

Jaden chuckled. "What's on the menu?"

The other vampire glanced at the tablet in front of him. "We're hoping to gather two thousand pounds of deer and elk meat for the humans and at least a thousand feet of copper wire. Some communications problem, I guess. I'm taking a team of ten." He glanced up at Jaden. "You don't have to go, you know. We've got it covered."

Jaden had little involvement in the logistics of these missions. Robert was perfectly capable of handling the details, and Jaden had bigger-picture things to concern him. That didn't mean he was going to sit inside while his buddies ran through the mountains gathering supplies.

"Are you kidding? I need this. I go a little stir-crazy if I don't get out of the city now and then."

Robert shrugged. "You're the boss."

"And don't you forget it," Jaden said with a smile.

Tonight, like most nights, they would be traveling by foot. Their destination was Colorado Springs, a once-great city that still held plenty of supplies. It was only a short run for vampires who could sprint the entire distance without tiring. Traveling under their own power was more satisfying than driving; it seemed to soothe the savagery that lived deep inside all of them. Besides, vehicles increased the chance of attracting Ferals.

Once the team was geared up, they headed for the exit. They stopped at the first set of blast doors and checked the cameras, to make sure the area outside was clear of Ferals before opening them.

At the second set of doors, they checked the monitors one more time.

"Looks like we're clear," Jaden said. "Shut down the auto turrets."

"Roger that." Robert did as ordered, and the twelve vampires exited Agartha.

With his first step outside, Jaden felt more alive. More *wild*. Though the cold wind didn't affect him, he could feel it brushing his skin, waking up his senses. The smells flooding his nose, the stars overhead, the rustling of the wind, it all felt right.

The team started slowly, jogging up the hill of dead Ferals that had been mowed down by the automated turrets over the past months. As they reached the perimeter, the vampires stopped. They saw something truly unexpected.

"What the hell?" Robert asked.

Fifty feet ahead of them, two naked men stood in the snow.

Jaden sniffed the air.

No, not men. These were vampires. But not Ferals. True vampires.

The two vampires took a few steps toward the team. One of them mumbled through frozen lips, "Help us."

Every vampire on the team turned slowly to look at Jaden.

"You heard him," Jaden said. "Help them."

As his team rushed to assist the two pitiful creatures, Jaden couldn't help but smile. For the first time in a long time, he was truly surprised. Maybe the world was still an interesting place.

11

JADEN AND ROBERT sat on one side of a table, and the two vampires sat on the other. They were in a locked room with vaulted doors, and the two strangers were wrapped in blankets to cover themselves.

So far Jaden hadn't been able to get much information out of the two. They hadn't even given their names; they'd just begged for blood. They'd gone berserk when they'd entered Agartha and smelled the humans. It had been all the team could do to drag them into the vault.

These two looked like true vampires, but they were behaving almost like Ferals. Jaden knew that could only mean one thing: they were starving.

"Please," the one with sandy-colored hair said, his eyes pleading. "Let me have one person. You have plenty to spare. I smelled them."

Jaden and Robert exchanged a glance.

"Who's your master?" Jaden asked.

"Please," the other vampire said. "We need blood."

Someone pounded on the door, and Robert went to answer. He came back a moment later with two packs of blood and a bundle of clothes. He set them on the table, and the two vampires snatched up the bags of blood.

They tore into them with their fangs and devoured every drop.

Jaden and Robert waited in silence while the vampires drank.

When they'd finished, they seemed more in control. The wild look was gone from their eyes.

"Thank you," the sandy-haired one said.

Jaden nodded. They waited in silence while the vampires dressed.

When they'd finished, Jaden asked for their names once again.

"I'm Mark," the sandy-haired one said.

"Aaron," said the other.

"Where'd you come from?"

Aaron shook his head slowly. "I'm not sure. We've been out there a while. We were turned during the third wave of the infestation. Then the humans got scarce. I sort of lost track of time."

"Me, too," Mark agreed.

Jaden paused a moment, considering how to continue. "The third wave was one hundred and fifty years ago."

Mark's eyes widened. "Jesus. You've got to be kidding me."

Jaden assured them he was not.

"This is insane," Aaron said.

"I'm sure it's disorienting," Jaden said.

"Disorienting? It's a hell of a lot worse than that." Aaron sat up straight and looked Jaden in the eye. "You have no idea what it was like. The starvation. More than a hundred years of perpetual pain and torment. My mind went away. It was like being an animal."

"Or being trapped at the bottom of a well," Mark added. The haunted look on his face confirmed how deeply he felt the words. "Sometimes, I could see a pinpoint of light. Like a glimpse of the man I'd once been. Most of the time, the pain blocked out everything else. The memories. Free will. I was operating purely on instinct."

"Same here," Aaron confirmed. "The memories of that time are more like snapshots of feelings. Almost like half-remembered dreams. Then I fed, and my mind came back."

"Fed?" Robert asked. "On who?"

Mark shrugged. "Just some guy. It was in a canyon about two weeks ago. I remember the feeling of surprise at sensing prey for the first time in so long. Then I did what came naturally. As I fed, my mind came back."

"Damn," Robert said. "That's intense."

Jaden nodded his agreement. Two weeks ago... there was only one person they could have fed on.

"Thank God you found us," Mark said. "There's no way we could go back to the way things were. We'd been searching for food every night. Even after only two weeks, our minds were beginning to slip a little."

Aaron said, "Our plan was to walk into the sunlight if we didn't find food soon. Like Mark said, there was no way we were going back."

"Well, I'm glad we were able to help," Jaden offered.

"You guys mind if I ask you something?" Mark nodded at the empty blood bag on the table in front of him. "You clearly have access to blood. You've got a whole herd of them locked up in this mountain, right?"

"It's not like that," Robert said, the hint of a growl in his voice.

"Well, you've got blood. Why aren't you helping the other vampires? Changing them back?"

Jaden thought a moment, considering how much to tell them. The answer came to him quickly. These two were vampires. They needed to know the truth. "Vampires have been around for a very long time, but our numbers have always been controlled. There were always one hundred of us, no more, no less. Then, the infestation happened. It was the first time the supply of humans couldn't keep up with the demand for blood. It was the first time there were ever Ferals, at least as far as I know."

"Ferals?" Aaron asked. "That's what you call them?"

Jaden nodded. "Until tonight, I didn't know they could be changed back. I thought their minds were lost forever. I was hoping they'd die out on their own, eventually. It was the only way to let them out of their misery."

"Huh," Mark said. "And now that you know? You're going to help them?"

Jaden frowned. "What could I do? Look, there's a lot you don't know about this world. There aren't many humans left, not nearly enough to bring all the Ferals back. If we brought too many back, they'd wipe out the humans and we'd *all* starve. So, no, I'm not going to help them."

"Damn," Aaron said. "That's cold. Especially when you haven't felt the hell of starvation firsthand. You're leaving them to a fate you can't understand."

"Maybe not," Jaden said, "but I have to do what's right for me and my people. I hope in time, you'll come to understand my point of view."

Mark and Aaron stared back at him, dour expressions on their faces.

"I know we've hit you with a lot of information," Jaden said. "We're going to give you time to process. You can spend today in here." He gestured to the bunks in the corner.

"We'll bring you more blood tomorrow, after sunset. Until then, try to get some rest."

Jaden started to rise, then he realized there was one more thing he hadn't said to them.

"Welcome to Agartha, gentlemen."

———

GARRETT "FIREFLY" Eldred finished his food and set his utensils on his plate with a satisfied sigh.

The meal had been delicious. How could he have expected anything less? It had been prepared by the best chef on *New Haven*, a woman who normally worked in the Hub's finest restaurant. The way she conjured such a rich array of flavors, textures, and aromas from the airship's limited food supply was a wonder. Tonight, she'd prepared a bean soup and pasta with a rich sauce. The taste of the sauce's slightly tart flavor, with a hint of sweetness, lingered on Garrett's tongue.

Tonight, the celebrated chef was cooking in Fleming's apartment rather than her restaurant.

And why not? It was a celebration. Sarah had finally been released from the hospital. She wasn't completely recovered from the gunshot wound that General Craig had inflicted on her—the doctor said she'd probably always have a bit of a limp—but she was free of the hospital and ready to return to work.

To celebrate, Fleming had invited her and Garrett to his home for dinner. His inner circle, Fleming called them.

Garrett was fairly certain you couldn't make a circle out of two points, but the phrase still filled him with pride. On the GMT, he'd been a member of the team. But he hadn't been Alex. He hadn't been Simmons. When CB wanted to bounce ideas off someone, he would never pick crazy old Firefly. And a promotion? Forget about it. Garrett would have been waiting decades before making captain, if not for Fleming.

He was grateful and excited to be part of Fleming's movement, the movement that would bring humanity back to Earth. Even if he didn't always approve of Fleming's methods.

Fleming raised his glass, a fifty-year-old red wine from his personal collection. "I'd like to raise a toast to the two of you. You believed in me before you had any real reason to think I could accomplish my lofty goals, and you both went to extraordinary lengths to help make our dream a reality. To you."

Garrett's smile wavered. He didn't like to think about those "extraordinary lengths" he'd gone to for Fleming. Still, he forced the smile back onto his face and clinked glasses with the other two.

Fleming took a small sip, then set down his glass. "I didn't just call you here tonight to celebrate."

"Shocker," Sarah said with a chuckle.

Fleming smiled. "So maybe I'm predictable. As we get closer to Resettlement, there's a threat we need to discuss."

"The GMT," Sarah said flatly.

Fleming nodded.

Garrett swallowed hard. They were right. He knew it in his heart. After what had happened with the Council and General Craig, CB would never accept Fleming as the true leader of *New Haven*.

At the same time, the GMT was Garrett's family. Whatever good was in him today was at least in part due to his time in the GMT. The years spent under CB. The battles fought next to Alex and Owl. He'd do what he needed to do when the time came, but it would rip his heart out to go against his friends.

"The GMT is our greatest threat," Fleming said, "but I believe they can also be our greatest ally."

Garrett sat up a bit straighter. Ally? That was a surprise.

"That's where you two come in." He turned to Garrett. "You're our way into the GMT. CB asks about you in every meeting. He still cares about you. That means you have leverage over him."

Garrett swallowed hard.

"The GMT has a lot of missions coming up. They're going to be busy little beavers in the coming weeks. I want you to take a small team, four or five of your most promising recruits, and accompany them on some of the missions."

"Wait, you want me on the surface?"

Fleming nodded. "Just a few times. The purpose is three-fold. One, I'd like you to watch Alex and the team on important missions. Their role is crucial to Resettlement, and I need to make sure they aren't purposely throwing a wrench in things. Secondly, I need you to get close to Alex. Rekindle your friendship. See if there's any way you can convince her to swallow her dislike for me in the interest of Resettlement. Finally—and this is the reason we'll give to CB and Alex for your presence—it'll give your people some much-needed field experience."

Garrett thought about that. Firefly, back with the GMT. He'd never been close friends with Alex, outside of work. In fact, outside of the GMT and the occasional group dinner or night at Tankards, he hardly spent any time with her. He wasn't sure they'd ever had a one-on-one conversation.

And yet, they'd been through so much together. The nuclear plant in Texas. The snowbanks in Colorado. If he could re-establish that bond, it could be his way in. Maybe he could win her over. She'd been a fan of Fleming, once. If he could convince her to get behind Resettlement, maybe he could save the GMT.

If not, Fleming would eventually decide it was time to crush them. There would be a tragic accident, the GMT would perish, and *New Haven* would move on without them. Their old teammate, Firefly, was their only hope.

"I'm on it," he said.

"Good." Fleming turned to Sarah. "I have an even more important job for you. Alex is the face of the GMT, and people love the GMT. But if something happens to her, she can be replaced, and Resettlement can still move forward. There's someone else we *couldn't* resettle without."

"Brian McElroy," Sarah said.

"Exactly. We can't proceed without his brilliance. That's why I need you back working in his lab as quickly as possible."

Sarah raised an eyebrow. "I thought you might have a more important position for me. I mean, after everything I've been through."

"There is no more important position." Fleming touched her arm. "Listen, I understand. The glory will come. You will receive the title and the attention you deserve. But there is real work to do first. I need you to learn everything you can from Brian. Starting with the daylights. I want you to become an expert. Follow him like a shadow. Siphon every brilliant morsel you can from his mind. Just in case."

He stopped for a moment, looking away.

"There's something else?" Sarah said.

Fleming nodded. "Just as importantly, we need to keep Brian happy. Show him that maybe there are other aspects of life just as important as science."

Sarah tilted her head, not getting it yet.

Garrett could see where this was going, and he suddenly felt a bit queasy.

"People like Brian McElroy get caught up in their own heads," Fleming continued. "They need something to connect them to the pleasures of the real world around them. They need something tangible to cling to. When that happens, things like politics start to seem a little less important. You're a beautiful and intelligent woman. I'm sure you can think of a few ways to put him in the right mindset."

For a moment, Garrett thought he saw a flush in Sarah's cheeks. Then it was gone, replaced by a smile.

"I understand," she said. "I'll do what I can—*everything* I can—to win Brian to our side."

"Excellent." Fleming put a hand on both of their shoulders. "My inner circle. That's what I love about you. You can see the big picture, and you're willing to do what it takes to make our dream a reality. That's how we're going to do it. That's how we're going to bring humanity back to the surface."

12

ALEX FOUND Brian in his lab, working on daylights. Now that she thought about it, he'd been in there every time she'd passed by for the last week. If he was sleeping at all, he was being pretty tricky about it.

He smiled brightly when he saw her, and the circles under his eyes seemed to fade a little with the smile.

"Hey, Captain! How you been?"

Alex shrugged. "Not bad. Busy saving the world."

"Same here." He leaned a bit closer and lowered his voice so the technicians working on the other side of the laboratory wouldn't hear. "Word is you're going down to see our friends in Agartha again."

She nodded. "Fleming says it's time for Jessica to come home. He wants her intel. That's sort of why I'm here. Is there somewhere more private we can talk?"

He led her to his office, an eight-by-ten-foot room with a single window that looked out on the lab. It was cluttered with stacks of paper and half-constructed gizmos that Alex couldn't identify. He hurriedly moved an old hard drive off of a chair so Alex could sit.

"I hear Sarah's coming back?" she asked, as he moved the junk off of his own chair.

"That, she is. Made a full recovery, I guess. I'll be glad to see her. I'll just have to make sure everything's nailed down before she gets here. Things have a way of walking off and showing up in Fleming's hands when she's around. No offense."

Alex held up her hands. "Hey, I'm guilty as charged. I own up to my role in taking those daylights."

"The difference is, you've changed. She hasn't." His expression turned dour for a moment, then he forced a smile onto his face. "What did you want to talk to me about?"

Alex scooted forward in her chair. "It's about the trip to Agartha. I need to figure out a way to speak with Jaden."

"The head vampire?"

Alex nodded. "I was wondering if you could help me arrange a plausible breakdown for the away ship."

He leaned back in his chair, lacing his fingers behind his head. "I see. You need to be there at night."

"Exactly. The ship's a backup. It shouldn't raise too many eyebrows if it breaks down, right?"

Brian frowned. "Fleming's a lot of things, Alex, but he's not an idiot. If you spend the night down there, he's not going to believe it's an accident. The guy's already suspicious of us. If you do this, he might stop playing politics and decide it's time to throw you in a cell. Or worse."

She sighed. "That's kinda what I was thinking, too. I was hoping you'd do your genius thing and come up with a workable solution."

Brian leaned forward, and his chair let out a high-pitched squeak. "Look, as good as you are at combat, as good as I am at mechanical engineering, Fleming's just that good at politics. He's three steps ahead of us. He'll see through any breakdown ruse."

"I guess you're right."

"I know I am. You said it yourself: I'm a genius."

Alex laughed.

"Look, you really need to talk to Jaden? You're going to have to do it during the day. Get into Agartha fast, get all the information you can, but make sure you get back here before sundown."

After Alex left Brian's office, she went to see CB. Technically, he had an office at the Hub to go along with his fancy colonel title, but he still seemed to spend all his time at GMT headquarters. She found him in his sparse old office, angrily tapping away at the tablet in front of him.

He didn't look up as she entered. He just kept typing with his index fingers. His fingernails made a loud click every time they came down on the screen.

"You don't have to type that hard, Colonel," she said. "You keep pounding away at it like that, you're going to either break the screen or your fingernails."

He grunted. "You know what the most significant change that comes with a promotion is, Goddard? It's not pay. It's not respect. It's paperwork. If I knew being a colonel involved filling out so many forms, I would have stayed a lieutenant."

Alex lowered herself into the seat across from him. "That bad?"

He set the tablet on the desk and looked at her. "I've got engineering up my ass wanting to know why we're using so much power, so I've got to fill out a report to keep them happy. Agriculture is requesting some damn seed found only in central Asia, so I've got to prioritize that request. The badges are so depleted from the way Firefly cherry-picked half their officers that they're asking for the GMT to pull shifts for them, and I need to put together a detailed breakdown of our time that proves we can't help. On top of that, Fleming is ordering more missions in the next few weeks than would be humanly possible for a team of fifty."

He gestured at the cast on his arm.

"And that's not to mention this damn thing. I can't wait for it to come off next week."

Alex whistled softly. "And to think, I thought fighting vampires was the tough part."

A slight smile crossed CB's face. "Speaking of fighting, I heard you had quite the evening the night before last."

She suddenly wished blushing was a voluntary action. "I'm sure I don't know what you're talking about."

"Oh?" he asked. "I received a report of an extremely drunk young woman causing a scene at Tankards."

"Not uncommon," she countered. "Why would you think it was me?"

"This young woman knocked out three bouncers."

She winced. "Guess that explains my bruised knuckles."

His face grew serious. "Alex, I'm here if you want to talk. And I don't mean that in some bullshit, theoretical way. I'm really here. Right now."

"I know that. Thanks, CB. I'm just not ready to talk about it. Not yet."

He nodded. "Okay. I can respect that. What time are you and Owl off to get Jessica?"

She sat up a little, happy the conversation had moved on from her emotional state. "About an hour."

"Good. And you will be back around eighteen hundred hours?"

Something about the way he said it made her think this

wasn't just a casual line of questioning. "Yeah. Why you want to know?"

He looked away. "No reason. I just thought I might meet you when you come back. To make sure you made it safely. And Owl. And, you know, Jessica."

It all clicked, and Alex smiled. "CB, why didn't you ever tell me you had a thing for Jessica?"

"It's not like that. I just want to make sure you get back safely."

She didn't have any interest in his coy games. Not after everything that had happened. "You should go for it."

For a moment, he looked like he was going to protest again, but instead he said, "You really think so?"

"I do. And don't wait. We both know nothing's guaranteed. Make the time you have the best it can be." She stood up and started to go.

Then CB called her back. "Alex, I need you to do something for me when you get back tonight. Something dangerous."

She turned back to him, her interest piqued. "What is it?"

"I need you to get a tape from a camera."

———

OWL BEGAN her descent toward Agartha about thirty minutes after sunrise local time.

Alex had been quiet for most of the trip, thinking about the covert mission CB had given her, and what it would mean for the future of *New Haven* if she could get that tape.

Now that they were getting close, she needed to focus on the task at hand.

"No facts this time?" Alex asked Owl.

Owl glanced at her, annoyed. "First, this isn't a real mission."

"How is it not a real mission? You owe me facts, Owl!"

The pilot ignored the comment. "Second, I don't know shit about this place. That's why we're here, right? To learn."

Alex couldn't argue with that. Instead, she picked up the radio and contacted Agartha. She smiled when the person on the other end handed the radio to Jessica.

"Alex! I can't wait to see you."

"Same here. *New Haven* is falling apart without you."

There was a pause. "Wait, really?"

Alex laughed. "No. Not yet, anyway. But it will eventually if we don't get you back there."

"Roger that, Lieutenant."

"I'm a captain now. But, listen, I have a favor to ask. I need to speak with Jaden."

She heard a bit of rustling on the other end, then a male voice came through. "Alex, it's George. Listen, I'm sure Jaden would be happy to talk to you, but it's a little sunny for his tastes. He'll be sleeping until tonight."

"I get that, but this is important."

"Really, Alex, I can't just—"

"George, I'm going to pound on his door until he answers. You might as well cut out the middleman and wake him up yourself."

She heard Jessica in the background say, "She'll do it, too."

George sighed. "I'll see what I can do."

An hour later, she was following George down a long, stone hallway. Jaden had agreed to see her, but only in his quarters, and only alone.

George cleared his throat. "It's really saying something that he agreed to this. He must like you."

"That, or he's hungry," Alex quipped.

"Uh, yeah, about that..."

Alex paused mid-stride. "Wait, I don't actually have to be worried about him trying to eat me, do I?"

"No, of course not! I just meant... Well, he's going to have day sickness. He might not exactly be at the height of good spirits. He'd never do anything to hurt you, but..."

"That doesn't mean he won't bite my head off."

George chuckled. "Metaphorically, yes."

He stopped in front of a steel door with an impressive-looking locking mechanism. "Here we go."

He rapped on the door three times.

"Come," a low voice said, through the door.

George pushed the door opened and gestured for her to go inside. "Have fun."

Alex walked into a dimly lit room. She blinked hard, trying to force her eyes to adjust, but she could only see vague shapes.

"Alex," Jaden said, in a shaky voice. "I hear you wanted a word."

"Thank you, I do. Any chance we can get some light in here?"

"Right. Sorry. Light isn't so necessary for vampires."

"Must be nice."

"It has its moments. Daytime generally isn't among them."

A light came on, illuminating the small room. It was adorned with nothing but a single bed, a desk, and a chair. Since Jaden was sitting on the bed, she took the chair.

He was shirtless, and he wore loose cotton pants. An odd choice for a meeting, but she couldn't exactly blame him. She'd woken him at an inopportune time.

"Sorry about all this," she said. "I needed to talk to you, and I can only come down here during the day, so—"

He held up a hand. "It's fine. Let's talk."

She looked at his face, at first, only to avoid staring at his sculpted chest and solid shoulders. But then she noticed something. The usual look of concentration was gone, as was the hint of laughter that normally lived at the corners of his eyes. He looked to be in a sort of daze. Even the way he moved was odd and exaggerated. Like he lacked fine-motor skills.

Day sickness, she realized.

As if reading her thoughts, he rubbed at his temples. "You'll have to forgive me for not standing to greet you. I didn't think you'd want to see me stumble around like an idiot. My legs don't work so well in the daytime. Or my hands. I can barely hold a pencil." He glared up at her. "A less trusting man might suspect you're trying to have this conversation while I'm mentally weak. Perhaps you think I'll let some useful information slip." There was a hint of a growl in his voice. "That's not what you're up to, is it?

"It's not like that," she quickly responded. "I agreed to meet you alone in your quarters. We both know you could kill me in five seconds, flat."

"I'm tired," he said. "It might take six."

"Regardless, I'm trusting you. I'm asking that you trust me in return."

"Fine. Then talk."

She swallowed hard, wondering if this had been a mistake. It wasn't just his movements he was having a hard time controlling. It was his emotions, too. Anger bubbled under his words, like he might lunge at her at any moment.

"I was wondering if you might be able to tell me more about vampires."

"That's why you woke me?" he snapped at her. "For a history lesson?"

"Yes. But there's a reason. The people of *New Haven* want to resettle the Earth."

He was silent for a long moment, then he said, "Go on."

She told him about the mission at the prison, being as honest and forthcoming as she could, in the hopes it would lead him to do the same. Jessica had already told him about Resettlement, so there was no need to hide it.

She told about the way the vampires had first gathered at the doors of the buildings, but had later stopped doing so. And, as painful as it was, she told him about Hope's death.

"I'm wondering if you can shed any light on what happened. How did the vampires work together so well? How did they know what was happening in other buildings? Why did that vampire start to change when it fed on Hope?"

Jaden was quiet a moment before answering. "Thank you."

"For what?"

"For putting your trust in me. I'll do the same. I'll tell you what I know."

Alex leaned forward, and as she listened to him speak, the bit of fear she'd been holding on to at being alone in a twelve-by-twelve room with a vampire slipped away.

He closed his eyes as he spoke, as if relaying this information clearly was taking all his concentration.

"Vampires have a sort of a psychic link," he said. "We can't communicate mentally with words, but we can share emotions. General concepts. For example, if you were to attack me right now, assuming I felt I was in danger, every vampire in Agartha would sense it and come running."

"I wasn't planning on it before," Alex said dryly, "and now I'm *really* not."

He opened his eyes and looked at her. "We can also communicate slightly more complex concepts. For instance, if I wanted the vampires to meet me in the control room, I could communicate that mentally, as well as a general notion of how urgent the request was."

"Huh. And Ferals can do this too?"

His face darkened. "Before this conversation, I wasn't sure. But from what you're saying, the answer must be yes. It could be even more powerful in Ferals than in true vampires. Their minds aren't clouded by complex thought. They live purely by emotion and instinct. It would make sense that they would be able to work as a group even more effectively. As to your other question, Ferals who feed can return to true vampire form."

Alex frowned. She'd suspected as much, based on what she'd seen in prison. "Have you or the other vampires here ever been Ferals?"

"No," he answered quickly, almost as if the question offended him. "Let me ask you something. Do you know how the vampires overtook humanity so suddenly?"

Alex shrugged. "They're stronger and faster than us. And we're very tasty, apparently."

A hint of annoyance crept into Jaden's eyes. "You're going to have to do better than that if you want to keep humanity alive."

Now Alex frowned. "Okay, so tell me. Only one of us was there."

"That, I was. In fact, I'm over one thousand years old."

She watched him for a long moment, trying to tell if he was joking. "Bullshit."

"It's not. The reason vampires never overran humanity prior to the infestation is due to a curiosity of our genetics.

A vampire has complete control over any human they induct into the vampire race."

"Wait, like mind control?"

"Of a sort. It fades over time, but for the first one hundred years or so, the new vampire is under the complete control of its master. I look at it as a defense mechanism built into our species. It prevents overpopulation. No young vampire can create a new vampire of his own unless his master allows it. We managed to keep the vampire population to exactly one hundred for centuries, only allowing a new one to be inducted when another died."

"So how did it go wrong? How did it go from one hundred to eleven billion?"

Jaden considered that a moment. "That's a very long story and it includes many small errors by many people, including me. And one massive error, committed by someone I trusted." He looked up, meeting her eye. "I'll tell you sometime, but not now. Not while I'm day sick. The important thing to know is that if a Feral turns a human, it will be under the complete control of that Feral."

"Holy hell." Alex considered the ramifications. "So, if you were to turn me right now, you could make me radio *New Haven*, have them send a transport into a trap, give them false information, anything."

Jaden nodded. "Now you know the real danger of humans coming to the surface. There were leaders on your ship with all of this information, and in a few generations, you have all but forgotten your lessons. It's insane. The good news is, the Ferals have been starving for so long, there is almost no chance they would have the restraint to turn a human. It's much more likely they'd drink them dry and leave them dead. Turning a human is difficult for any vampire; you have to fight the instinct to drain them fully."

He said it flippantly, as casually as a human might talk about the weather.

In that moment, Alex could no longer ignore what he was. In a thousand years of life, how many humans had he killed? Hundreds? Thousands?

He looked at Alex, seeing the disgust on her face. "You are so very young, but I like you. Your heart is in this thing, I can tell. I am your ally in this mission to save the human race. Now take this information back to *New Haven*, and make your leaders see. I need to sleep."

13

"You wouldn't believe it. It's like they've had this technology so long, they don't even realize how incredible it is. It's like if someone from a city without electric lights came to *New Haven* and we were like 'yeah, electric lights, no big deal.'"

"Yeah, Jessica, sounds fascinating." Alex looked at Owl and the two exchanged a glance, confirming that Jessica's monologue about Agartha's use of electromagnetics was going over both their heads.

They were on their way back to *New Haven*, and Jessica was talking a mile a minute, beyond excited about the things she'd seen in Agartha. The three of them were crammed into the cockpit, Owl in the pilot's seat, Alex in the copilot's seat, and Jessica in the rarely used jump seat that was normally folded into the wall.

"The electromagnetic elements they use for railguns have so many other uses," Jessica said. "The fact that they haven't considered how it could be used to increase the efficiency of motor relay systems is just silly." She let out a laugh, as if she couldn't believe the ridiculousness of it all.

"Yeah, it's so obvious," Owl said.

Jessica didn't seem to notice her sarcasm.

Owl tapped Alex on the arm. "Hey, you okay? You've been staring off into space for twenty minutes."

Alex looked up and forced a smile onto her face. In truth, she'd been lost in thought, only partly paying attention to Jessica's techno-babble. "I'm fine."

For a moment, it seemed like Owl was going to accept that answer. Then she said, "No you're not. What did Jaden tell you?"

"A lot, actually." She gave them a summary of what she'd learned about the vampires' mental connection, the way Ferals return to human-like form, and the way that masters could control the former humans that they turned.

"Damn," Owl said when Alex had finished. "That all sounds like information that would have been good to know before we went on our first mission to the surface."

Jessica chuckled. "Would you still have joined the GMT?"

"And risk being some vampire's mind-controlled puppet?" She shrugged. "I don't know. But I certainly would have more seriously considered my mother's recommendation of going into agriculture."

Alex forced a laugh.

"We have to tell Fleming," Jessica said. "We can make him understand."

Alex shook her head. "We should try, but I'm not hopeful. Fleming sees himself as this great savior of humanity. We can throw all the facts at him we want, but he's still going to go forward with Resettlement. We can't trust him to stop it. It's up to us."

Owl glanced at Alex nervously. "How the hell are we supposed to do that?"

"CB and I have a plan, but we have to play our cards right. The two of you are going to be key to pulling this off."

Two hours later, Alex, CB, and Jessica sat down in Fleming's office in the Hub for Jessica's debriefing. They were seated around a large round table.

It took all of Alex's willpower to not let out a laugh when CB took the seat next to Jessica.

"Should we get started?" CB asked.

"Not yet," Fleming said. "We're waiting for one more."

Alex and CB exchanged a curious glance, both wondering who it might be.

A moment later, the door opened, and Firefly walked in.

"Sorry I'm late." He nodded hello to Alex and CB.

For the second time in a minute, Alex stifled the urge to laugh. This was the first time she'd seen Firefly since his promotion. The captain's uniform looked odd on him, and he had an air of formality that didn't seem to fit with the man she knew.

"How you been, Firefly?" Alex asked.

He glanced awkwardly at Fleming before answering. "I've been good. But I'm, uh, not going by Firefly anymore. Call me Garrett."

Alex raised an eyebrow. "Garrett?"

He smiled weakly. "That's my first name."

"Huh."

Fleming rapped a knuckle on the table. "As fascinating as this all is, I'd prefer we spend our time talking about the city of intelligent vampires. Jessica, give us the rundown. What did you learn in Agartha?"

Jessica smiled. "A lot. Agartha has an electromagnetic component they're using for weapons. I believe we could use the same technology to improve the efficiency of our motors up to twenty percent. And that's just the start. The agricultural techniques they use could allow us to increase our crop output and actually use less resources and square footage."

As she spoke, Fleming's face darkened. "I'm sorry, maybe I didn't state my question clearly. I'm glad you learned about some new technologies, but that's not what I was asking. In case you hadn't noticed, our focus isn't on improving the ship; it's on getting off it. What did you learn about our potential enemies?"

Jessica blinked hard, taken aback. "I *am* telling you what I learned. And you might think of them as enemies, but they don't see us that way. They were happy to share."

"How very naive of them," Fleming commented.

"Regardless, we should learn everything we can. We have to get Brian down there as soon as possible. It would blow his mind. He might never sleep again, he'd be so excited."

"I don't think we should put the greatest mind in our community at risk by sending him to a foreign and possibly hostile city."

Jessica's face reddened. "Yes, but you'll gladly send your top engineer."

Fleming paused, gathered himself. "I apologize, Jessica. I didn't mean to imply you are expendable."

"That's okay," Jessica replied. "I didn't mean to imply 'fuck you.'"

CB cleared his throat. "Okay, let's all focus on why we're here."

"Yes, let's." If Fleming was thrown by the comment, he didn't let it show. He'd lost control of the conversation for a moment, and it had clearly rattled him. But he was back now. "I don't mean to diminish the engineering marvels, but what other, non-technological information did you learn? Tell us about the city."

Jessica hesitated, her face still flushed with anger.

Alex tried unsuccessfully to catch her eye, willing her to keep things civil. They needed to keep the peace with Fleming. At least, on the surface.

After a moment, the engineer spoke. "The people in the city seem happy. They interact with the vampires as much as their conflicting sleep schedules allow. The vampires feed off blood donated by humans, never directly from the people."

Firefly leaned forward. "Did they give any indication of their feelings toward *New Haven*?"

"No, they didn't reveal any secret plans to attack us, Firefly," she snapped.

"It's Garrett," he reminded her. "Do you really think they have our best interests in mind?"

Fleming held up a hand, stopping his captain. "No need to speculate. If they were planning something, they wouldn't be dumb enough to share it with someone from *New Haven*. What I'm more curious about is their defenses."

Jessica hesitated again, but not as long, this time. "Their security is insane."

"Care to be more specific?" he asked.

"Sure. Fifty-caliber railguns around the perimeter. Cameras everywhere. The place is built into the side of a mountain. And if you somehow did manage to get inside, you'd have one hundred intelligent vampires waiting to rip out your throat."

Alex looked at Fleming. "Tell me you're not considering an assault on Agartha."

"Of course not, but it is smart to be prepared for all possibilities."

CB turned to Jessica. "What's your gut feeling on the city?"

"It's filled with people just trying to get through the day. People with families. People with dreams. All of them doing whatever they can not to think about the horrors that live outside their city. In other words, they're just like us."

Fleming thought a moment. "Their head vampire, this Jaden, he contacted me early this morning, just before sunrise their time."

CB and Alex exchanged a surprised glance.

"I spoke to him briefly. It was fascinating. He sounded almost like a real person."

"What did he want?" CB asked.

"He had the ridiculous idea that one of their people should come spend time on *New Haven* the same way Jessica spent time in their city."

"What did you tell him?" Jessica asked.

"I said I'd think about it. Needless to say, that's one call I won't be returning. They may be dumb enough to let a spy into their midst, but we are not."

———

AARON HADN'T KNOWN what to expect when Jaden told him he and Mark would be starting their new jobs that night. He'd imagined it would involve venturing out of the city to gather supplies. Or to hunt. But he certainly hadn't expected this.

They stood in a storeroom the size of a football field (ah, football, how he missed watching it on Sundays), surrounded by large shelving units filled with carefully labeled crates.

If Mark's crossed arms and dour expression were any

indication, he was just as unhappy about their current situation as Aaron was.

Jaden and Robert stood in front of them, along with a vampire whose name Aaron couldn't quite remember. Toby? Tommy? Something like that.

"Your training begins tonight," Jaden told them. "Every human and every vampire in Agartha needs to earn his or her keep. You two are no exception. You will be expected to pull your weight, and that starts now."

"In the storeroom?" Mark asked.

Jaden nodded. "As vampires, you fall under my jurisdiction. So, your duty is whatever I say it is. Be happy I don't have you scrubbing toilets." His tone softened a little. "Do what's asked of you without complaint. Earn our trust. If you can manage that, you'll move on to more fulfilling tasks in time. You're immortal—be patient."

Robert then explained their duties. They'd be performing maintenance in the storeroom, as well as moving and cataloging the supplies that came in and out. Toby would train them, and eventually, he'd move on, leaving them in charge of the storeroom.

"Lucky us," Mark muttered.

Thankfully, neither Jaden nor Robert seemed to notice the comment.

"Like Jaden said, work hard and you will be rewarded," Robert told them. "Any questions?"

"Yeah." Mark turned to Jaden. "What's the long-term plan, here?"

Jaden glanced at his watch as he answered. "What long term plan are you referring to?"

"I'm talking about the Feral vampires suffering right outside your door." There was a hint of anger creeping into

Mark's voice now. "When are you going to help them? What's the plan to rebuild society?"

Jaden regarded Mark for a long moment before answering. "Let me ask you a question. Do you like your accommodations? Do you like having a regular supply of blood delivered to your door every night just after sunset?"

Aaron answered before Mark could. "Yes. We do."

"Good. You need to understand that these things are only possible because of the careful balance we're maintaining. We've kept that balance for one hundred and fifty years, and it's kept both the vampires and the humans alive and well fed."

"Some of the vampires," Mark clarified.

"Sure. But you have to remember we're playing the long game here. For now, you can either choose to be part of this city and assist in its operation, or you can go try your luck elsewhere."

"We're staying," Aaron said quickly. He wanted to hit Mark. As much as he agreed with the other vampire's sentiments, there was no need to say it out loud. Not when he knew it would piss off their benefactor.

"Okay, then," Jaden said. "We've already upset the balance by adding two more vampires to the mix. Don't make me regret it."

"You won't," Aaron assured him. "We're going to be great assets to Agartha. Thank you for the opportunity."

Eight hours later, they finished up their work and Toby escorted them back to their shared quarters.

"You did well," Toby told them once they reached the solid steel door. "You're going to like it here. Keep up the good work."

After they were inside and Toby left, Mark said, "Yeah,

we did well, but not so well that they aren't going to keep locking us up every day. This place is bullshit."

Aaron walked to his bed and sat down, saying nothing. Morning was fast approaching, and he wanted to sleep.

"We have to do something," Mark continued. "Doesn't it drive you crazy thinking of all those poor starving bastards outside the city?"

"Of course, it does," Aaron snapped. "You think I don't want to help them?"

Mark plopped down on his own bed. "I wouldn't have known it by the way you clammed up in front of Jaden. You could have had my back."

Aaron leaned forward and looked Mark in the eye. "You really think pissing off the ancient asshole who runs this city is the best way to help the other vampires out there?"

"You have something better in mind?"

A sly smile crept across Aaron's face. "We need to do exactly what Jaden told us to do. We need to earn their trust. We're going to be the best little worker bees Agartha has ever seen."

Mark nodded slowly, starting to understand. "Get them to let their guard down."

"Exactly. Then, once we have a plan *and* have their trust, we make our move. Then, and only then."

"I like it. You know, I'm glad we happened to bite the same guy."

Aaron chuckled. "Think about it, though. This city could be the first step in rebuilding the vampire race for the long haul. We already have a nice food supply. If we cultivate it, breed them, we can expand. But step one is getting access to other parts of the city."

"And that requires Jaden's trust," Mark repeated.

"You got it. That means no more of this mouthing off like

you did tonight. You need to be respectful to Jaden and the others."

"I can do that," Mark said. "I'll happily kiss ass and wait for our moment. But I do have one request."

"What's that?"

"When we take over, I want to throw Jaden in a cage and let him starve for a couple centuries. I want him to know firsthand the hell he's let every Feral vampire experience. Then, I want to bring him back and do it all over again."

———

ALEX WAITED until the wee hours of the morning to make her move. Of course, in *New Haven*, the wee hours were just as bright as any other time. There were far fewer people awake, though. Even in a city that was always in sunlight, people observed day and night.

As soon as she reached the Hub, she scurried up the first fire escape she saw. The buildings in the Hub were all built to be a uniform height, which made traveling from rooftop to rooftop an ideal way to get to the City Council headquarters without being noticed.

It felt odd running a covert mission on *New Haven*. Unlike her usual operations, there was no risk of encountering a vampire today. So why did she feel so nervous?

She leapt to the rooftop of the City Council building and made her way to the fire escape on the northeast end. Taking a deep breath, she headed down to the third floor, jimmied the window open, and slipped inside.

She found herself in an unoccupied office. After listening at the door for almost a minute, she crept into the hallway and made her way to the conference room where the City Council held their meetings. The room where they'd died.

Just as she'd expected, the door was locked. That was okay; she'd come prepared. She reached into her pocket and pulled out a key card.

As colonels, CB and Kurtz both had access to open most of the doors in this building, but using one of their key cards would have been risky. If Alex did her job correctly, Fleming wouldn't know anyone had been in this room until it was too late for it to make a difference. But it was possible he was tracking the movements of his colonels, and they didn't want to throw up any red flags.

Thankfully, Kurtz had come through and provided her with General Craig's keycard. The badges had taken it along with the rest of his personal effects when he was arrested. Granted, if someone looked at the access logs, it would seem awfully strange that a man currently locked in jail had entered the City Council chambers at three in the morning, but it seemed unlikely anyone would check. And even if they did, it would take time to figure out Alex had been the one using it.

She opened the door and entered the chamber.

Even more than two weeks after the explosion, the devastation in this room shook her. The furniture and carpet had been removed. The western wall had been stripped down to the studs, but there were still telltale scorch marks on the ceiling and some of the other walls. The thought of what had happened here made her shudder.

The north wall was still intact, and she saw the removable panel with the small hole in it just where Kurtz had said it would be. Taking a screwdriver out of her pack, she went to work. Unlike most security cameras which fed to the network rooms on each floor, Kurtz had told them that the hidden camera had a separate storage mechanism kept in the hidden compartment with the camera.

In less than a minute, she was able to confirm that for herself. She quickly had the camera exposed, and a few seconds after that, she was holding the tape in her hand.

She suppressed the urge to laugh. She couldn't believe it had been that easy. After all the scheming Fleming had done, he was going to be taken down by this little video tape. The thought made her giddy.

On the way out, she stopped at the network room at the end of the hall and pulled the tapes for every camera in the hallway, thus erasing the evidence she'd ever been there.

Then she went out the window, up the fire escape, and started back toward GMT headquarters.

14

GARRETT ELDRED WATCHED from the doorway as Councilman Stearns sat down at the table and looked around at the other Council members, a wide smile on his face. "Ladies! Gentlemen! It's been too long."

"Indeed, it has," Phyllis said. "How've you been, Stearns?"

"I can't complain. Shall we get to it? We're here to discuss the future of our great city. I think you'll all agree that there's more we could be doing—"

He stopped mid-sentence and looked at Garrett. "Firefly. You again?"

But it wasn't just Stearns who was staring. It was all of them. Phyllis, a woman in her sixties who represented the agricultural sector. Vernon, a man in his late thirties who'd been elected to represent the engineering sector only earlier that year. On and on it went, every Council member staring at him, as if waiting for him to say something important.

Garrett opened his mouth and felt his vocal cords tighten as he tried to speak, but no sound came out. He wanted to warn them, to tell them to run. He knew what was coming next.

It started at the far end of the table with Councilman Vernon. Thin tendrils of smoke rose from his sleeves, quickly thickening, and followed shortly by flames as the man's clothes caught fire.

The strange phenomenon traveled down the table, and it became more violent as it progressed, changing from a strange fire to an explosion.

Garrett found himself unable to move, unable to speak, forced to watch in horror as these people burned.

The councilmen and councilwomen didn't scream. They made no move to dampen the flames. They sat still, resigned to their fates as the slow-motion blast tore flesh from bone, leaving only charred, blackened patches of skin. The exposed teeth left behind after their lips disintegrated made them look like they were wearing ghastly smiles.

The slow-motion blast reached Stearns, and as his eyeballs liquefied in their sockets, he spoke to Garrett in a calm voice. "Am I pretty now? Do the ends justify my makeover?"

Garrett screamed as loud as he could, straining his vocal chords, but no sound emerged.

Until it did.

He heard himself crying out and opened his eyes to see his bedroom. For a few moments, he just lay there, breathing deeply and waiting for his heart rate to return to normal. Then he glanced at the clock and saw it was nearly morning.

Twisting himself out of the tangle of sweat-drenched sheets, he got up and walked to the bathroom. He looked at himself in mirror for a long moment, and he couldn't help but remember the vivid way Councilman Stearns's eyes had been destroyed in his dream.

"Fuck you, Stearns," he said, still looking into the mirror.

An hour later, he was outside the GMT facility. He waited by the doors where he'd instructed his handpicked recruits to meet him. Thankfully, none of them were there yet. As the boss, he made it a point to always be the first in and the last out.

He hadn't been to this building since he'd left the team, and it felt odd being here as an interloper who'd been forced upon them. But that was his role, and he'd play it out.

Shirley arrived three minutes later, followed by Henry and Mario. These were the top three recruits. All of them were honored badges, and he was hoping to give them this experience to help prepare them for leadership roles on the surface.

"You ready for this?" he asked them.

Shirley was the first to respond. "Captain, I've been waiting for this all my life."

"Good," Captain Garrett Eldred said. "Then let's go. It's time for your first mission to the surface."

———

CB, Owl, and Alex huddled around the monitor as Brian scrubbed through the security footage Alex had brought back.

"Whatever we find on this tape, we still have to proceed with caution," CB said. "This is our smoking gun, but we need to make sure everything is in order before we reveal it. Kurtz is still working on his badges, and I still believe we need Firefly."

"Of course," Alex said, but she was barely listening. In a

few moments, they would see the hard evidence against Fleming. And then, whether he knew it or not, Fleming was finished.

CB frowned at her, clearly able to tell she wasn't paying attention. "I'm just saying, we can't show our cards until—"

"Hang on, CB," Brian said, his brow furrowed in concentration.

"Is there a problem?" CB asked.

"That's what I'm trying to figure out."

They waited in silence, watching the images on the screen flicker past in fast motion.

"Okay, there's a problem," Brian said.

"Explain." CB's voice was tense.

Brian paused the video on a shot of the empty Council room. "This is two days before the explosion." The picture flickered to a very different, burned-out image of the room. "This is the day after."

"Where's the footage from in between?" Owl asked.

Brian looked up at them, his face drawn with concern. "It's not here. Someone erased it."

Alex felt sick.

For a long moment, no one spoke.

Finally, CB cleared his throat. "I don't want anyone to panic. This is a dead end, but we'll find another way."

"What way?" Alex asked, her voice weary. "Fleming's two steps ahead of us. Again."

"There's evidence out there. We just need to find it. In the meantime, winning Firefly over to our way of thinking is more important than ever. Today's a great opportunity to start working on him."

Alex nodded absently, barely registering the words. She'd been so sure this was how they were going to take

Fleming down. She'd been so confident. And now the tape had proven itself worthless.

"I know this is disappointing," CB told them, "but don't give up. You keep doing your jobs. Kurtz and I will do ours."

———

The GMT away ship cruised toward their target location.

"Ladies and gentlemen," Owl said in their headsets, "you will soon be planting boots on the fertile soil of a rainforest in the pre-infestation country of Columbia. It's a diverse landscape filled with more species of bird than any other place on Earth."

"We're really doing this again?" Patrick grumbled. "Every time?"

"Spanish was the primary language of the region," she continued. "The economy was agrarian for most of its history."

"What the hell is that?" Ed asked.

"Means they farmed and shit," Chuck said.

"In the late twentieth and early twenty-first century, the country was engaged in ongoing warfare between the government and guerilla groups. I assume that's the source of the weapons stash we're after today. Columbia was also part of the region that scientists called the Ring of Fire, because of the frequency of earthquakes and volcanic eruptions."

Patrick put a hand to his earpiece. "Hang on. Did she just say, 'volcanic eruptions'?"

Alex raised an eyebrow. "Now you're paying attention?"

"I signed up to fight vampires. I don't mess with volcanos. Lava is liquid rock."

"If any volcanoes erupt, we'll let you get back on the ship."

The purpose of the mission was to recover a large weapons stash they'd identified from the NSA records. As disappointing as Brian's news about the tape had been, it felt good to have a straightforward mission for once. Go to a building and find some guns. No politics, no electricians, just her team and a clear-cut objective. The only thing that had her on edge was their companions.

Firefly—she couldn't bring herself to think of him as Garrett—and three of his top Resettlement recruits were accompanying them on this mission. At Fleming's orders, of course. Fleming had informed CB and Alex in no uncertain terms that this was not optional. They were to take the Resettlement crew along to give them some experience on the surface.

Alex was doing her best to hide her frustration at the situation, but she was pretty sure the others could see through it.

Here she was, still trying to break in this new team, trying to help them establish good habits and trust her as a leader, and now there was a whole new group of rookies she hadn't even been allowed to vet.

Not that she minded having Firefly. As much as they'd clashed over Resettlement, she respected him as a soldier. She'd fought back-to-back with him, sometimes literally, and she knew he could hold his own in a fight. And, as CB had made painfully clear, this was a good opportunity to try to win him over.

And yet, his mere presence confused things. Technically, she and Firefly were equals, both captains. CB had made it clear that Alex would be in charge on this mission. But everyone aboard the away ship knew Firefly held the more important position as head of the entire Resettlement operation.

Not only that, but it didn't take a genius to realize Firefly wasn't only there to give his troops experience. He was there to watch her. To make sure she didn't throw the mission.

Chuck looked out the window and whistled. "Would you look at that? I've never seen anything like it."

Alex had to admit it was breathtaking. Even though she'd been on dozens of missions to various climates and regions of the Earth, the sight of the surface never failed to awe her. Especially rainforests.

She supposed it was a result of spending her life on an airship where most of the surfaces were made of cold metal and every square inch was carefully planned and engineered for optimum usage. The rainforest below was the exact opposite. It teemed with life, and the vegetation sprawled, each living thing limited only by its own ability to survive. If something could get the sunlight and water it needed, it grew.

The sprawl of the surface boggled her *New Haven*-bred mind.

The away ship slowed to a stop, hovering a hundred feet over the canopy of trees below.

"What's going on, Captain Eldred?" a recruit named Shirley asked. Alex couldn't help but notice the recruit had quickly taken the seat next to Firefly and had barely stopped staring at him during the flight.

"Don't know," Firefly said. "Alex?"

Alex touched the radio on her chest. "What are we doing, Owl?"

"That's what I'm trying to figure out, Captain," came the reply. "These are the coordinates we have, but I don't see anything down there but trees."

Alex stared out the window. She saw nothing below them but green. "This weapons stash was supposed to be secret, right? I guess it makes sense that it would be camouflaged from the air." She thought a moment. "Owl, get us as low as you can. We'll use the ropes to get down there."

Firefly frowned. "We're going into that jungle blind?"

Alex stood up and started back toward the cargo door. "My team is. You can do what you want."

She was gratified to see Chuck, Ed, and Patrick immediately rise and follow her to the back.

After a moment, Firefly nodded to his crew. "You heard the captain. Let's move."

It took a few minutes to get everyone rigged up, but they were soon being lowered down, two by two through the thick canopy to the jungle floor. Alex and Chuck went first, followed by the Barton brothers. Firefly and his three recruits were the last down.

The jungle floor was dim, but Alex was relieved to see there was enough sunlight coming through the canopy that a vampire encounter seemed unlikely. On a less positive note, there were no structures in sight.

Alex looked around, hands on hips, searching for anything that might have been made by human hands. She was already sweating. The humid air felt like a wet blanket over her. She could see in her crew's faces that they were surprised at the weather, so much different than the arid, cold Colorado weather they'd experienced at the prison.

The sounds of life were all around them, from the songs of birds to the distant calls of unknown animals. The team looked a little spooked. She could hardly blame them, after a life lived on the sterile environment of *New Haven*, where the only nonhuman sounds were those of machinery. She should have prepared them better for this. But as long as they kept their fingers away from the triggers, they'd be okay.

A gunshot split the air.

Alex spun, drawing her pistol as she turned.

Ed stood with his weapon pointed toward the brush, his eyes wide with fear.

"What the hell?" Alex shouted.

Ed's stare remained fixed on the brush. "Something was looking at me, Captain. From the bushes. It had yellow eyes. Pretty sure I got it."

Alex glanced up at the sky and saw once again plenty of sunlight was streaming through the leaves. "Hold your fire. Patrick, with me."

She slowly crept forward, pistol at the ready. Patrick was close behind her. It took them nearly a minute to make it ten feet through the dense foliage, but they soon found Ed's enemy combatant.

She sighed. "Well, at least your aim was true."

The creature lay dead at her feet, a single bullet hole in the center of its skull. She recognized it from the picture books she'd obsessed over as a kid. It was a jaguar.

"Are you kidding me?" Patrick muttered when he saw it. He turned back and shouted to his brother, "You dick! You killed a cat."

Owl's voice came through her headset. "Hey, Captain, I ran a scan of the area, and I think I found something."

———

"I'M NOT GOING TO LIE," Chuck said. "This is a bit anti-climactic."

Alex couldn't disagree.

The entire expedition, including the four GMT

members and Firefly and his three recruits, stood in front of a small structure. The single-story building was made of brick, though thick moss and crisscrossing vines hid most of it from view. The remains of a few other structures stood nearby, but time and exposure had reduced them to little more than piles of rotting wood and scraps of metal.

The building in front of them couldn't have been more than ten feet by ten feet. If there was a weapons store in there, it would be a very small one.

"Wonderful," Firefly grumbled.

Judging by the condition of the exterior, Alex couldn't imagine anything inside would be in usable condition, but she kept her feelings about the situation to herself. "Well, we're here, aren't we? Let's open her up."

Chuck tried the door. "Seems to be rusted shut, Captain."

Alex looked at him, her face expressionless. "Shame we don't have an explosives expert who might rectify that situation."

"Yeah it is." He paused a moment, then turned red. "Oh, right." With that, he took off his backpack and began rifling around inside.

Alex suppressed a chuckle. This was the man's first mission in charge of explosives, so she couldn't fault him too much. She glanced at Firefly, who wasn't making any effort to hide his annoyance at the way Chuck was slowly going through the backpack.

"Use a charge," he said. "A small one. We don't want to risk anything large if there could be weapons inside."

"Yes, sir," Chuck answered.

Alex nodded toward the backpack. "You miss it, Firefly?"

"It's Garrett," he said, almost under his breath. "Getting to blow stuff up? Hell yeah, I do."

Alex turned to the recruits. "You should have seen this guy in action. There was this one time we were trapped in this tiny control room in a nuclear reactor building, surrounded by vampires on every side. Your captain pulls out the cutter and goes to work, cutting a hole in the damn floor. We dropped down to the next level and ran right out from under the bastards."

Firefly laughed. "Cutting the hole in the floor was your idea, if I remember correctly."

"Team effort. That's how we worked best."

Firefly nodded. He glanced at the recruits, and the smile slipped from his face. "Anyway, that's enough war stories for now. Got that charge ready, Lieutenant?"

Alex chuckled. At least she'd gotten Firefly to drop his bigwig routine for a second. That was a step in the right direction.

"Ready," Chuck said. "Stand clear."

He pressed a button and the charge exploded with a loud *pop*, knocking the door off its hinges.

They waited for a tense moment for the familiar angry howl of a woken vampire, but none came.

Patrick said, "Not a lot of room in there, Captain. Unless you want us all standing shoulder to shoulder—"

"I got you." Alex started toward the door, intending to check the small building with one of the others, but then she stopped. It was time to start trusting her team. "Patrick, Ed, clear the building."

Ed grinned. "The Barton brothers are on it."

She stopped herself again just as she was about to remind them to check the dark areas for vampires. They knew their jobs. It was time to let them do them.

Patrick awkwardly clutched his shotgun. After Hope's death, he'd asked Alex if he could start carrying her favorite weapon instead of his usual carbine. She'd quickly agreed. Having a shotgun on the team came in handy, and it was a great way for him to honor Hope's memory.

The brothers entered the building and gave it a quick sweep.

"There's nothing here, Captain," Patrick called. "Total waste of ti—"

His words were cut off and a clanging sound split the air, like something heavy had been dropped onto a metal surface.

"What happened?" Alex paced toward the building.

"He fell through the floor," Ed answered. "Patrick, you okay?"

Alex walked through the door just in time to hear an echoey response.

"Yeah, I'm good. But I think I found something. There's a big steel door. Like a vault, maybe."

That sounded promising. Maybe this mission wasn't going to be a bust after all.

"It's locked up tight!" Patrick called. "We're going to need the cutter."

Alex turned back to the group waiting outside. "Chuck?"

Once again, Chuck turned crimson. "Yes, ma'am. The thing is, I didn't think we'd need the cutter. I haven't learned how... you know."

Alex took a step toward him. She couldn't believe what she was hearing. "You don't know how to use it? I told you to spend time with Brian's team, learning the gear."

"I did, Captain. It's just, after learning all about the explosives, my brain was fried. I asked if we could wait until—"

"I don't want to hear it." She turned to Firefly. "Remember that teamwork we were talking about?"

Firefly smiled, and for a moment she saw a glimpse of her old teammate. "On it." He walked to Chuck's backpack and picked it up, slinging it over his shoulder. "Lower me down, rookie."

Ten minutes later, he was through the door and the team followed him into what lay beyond.

"Now, this is more like it," Ed said.

The vault was a forty-by-forty-foot room with ten-foot-high ceilings. The walls and floor were made of steel. Much like the prison, it looked pristine. More importantly, the room was lined with large shelving units filled with crates.

"Sweep the room before we dig in," Alex reminded them.

It didn't take long to ensure there were no vampires, and then Ed cracked open one of the crates.

"This...this is the most beautiful thing I've ever seen," he said.

Alex looked over his shoulder and saw the crate was full of rifles.

Firefly grinned. "This is a huge find. What else do we have?"

The Barton brothers ran through the vault, prying open crate after crate, cheering each time they uncovered a new type of weapon. They discovered a massive variety of rifles and pistols. They found grenades and landmines. One crate even had missile launchers.

As each crate opened, Alex felt like a weight was pressing harder against her chest. They'd accomplished their mission, but what would the consequences be? Each weapon here would make Fleming a little more confident. Each gun brought them one step closer to Resettlement.

She felt like screaming. Her every success was bringing her enemy one step closer to victory.

There was only one way forward. Firefly. She needed to win him over, and she needed to do it soon.

He grinned at her. "Looks like we're going to need that pretty new rover they built you."

"One problem," Chuck interjected. "Owl can't land. How are we going to get it down here?"

Alex nodded toward the backpack Firefly was still wearing. "You got enough explosives in that thing to clear a landing site?"

"I sure do," Firefly answered.

Ed and Patrick both stopped what they were doing and looked up.

"Um, can we help?" Patrick asked.

It took four hours to clear a landing zone and load the ship. In the end, they only had room to take a small portion of crates. It would take four or five more trips down here to get the rest of the weapons.

As the away ship took off, Firefly nudged Alex. "Hey, that was a great mission. We should celebrate. Want to have dinner with me tonight?"

She blinked hard, taken aback. "Um, are you..."

"No! I mean, not like that. Not a date or anything." His expression grew more serious. "But we need to talk."

She hesitated only a moment before answering. "You're right. We do need to talk, Garrett. Dinner it is."

15

ALEX DREW in a deep breath and stepped through the dim doorway. It took her about three seconds to realize she was wildly underdressed.

She'd come straight from the debriefing room, and she wore an old flak jacket over a ratty T-shirt and pants that hadn't seen a washing machine in a week. And the people around her...the only times she'd seen people dressed this nicely were weddings and City Council meetings.

But what could she do about it now? She was committed.

She spotted a man waving to her from a table across the room, and it took her a moment to recognize him. When she did, she had to stifle a laugh. The sharply dressed man with slicked-back hair didn't looked much like her old GMT friend. No wonder he'd left the debriefing early.

She walked to the table and sat down across from him.

"Welcome," Firefly said. "You ever been here?"

"I've never even heard of this place. I don't make it to the Hub often. Except for meetings." She took another look around, hoping she didn't look as uncomfortable as she felt. "Is this really necessary? We could have met at Tankards."

Firefly raised an eyebrow at the mention of their old favorite dive bar. "Why would we do that? Alex, you deserve to reward yourself. We both do. That was quite the haul we brought back today."

"Maybe your idea of reward is different than mine. Besides, we didn't even run into any hostiles."

"Yeah, but we got results. That's what matters. You should try the wine. The waiter said it's from one of their best barrels. It's been aging longer than we've been alive."

Alex took a sip to humor him, hoping it would make her feel less out of place. She needed to focus. She needed to talk to Firefly, and this was the prime opportunity to do so. "I can't believe all those weapons. It's tough to imagine anyone would ever need that many."

"Yeah, I hear you. A few months ago, I would have said the same thing. But we sure as hell need them now. Nights are going to get cold on the surface, and I'll feel a lot better if every one of my people has a warm rifle in their hands."

She resisted the urge to launch into a diatribe against Resettlement right then. She had to be smarter than that. She needed to play this like Fleming would.

"Anyway," he continued, "all I'm saying is, you're kind of an important person in *New Haven* now. Enjoy it. God knows you've earned it."

"Is that what you're doing? Enjoying it?"

The skin tightened around his eyes as he frowned. "What I'm doing is working my ass off. In my few hours of free time, yeah, I'm trying to enjoy a few of the perks. Is there something wrong with that?"

"Of course not, Garrett." She almost tripped over the name as it fell heavily past her lips, but she needed to be nice. "Listen, there's something I need to talk to you about. Something that could change the plans for Resettlement."

She went on to tell him about the conversation with Jaden and the things she'd learned. About how masters controlled turned vampires. About how Ferals who drank from humans returned to their intelligent forms. About how vampires could communicate simple ideas psychically.

She spoke in hushed tones, leaning in close so only he could hear her. As she spoke, the color slowly drained from his face.

"You understand what I'm telling you, right?" she said when she'd finished. "I'm not saying Resettlement should never happen, but we need to learn more about the Ferals first. Doing it now will be suicide. The Ferals will learn, over time. Individually, they're dumb animals, but each failure will make the survivors smarter. Eventually, they'll launch a coordinated attack, like they did to us in Texas. And if even one Feral gets into your settlement and turns someone without your knowledge, it's over. They'll have a slave on the inside."

"Damn." He was quiet a moment, staring into his wine glass. "There's only one thing we can do. We've got to tell Fleming. Now."

He started to stand, but Alex put a hand on his arm.

"We already did," she said.

He stared back at her in disbelief. "You did?"

"Do you think I'm an idiot, Firefly? The first thing I did when I got back to *New Haven* was tell CB. He walked directly over to Fleming's office to tell him. Judging by your reaction, Fleming didn't exactly rush out to tell his favorite captain."

Firefly's lips tightened in a thin line.

"Listen to me," she said, speaking even more softly. Her

voice cracked with emotion when she continued. "Fleming *does not understand*. You and I have been on the surface. We've fought them in the day and in the night. We've watched as they tore our friends to shreds. You remember what they did to Drew? What they did to Simmons?"

He broke eye contact, looking down at the table. "Of course, I remember."

"Now, imagine that happening to every man and woman who settles in that damn prison. How many people is it going to be? Two hundred?"

"Try three."

Alex cursed under her breath. "Fleming trusts you. He respects you. You have to convince him to put this thing on pause. He's so blinded by his confidence that he isn't seeing the obvious. The people he sends down there? They won't last a week in that prison."

"Fort Stearns," Firefly said softly.

"Excuse me?"

"He wants to name it Fort Stearns. In honor of the former head of the Council. He says it'll be a nice gesture. After the accident and all."

"The accident?" Alex said. Her voice sounded distant in her own ears as the anger boiled up in her. Firefly suddenly couldn't meet her gaze.

He raised his glass with a shaky hand and took a big swallow of red wine. When he set it down, he looked her in the eye. "The accident, whatever it was, I'm sure every person involved wishes it hadn't happened. But it did. We gotta find a way to move on from it."

"What about justice?" Her voice was cold, her initial plan to remain friendly forgotten.

"It's time to grow up, Alex. If Fleming knows about what Jaden told you, we have our answer. Resettlement is moving forward. Get onboard. I'm telling you this as a friend. You have a good position here, but Fleming has powerful supporters. People who go up against Fleming don't keep their jobs too long. Ask General Craig."

Alex took a deep breath, trying to calm herself, but her very surroundings made her even more angry. "The people in this restaurant, the ones you're enjoying the good life with, they won't be the people he sends to 'Fort Stearns.' It'll be the badges. The worker bees. The people from the Ridge. The ones Fleming claimed to be fighting for when he rose to power. These people here in the Hub will be the last ones to soil their fancy shoes with the dust of the Earth."

"Alex, please."

The panic in his eyes made Alex realize how loudly she'd been speaking. She looked around and saw that the people at the surrounding tables were staring at her. Some were even whispering. All of which served to make her even angrier.

Firefly leaned close and spoke softly. "Listen, I understand your concerns. I swear to God, I do. You think I haven't considered this stuff? There are huge risks to Resettlement. But staying up here isn't any better. We're one major system failure away from this ship crashing and every person aboard dying. There is no safe option. But in Fort Stearns we'll have the walls."

"You know as well as I do that a vampire at night could hop that wall."

"And it'll get burned by the daylights if it tries. Or lit up by our armed guards."

"What about silver mail? How are they going to make enough for three hundred people in less than a month?"

"We won't need it. Not with our other defenses."

"You're delusional." She pushed back her chair and stood up.

"We haven't even ordered yet," he said, the shock clear on his face. "You're not going to eat?"

"No. I'm not hungry. I'm going to grab a beer in the Ridge. Enjoy your wine, Firefly."

————

AARON VIVIDLY REMEMBERED his first thought after he'd become a vampire, during the third wave of the great infestation.

He remembered the feelings, too: the hunger, the irresistible compulsion to follow his master's commands, the electric feeling of power racing through his veins where blood had once flowed.

But mostly he remembered the thought: now anything is possible.

In that imagined glimpse of his limitless future, he'd never imagined that he'd spend every night in a musky storeroom, moving boxes and filling out spreadsheets. And yet, here he was, hunched over a computer at a little after two in the morning, entering the updated grain inventory into a color-coded cell on a spreadsheet. The color was Orange, Accent 2. He knew because he'd used it approximately eighteen hundred times over the past four nights.

To make matters worse, not only was he forced to do mindless labor, but they didn't even trust him to do it correctly. Toby, their trainer/chaperone, watched over his shoulder as Aaron keyed in the information. Aaron idly wondered how long it would take him to rip out Toby's throat. Would Toby even have a chance to put up a fight? Aaron guessed he wouldn't. He speculated that he could kill

Toby before the other vampire even knew what was happening.

Of course, Aaron's own throat would probably be ripped out by Jaden and his vampire disciples, shortly thereafter. If they were feeling generous. If not, they'd throw him back out in the snow to starve.

So, Aaron kept a forced smile on his face even while working on his meaningless tasks.

He saved his spreadsheet and yelled, "Yo, Mark! You got those gears stocked?"

Mark raced up a ladder, a box under one arm. He moved at a pace that would have been shocking if he'd been a human. He quickly reached the top and placed the box on a shelf.

"Done," he said.

"Excellent." Aaron turned in his chair to look at their chaperone. "What else you got for us, Toby?"

Toby laughed and shook his head. "You guys are like kids running around, always in a hurry. In time you'll learn to pace yourselves."

"Kids?" Mark asked, climbing down the ladder. "We're nearly two hundred years old. How old are you?"

"Four hundred thirteen."

Aaron didn't know how to respond to that. Toby looked to be in his forties. Did age mean anything in a world where your looks never changed? "There's got to be some more work we can do. We've got four hours until dawn."

Toby shook his head again, then pulled the radio off his belt. "Griffin, you there?"

"Yeah, buddy," the reply came. "What do you got for me?"

Toby glanced at Aaron. "Two eager vampire cubs looking for work. You need a couple pairs of hands?"

Aaron and Mark spent the rest of the night helping five other vampires install new piping for the water system. They were still away from the humans, and the crew boss, Griffin, kept a wary eye on them throughout the night, but it was nice to get a change of scenery.

They learned quite a bit by simply keeping their mouths shut and listening. They learned about how Jaden often left with a team to get supplies for Agartha. Maybe just as importantly, they learned there was another human city, one that was built on an airship. Apparently, the people on the airship were trying to resettle onto the surface.

A half hour before sunrise, Toby showed up to take them back to their quarters. He had a surprise for them: two blood packs.

"Reward for a hard night's work," he told them.

Back in their quarters, Aaron and Mark drank from the packs as they lounged on their beds. Normally, they each got one packet a day, delivered just after they woke, so this was a rare treat.

Aaron set down the empty packet and lay his head on his pillow. The combination of a full belly and the approaching dawn had left him tired and happy. "We did well tonight, Mark. Toby is starting to like us. I'll bet they give us access to more sections of the city soon."

"Yeah, well, it's a good thing I had this blood to wash the taste out of my mouth after kissing ass all night."

Aaron chuckled. "Stay strong, buddy. It won't be forever. Once we're free of Toby shadowing us everywhere, all we need is access to the security control room. If we turn the humans who work in there, we're golden. We'd control the blast doors, the gun turrets, the alarm systems, you name it."

"What do we do, then?"

"We force them to send out an emergency signal and get

the vampires running for the blast doors. I figure if we trap Jaden's disciples between the blast doors, we'll have time to turn a bunch of the humans into disciples of our own."

"Huh." Mark was silent so long, Aaron thought he might have fallen asleep, but then he spoke again. "I don't know, man. That all seems pretty complicated. Who knows when they'll even let us out without Toby watching us? Things seem to move damn slow around here."

"Relax. It's good that things are moving slowly. Means we have time to plan. For now, we just have to concentrate on getting Jaden's trust. Once we have that, everything will fall into place."

"And what do we do once we take over?"

"We do what Jaden won't," Aaron answered. "We help the Ferals. With ten thousand humans in this place, I'll bet we could feed four thousand vampires. And that's just the start. Once we get the humans breeding, every female pumping out a kid a year, that number will jump up fast in just a few generations. Vampires could have a world worth living in again. All vampires, not just one hundred assholes who think they're better than the rest of us."

"Heh. I'd like to see that."

"You will see it. And the best part? We're going to rule it."

16

THE NEXT TWO weeks were a whirlwind. Fleming sent the GMT on fourteen missions in as many days.

Today was their fifteenth. Alex had promised her team they'd get a much-needed break after this one, and it was a promise she intended to keep, no matter what Fleming had to say about it.

The two previous weeks had been an assortment of failures and successes. They'd managed to bring back all the weapons from the Colombian rainforest. It had taken five trips, and they'd encountered a few vampires waiting in the vault on their fifth trip, but they'd managed to recover every damn crate.

Alex had hoped that this would earn them a short reprieve, but she'd been incorrect. First, the team had been sent to salvage as much as they could from the away ship that had crashed near Agartha. The backup ship was serving the team well enough, but Fleming had a team working on building a larger transport that could get big groups to and from Fort Stearns.

Then, there had been the daylights. Brian needed more

supplies to continue making them in the numbers and sizes Fleming demanded. The parts he needed would have been used in large lighting systems in the pre-infestation days, so the GMT had gone to retrieve them. Though they'd visited various sports stadiums around the world, they'd so far come back empty-handed. It turned out that the stadiums hadn't held up well without anyone to maintain them. The rusted-out and deteriorated lighting systems had been useless.

And then, there was Firefly. Things had been contentious between Alex and Firefly since their ill-fated dinner. He and a few of his best recruits had accompanied them on about half the missions, and Firefly seemed to flex his leadership muscles a little more on each trip. The last time, he'd actually tried to override one of Alex's commands, a move that had almost earned him a punch in the face. He'd apologized after the mission and had promised to let her take the lead on this next mission, but she'd believe it when she'd seen it.

It hadn't been all bad, though. As hard as the nonstop schedule had been on her team, it had hardened them like a refining fire. She almost couldn't believe how far they'd come in such a short time. They operated with poise and instinctive teamwork that most units took years to develop. The Barton brothers were absolute monsters in the field, eradicating hostiles with a ruthless efficiency. Chuck had come into his own, too, now that he'd been moved back to reconnaissance.

The other bright spot was their newly returned team member, the one who'd taken over the explosives specialist job from Chuck. He still had a slight limp and probably always would, but it didn't restrict his movement. It was damn good to have Wesley back on the team.

Though there were no backup GMT recruits at the moment—Fleming was supposedly working on that—they had a full team again for the first time since Hope's death.

Now they were back on the away ship, heading toward yet another mission. They were going after another lighting system and the stakes were high; Brian was out of components, and he wouldn't be making any more daylights for Fort Stearns until the team brought him some.

Alex looked out the window and tried not to let her confidence falter at the sight of the landscape stretched below her. Nothing but sand and mountains as far as she could see. She couldn't imagine a large lighting system down there.

Owl came over the speaker when they were five minutes out from their destination. "Okay, ladies and gentlemen, I hope you're ready for some fun in the sun, because we will soon be arriving at the location formerly called Las Vegas. Also known as Sin City."

Patrick sat up a bit straighter at that. "Sin City, huh? That doesn't sound half bad."

The ship banked left, and Alex noticed some columns protruding from the sand; it took her a moment to identify them as the tops of buildings. There were no other signs that a city had ever been there. If there were roads and houses down there, they were buried beneath the sand.

"Las Vegas means 'the meadow' in Spanish," Owl continued. "In actuality, the city is situated in a basin in the Mojave Desert. It's surrounded by mountain ranges on all sides. This area also had the third greatest seismic activity of anywhere in the United States. Whether it was an earthquake, or simply the passage of time that led the city to being covered in sand, I do not know."

Chuck let out a laugh.

"What's so funny?" Ed asked.

Chuck nodded out the window. "We're going into a desert, one of the sunniest places on Earth. And yet, we're going to be digging down into the darkness under the sand."

Ed chuckled. "Let it never be said the GMT doesn't go to great lengths to find and exterminate the enemy."

Firefly touched his radio. "Hey, Owl, how many people lived here, prior to the infestation?"

"Patience, Captain," she said. "Las Vegas was known for its casinos, which were gambling establishments, where visitors could wager their money against long odds in the hopes of winning even more."

"Long odds, huh?" Patrick interjected. "This is my kind of town."

"And to answer Captain Eldred's question, the population of the city was eight hundred thousand people, prior to infestation."

"Great," Firefly muttered. "So, we're looking at over three quarters of a million vampires under that sand."

"That is all the information I have for you today," Owl said. "My apologies. With our frantic schedule, I haven't had much time to spend in the library."

The ship touched down next to three towers that stuck out several stories from the sand.

Alex led the team off the ship and out onto the sea of sand.

Firefly put his hand in his hips and grunted. "I thought Brian said the lights we're looking for are in a stadium."

"They are," Alex answered. Then she pointed downward.

"Great," he said. "So, we take the tower down?"

"Yep," Owl said, stepping out of the ship. "There should be a system of tunnels that connect this tower to the stadium. Assuming it hasn't collapsed under the weight of the sand."

"No time like the present," Patrick said. "Let's go inside." He walked up to the tower and slammed the butt of his shotgun against a window. The gun bounced off, the window still intact.

Ed barked out a laugh. "Let me show you how it's done." He slammed the butt of his gun hard against the window, grunting with effort, and he got the same result.

"Son of a bitch," Ed muttered. He swung his gun around and fired into the window. That did the trick.

Alex glared at them both. "Wait for orders before you fire at a non-hostile target. I would have preferred not to let every vampire in the building know we were coming."

"Sorry, Captain," the brothers muttered in unison.

Alex walked toward the window. "Nothing to do about it now. The damage is done. Let's go inside."

———

THE TEAM MADE their way into the room, past the ruins of old furniture and out into the hallway beyond. Firefly brought up the rear. He stepped into the hallway and the door swung shut behind him with a *thump*, instantly darkening the space. They were truly in the vampires' territory now—a cold, dead place cut off from the light of the sun.

They all turned on their headlamps, and Firefly tried the doorknob. It was locked.

"No worries," Alex said. "We can always bust through it, if we need to."

As they walked down the hallway, a low rumble came from the distance. The team froze.

Alex felt goosebumps spring up on her arms as she

stood stone-still, listening. It didn't sound like a vampire, but it took her a moment to figure it out. "It's the wind. Rushing through the halls."

The team let out a collective sigh of relief. "Not vampires," Chuck said, "but still damn creepy."

Owl pointed to a sign—it showed a simple depiction of a staircase and an arrow pointing left.

"Left, it is," Alex said.

As they made their way down the hall, she noticed that Firefly's three recruits—Shirley, Mario, and Henry—stuck close to their captain. It had been that way on every mission, and Alex had gotten used to it. Firefly's people wore the same equipment as the rest of the GMT, complete with silver mail and jetpacks, so it was easy to look past them. The three had proven themselves competent, if still a little jumpy, but they worshiped Firefly a little too much for their own good. For the most part, they tended to hang back and let the GMT do the real work, which was fine with Alex.

"This place looks pretty great for having been abandoned for one hundred fifty years," Patrick said. "Unless the vampires are keeping things tidy."

"It's the dry climate," Owl said. "This place was sealed up like a tomb."

"Not a wonderful analogy," Patrick complained.

After a few minutes of walking, they reached the end of the hallway and a door marked "Stairs."

Chuck tried the door, but it was stuck. Alex nodded to Wesley, who took out his cutter and went to work.

He cut slowly and carefully, making as little noise as possible, but even the quiet whir of the blade sounded loud in this dead hallway. The team waited in silence.

When Wesley was just about finished, the locking mechanism slid, then fell, cut free from the door.

Alex froze, dreading both the sound it would make when it hit the floor and the vampires the clang would bring. But Chuck reached out and plucked the lock out of the air.

Alex raised an eyebrow, impressed. "Nice."

Chuck just smiled.

They stood gathered at the doorway, looking through to the sign over the stairs. It read "20."

"I take it that means this is the twentieth floor?" Mario asked.

"Looks like," Alex said. "You got the layout of this place, Owl?"

The pilot pulled her tablet out of her bag and tapped the screen.

"There are three towers. We're in the westernmost one. There's a central area that connects all three towers at the base. That's where we'll find the stadium."

"The bottom," Firefly said. "Of course."

Alex glanced back down the hallway. "I do like the setup in here. Narrow hallways. Narrow staircases. That'll help, if we get outnumbered. Hopefully it'll be the same way below. Let's head down."

They descended the stairway quickly, but carefully. With each floor they passed, Alex tried not to think about the layers of sleeping vampires that were likely stacked on top of them.

They reached the doorway to floor one and stopped. Alex looked at the group. "Tight formations. Stay alert, but be damn sure before you fire at anything. The last thing we want to do is wake up any vamps in this place. Chuck, you're with me. Barton brothers, you're anchor."

"And us non-GMT weenies will huddle in the middle," Firefly muttered.

"I'll be huddling right with you," Owl said.

On Alex's signal, Firefly pulled the door open, and she and Chuck went through. They both immediately froze.

She wasn't sure what she'd been expecting, but it certainly wasn't this.

Their headlights weren't bright enough to see to the other side of the vast space before them, but they saw enough. Stone columns. Marble sculptures. Spiral staircases that led up beautifully adorned balconies.

"Damn, what the hell was this place?" Patrick asked as he came through the door and joined the group.

"A king lived here," Ed answered.

Patrick frowned at him. "How do you know that?"

Ed turned, shining his headlamp on a large sign mounted on the wall.

Caesar's Palace Hotel and Casino.

"Stay quiet," Alex told them sharply. "Owl? You know where we're headed?"

The pilot smiled. "I don't even need my tablet for that." She pointed to a smaller sign on the wall. It listed a number of locations with arrows next to each of them. The one they were interested in was on the bottom.

The Colosseum at Caesar's Palace.

"That's where we're headed," Owl confirmed.

"Okay. Team, let's follow the helpful arrows."

The group kept in tight formation as they crossed the expansive floor. The area they were passing through was cluttered with rows and rows of metal machines, which limited their visibility. The poor line of sight made Alex nervous; for all she knew there could be vampires huddled behind every one of those metal monstrosities.

They'd been walking for two minutes when Wesley

suddenly stopped and spoke in a low voice. "Captain. Two o'clock."

Alex looked to her right and saw it: a vampire was huddled against one of the machines, sleeping.

She held up a hand, indicating to her team not to engage. Then she started walking again, gun at the ready.

A few minutes later, they made their way through a massive arched hallway. Chuck looked up, illuminating the ceiling, and let out a barely audible whistle.

Alex followed his gaze and saw that the ceiling was painted to resemble a blue sky with a smattering of clouds. She couldn't believe this place. It was at once awe-inspiring and sickening. To think people had once lived with such extravagance made her both envious of the past and angry at how far humanity had fallen.

She looked around and her headlamp illuminated a window that seemed to lead to some sort of shop. A vampire was sleeping against the glass. She gestured toward it, making sure her team knew it was there, then kept moving.

"This is it," Owl whispered as they reached a wall with a set of double doors.

Alex pulled them open and led the team inside. The longer they were down here, the more nervous she was becoming. She didn't want to spend any more time under the sand than they had to.

The feeling of paranoia only increased as they stepped into the Colosseum. It was a massive space filled with stadium seating that led to a large stage at the bottom of the room.

There might be worse places to get into a fight with a large group of vampires, but Alex couldn't think of one. If a horde attacked them here, it would be all too easy for the vampires to surround the team.

She pushed the thought out of her mind. She didn't usually think like this, but something about being down here under tons of sand was stoking her nerves.

Owl touched her arm and spoke softly. "Alex, look. It's everything Brian needs."

Alex followed her friend's gaze upward to the impressive lighting system. Owl was right. If the lights were in as good condition as everything else in this palace, they'd make Brian a very happy man.

"Excellent." She thought for a moment. "Owl, Wesley, Ed, you're with me. We're going up to that catwalk to get the lights. The rest of you, hold formation on the stage. Everyone, work as quietly as you can."

Alex activated her jet pack and shot up toward the catwalk. The jet packs were relatively quiet, but the noise they made seemed amplified in the large, empty room. Still, the four of them made it to the catwalk without bringing any vampires down on them, and they immediately went to work.

The first few lights went slowly as they figured out how to remove them. To Owl's delight, the lights were in even better condition than they could have hoped.

Alex, Ed, Wesley, and Owl worked quickly and quietly, communicating with hand signals or whispers when necessary, but mostly just flowing through the job. Before long, they'd each removed twelve of the large lights and lowered them to the floor where Chuck, Shirley, and Henry were organizing them while the others stood guard.

Alex eyed the pile on the floor far below her. They wouldn't be able to safely carry out much more than what they had. She decided she'd let them each get one more light and then call it.

She was starting toward the next light when she heard

Owl gasp. Alex spun, and saw Owl staring down in horror at the light that had just slipped out of her hand and was falling toward the floor.

Chuck saw it too, and he raced for the spot, trying to get under Owl so he could catch the falling light. He stretched out his hands, but he was a good three feet short of the spot.

The light slammed onto the ground with a thunderous crash.

For a moment, the Colosseum was silent. The team waited, no one even daring to breathe.

Then a howl came from the lobby, splitting the air with its piercing cry.

Immediately, the nerves Alex had been wrestling with since they'd entered the tower were gone. The thing she'd most feared had happened. There was no longer any reason for dread. It was time to act.

She shouted down to the team on the stage below. "Eyes on the exits. Form up and watch your lines."

A door on the north side of the Colosseum burst open, and a vampire charged down the aisle toward the team.

Patrick immediately fired, dropping the charging vampire with his shotgun.

The vampire fell, but no one celebrated. Their headlamps were all pointed toward the now open door, and their lights reflected off dozens of sets of eyes in the darkness beyond.

17

ALEX TORE her gaze away from the eyes shining from behind the door and looked up at the ceiling above them.

"Owl! How high up is that?" she asked.

Owl shot her a confused looked.

"How high's the ceiling? Your best guess."

The pilot shifted her gaze upward. "Over one hundred feet. Maybe one twenty."

Alex nodded. That was about what she'd figured, too. She'd just wanted someone to give her a sanity check before she risked all their lives. She hurried across the catwalk to Wesley, addressing the team as she went.

"Make sure nothing gets through those doors. We have them bottlenecked now, but that won't last. Hear me?"

"Yes, ma'am," came the chorus of replies.

By that point, she'd found what she'd needed in Wesley's pack. "Good. Then light 'em up."

She took one last look at the domed ceiling, trying to decide whether what she was about to do was crazy. The answer wasn't hard to come by; of course, it was crazy. But there was no way they were getting out of this room the way they'd come in. This was their only shot.

She activated her jet pack and rocketed upward.

As she flew, she kept one eye on the team working below. Owl, Wesley, and Ed had taken sniper positions at various spots in the rafters and were methodically picking off the vampires that squeezed through the doors. Patrick and Chuck were making their way closer to the doors, giving themselves a better position from which to attack. Firefly had his people in tight formation around him on the west side of the stage, waiting to take out any vampires that came from that direction.

Another set of doors burst open, and two dozen vampires piled into the doorway, all fighting to get through to their prey.

Patrick and Chuck opened fire, sending a barrage of ammunition tearing through the vampires squeezing past their brethren and into the Colosseum.

Yet another set of doors burst open, these ones on Firefly's side of the auditorium. Two vampires immediately fell, victims of precise headshots by Ed and Wesley. Firefly's recruits went to work on the rest.

Despite everything that was happening, Alex flushed as a rush of pride hit her. This was her team, taking care of business. This wasn't just some collection of fresh recruits with potential—not anymore. This was the GMT. They were staring overwhelming odds in the face and never flinching.

Still, a few vampires were breaking through. Only one or two at a time now, but that wouldn't last long. Which was why Alex needed to finish her work as quickly as possible.

"Alex, we need you down here," Owl called up to her. "There are too many of them."

"Just finishing up," Alex said. Another moment, and she was ready to join in the fray. And none too soon.

She dropped down from the ceiling, using a small burst from the jet pack to control her fall. She held her pistol in one hand and a detonator in the other.

"Wesley, Ed, Chuck!" she shouted. "Get on the ground."

They obeyed her order without hesitation, immediately leaping off the rafters and gliding to the floor.

Alex touched down just as three vampires rushed at Firefly's right flank. He didn't see them, but that was all right. She did.

She sprinted toward them, weapon raised. Three shots and three kills. In the chaos, Firefly didn't even know she'd saved his life.

With those three taken care of, she spun back toward the door, and what she saw made her heart sink. Vampires were pouring in by the dozens now, through six different sets of doors. There was no fighting them off. It was time.

She looked at her team, and time seemed to stop. She couldn't have been prouder of them. And now she was either going to end their lives or save them. She took a deep breath, held it for just a moment, then pressed the detonator.

The force of the blast hit her like a punch to the chest even though the explosion was a hundred feet over her head. She was knocked back and landed on her ass. As she pulled herself to her feet, she looked up and saw that her plan had worked.

She'd blown a thirty-foot hole in the ceiling of the Colosseum.

The edges of the hole bent under the pressure as sand poured into the room. Hitting the center of the stage in an unceasing cascade, it began to pile up, filling the air with dust.

Alex cursed herself for not anticipating that. She'd made sure her team was far enough from the stage to avoid being buried, but she hadn't considered what the influx of sand would do to the air.

She touched her radio and shouted into her headset. "Gas masks! Now!"

She pulled on her own mask, then scanned the room for her teammates. It was difficult to see through the dusty air, but she spotted a few of them straight away. She also spotted the vampires.

To her amazement, they appeared to be gathering together near the doors. It was like they were regrouping, considering how to continue their assault.

The GMT didn't give them time. As one, the team resumed their attack, firing on the gathered vampires, taking them down and whittling away at the horde, even as more vampires poured through the doors to join it.

Alex felt something touch her ankle as she downed another vampire, and she spun toward it, expecting to see a hostile clawing at her leg. But it wasn't a vampire; it was the sand. She gazed at the stage in awe, shocked at how massive the pile of sand had become and how far it had spread.

Then it happened, the thing she'd been hoping for since she'd thought of blowing a hole in the ceiling—the sun broke through the dust and sand, bathing the Colosseum in daylight.

The vampires began to shriek and jump back toward the doors. The sand coming through the hole had slowed to a dribble from just the right side, now.

"Team, form up!" Alex shouted.

They gathered below the edge of the stage, well within the safety of the light.

"Holy shit, Captain," Patrick said, his voice gleeful. "That was awesome."

Alex scanned the group. Her entire team was accounted for and uninjured. Most of them were laughing as the combination of adrenaline and the euphoria of having survived such a close brush with death overtook them. Even Firefly was smiling. As were Henry and Mario.

Then it hit her. "Firefly! Where's Shirley?"

Firefly blinked hard. "I... I don't know."

The team stood in shocked silence for a long moment.

Then Henry pointed to a large pile of sand on the west side of the auditorium near the stage. "She was standing over there."

"Come on." Alex marched toward the spot and immediately started digging. The rest of the team quickly joined her.

Firefly was the only one who held back. "Alex, you don't know what that exposition might have done to the structural integrity of this place. We can't stay here long. If Shirley got covered in the rush of sand, there's no way—"

She whirled toward him, her teeth bared. "Shut up and dig."

He stared at her in disbelief, and for a moment she thought he was going to argue. But then he nodded and got to work.

"Here!" Ed shouted. "I've got something!"

Alex rushed over, and sure enough, he'd uncovered a hand, the fingers opening and closing frantically, grasping at the sand as she futilely tried to pull herself out.

The team converged on that spot, quickly uncovered her arm, then her torso before finally pulling her free.

Shirley's eyes were filled with confusion and wide with terror. She immediately stood up, then stumbled forward and fell on her face in the sand.

Alex dropped to her knees and put a hand on the woman's shoulder. "It's okay. You're safe now. Lay here a moment and just breathe."

Firefly kneeled next to her. "Alex, thank you. If you hadn't—"

"Don't talk to me right now, *Captain*," she said, spitting out his title like a curse.

As angry as she was with him, she had to admit that he hadn't been wrong. There was no telling whether this room was safe, and they shouldn't dawdle.

But they had the lights. They had jet packs and there was a hole in the ceiling. Most importantly, they were all alive.

It was time to go home.

————

"YOU BOYS HAVE A GOOD SLEEP?" Toby asked Aaron and Mark.

Aaron nodded. "That, we did. You?"

"No worse than last night, and no better than the night before that."

Aaron suppressed the urge to roll his eyes. Toby was full of dumb sayings like that, things that were needlessly confusing and barely made sense once you'd untangled them. It reminded him of the way his grandfather had talked. He supposed that made sense, though Toby had been born a couple hundred years earlier than Aaron's grandfather.

For a while, the way Toby talked had nearly driven

Aaron crazy, but now he'd come to terms with it. In fact, *everything* seemed a little easier to deal with, now that they had their key cards.

Jaden had presented them to Mark and Aaron himself three days ago, two little squares of plastic that meant the difference between captivity and freedom in Agartha.

They hadn't used them yet except when they were required for their job duties—that would have been foolish. Aaron had instructed Mark to do his best to forget he even had it. They would only use the key cards without authorization one time: when they made their move. And they were still waiting for that opportunity.

"I hope you don't mind a little variety," Toby said. "You're going to have to run the storeroom without me tonight."

Aaron could practically feel Mark looking at him, but he willed himself to keep his eyes focused on Toby. In as casual a voice as he could manage, he said, "That so?"

Toby nodded. "Jaden's taking a scavenging crew out tonight. That means the rest of us get temporarily bumped up one slot. Robert is in charge. My boss is handling Robert's usual duties. That means I have to handle his."

"And we have to handle yours," Mark said. "I think we can manage."

"Good." Toby pulled the radio off his belt and held it up. "You know how to reach me if you need me." With that, he walked out the door, and they were alone.

Aaron tried to calm his spinning mind. He knew the patrols normally consisted of ten to twelve vampires. That left around ninety in Agartha. Still a lot to contend with, but slightly better odds than one hundred to two.

They waited three hours, both knowing this was their opportunity to take Agartha, but neither even daring to speak it aloud to each other.

At the three-and-a-half-hour mark, Aaron turned to Mark. "It's time."

They left the storeroom without another word. Aaron was aware that whatever happened tonight, they would never work in that storeroom again.

They walked hurriedly down the hallway, working their way toward the security control room.

Aaron spoke in a low voice. "Once we have the control room, everything else will fall into place. We turn the security people first. Then, we have them send out the emergency signal that Ferals are overrunning the defenses and all vampires are needed at the blast doors. When that happens, we can start turning more humans."

"We open the outer blast doors, right?" Mark asked.

Aaron nodded. "Let the Ferals take out as many of the vampires as they can. Use the railguns to take out some of the stragglers. The humans we turn can wipe out the rest of them."

"Sounds like a plan," Mark confirmed. "I can't wait for Jaden to get back with his team and see that we've taken over the city. That'll wipe the smug smile off his stupid face."

They reached the first set of locked doors they'd need to pass through in order to reach the security control room. Aaron held his key card up to the reader. Part of him was convinced alarms would immediately start blaring and vampires would drop from the ceiling to arrest them. Instead, the tiny light on the reader turned green and a soft click indicated that the door was now unlocked.

They passed through two more sets of locked doors before they reached the security room. With each door, Aaron grew more confident. The feeling that Jaden or

Robert was going to jump out at them faded, leaving determination in its place.

They paused just before they reached their destination.

"You ready?" Aaron asked.

Mark hesitated. "We each get to turn half the people in that room, right? I want vampire slaves, too."

"Yes, even split."

"Then I'm ready."

Aaron slowly raised his key card, acutely aware that once they opened that door, there was no turning back.

Mark bent his legs slightly, preparing to leap inside the moment the door opened.

Aaron took a deep breath, used his key card, and pulled open the door.

Mark's eyes widened, and he froze, still partially bent down. Aaron followed his gaze into the security room, and he, too, froze.

Jaden and a dozen other vampires stood in the middle of the room, their expressions hard.

"Good evening, gentlemen," Jaden said. "We've been expecting you."

———

JADEN STOOD STONE-STILL, his arms crossed, as the two young vampires entered the security control room. Mark look dumbstruck; he wore the expression of an animal that knew it had been spotted by a predator. Aaron, on the other hand, had a hungry, desperate look on his face. Jaden could practically see the wheels spinning in his mind.

"Jaden!" Aaron said. He spoke quickly, almost frantically. "What are you doing here? We thought you were out on an expedition tonight." He gestured toward Mark. "His radio broke, so we were just coming to switch it out with a new one."

Jaden ignored the obvious lie. "We've been watching you two closely, and we were well aware of your plan."

The look in Aaron's eyes shifted from one of desperation to one of defiance. "That so? Then how'd we get this far?"

"You didn't get far at all. Your key cards don't even work." He cocked a thumb toward the bank of monitors. "We had Theresa here watching you on the security cameras and manually unlocking the doors when you swiped your cards. You were never actually free to move about the city. I just wanted to see what you'd do. Now, I see we need to beef up security around our control room. So, thank you for that."

Aaron's lip quivered as he fought the instinct to bare his teeth.

A casual smile appeared on Robert's face. "You know what your problem is? You need to learn patience.

"Patience?" Mark asked. "We waited over a month."

Jaden chuckled. "That's what Robert's saying. A month is nothing. If you wanted to earn our trust, you should have waited a decade or two. Then you might have had a chance of catching us off guard."

After a moment, Aaron said, "What happens now?"

"That's up to you," Jaden said. "I'm a big believer in letting a vampire choose his own fate. So here are your options. We can kill you here and now, and it's over quickly. Or, you can choose banishment. We let you loose outside the city, and you take your chances in the wild."

Mark let out a wild laugh. "That's no choice at all. If you think I'm becoming a Feral again, you're even stupider than you look."

Aaron whirled toward Mark. "Shut up!" Turning back

toward Jaden, he continued. "I want to go out on my own terms. So does Mark, though he's too stupid to realize it yet."

"What? We said we'd never—"

"We'll enjoy the world for a couple more weeks. Then, when our minds start showing signs of slipping, we'll let the sun end things. Easy as that."

"So that's your decision?" Jaden asked. He looked at Mark. "Both of you?"

"Yes," Aaron said immediately.

After a moment's hesitation, Mark nodded.

"All right. Come with me." Jaden didn't bother restraining them. He knew if they tried anything, he could subdue them in seconds. That wasn't even taking into account the nineteen vampires who had his back.

He led them to the blast doors. No one spoke; what was there left to say?

As the blast doors opened and the cold wind rushed in, he gave them one final warning. "If we find you anywhere near the city, we'll kill you."

Then Mark and Aaron walked out into the night.

18

ALEX MARCHED INTO THE HUB, trying to ignore the sore muscles that were trying to slow her steps and the weariness trying to cloud her mind. The two weeks of daily missions to the surface had taken their toll. Fleming had asked to meet with her to discuss logistics for upcoming missions, and she intended to use this opportunity to tell him in no uncertain terms that the team needed a break. It was both cruel and unwise to push them this hard. They needed to be sharp on the surface. Keep this up, and they'd be looking for more replacement GMT members soon.

Besides, all these missions left little time for plotting with CB and Kurtz.

Technically, she probably should have alerted CB to this meeting. He was her superior officer, and she knew that he'd want to be present when she met with Fleming. But she knew that CB was being run just as ragged, though his over-work came in the form of endless meetings and reports. She didn't want to bother him with this. Also, Fleming's invitation had been so unexpected, it had caught her off guard.

She hadn't even seen Fleming in weeks. All of his orders had come to her through Firefly or CB.

She reached Fleming's office and the secretary immediately ushered her in. Alex was surprised to find the office alive with activity. Two sets of cameras were pointed at his desk. Fleming stood behind the desk, and a young woman was applying powder to his face.

Fleming's eyes lit up when he saw Alex. "Ah, Captain Goddard!"

"Hi. What's all this?"

Fleming let out an embarrassed chuckle. "I'm so sorry, but my secretary double-booked me. I have to give a very brief address. Do you mind hanging out for fifteen minutes or so? Then we can talk."

"Uh, sure." She looked around the crowded room, wondering where she'd even sit. "Do you want me to wait outside?"

"Don't be silly. Actually, would you mind terribly, being here for it?" He waved her over.

Before she knew what was happening, she was standing next to him, and the short woman was patting powder on her face.

"Fleming," she said, "I'm not sure I'm comfortable with this."

He waved his hand dismissively. "Nonsense. It'll only take a moment."

The makeup woman slipped away, and the cameraman said, "We're live in five, four, three…"

A brilliant smile appeared on Fleming's face and exactly two seconds later, he started speaking. "Good afternoon, *New Haven*. As director of the city, I've had the opportunity to address you many times, but I've never been more excited to do so than I am this morning. And I'm delighted to be standing next to *New Haven*'s favorite daughter, Captain Alex Goddard of the Ground Mission Team."

Alex smiled dumbly, her gaze frozen on the intimidating black eye of the camera in front of them. A heavy ball of worry grew in her stomach as she realized she'd been duped by Fleming, yet again.

"Captain Goddard returned only yesterday from another successful mission. Her team brought back components that will allow us to step up our efforts to defend our new settlement on the surface. Her team has been to the settlement a number of times and they are working hand-in-hand with Captain Garrett Eldred to ensure it is safe and secure."

Alex went cold as she realized Fleming's game. By standing beside him, she was implicitly giving her support and agreement to every word he said. And yet, she couldn't force herself to run, to argue, or to even speak. That camera lens held her frozen.

"Captain Goddard is one of the true heroes who is going to help humanity to reclaim the Earth. That's why I wanted her to be here today for two important announcements. First, I'd like to make public a name we've been using internally for some time now. As you know, Councilman Stearns was a true patriot who lived for the betterment of our great city. Since his tragic death, I've missed him every day. We certainly clashed in the Council room a time or two, but I know he would have given anything to see the safe Resettlement of Earth. That's why we've decided to call the first human settlement on Earth in one hundred and fifty years Fort Stearns."

He paused for a moment, apparently overcome with emotion.

"It's a fitting tribute to a great leader and it ensures that his legacy will live on long after we're all gone."

Alex wanted to throw up. She'd heard Firefly using the name Fort Stearns for weeks now, but she finally understood its significance. It wasn't a tribute to Stearns; it was the ultimate indignity for a man who had vehemently opposed Resettlement. Now, his name would forever be linked with it.

Fleming put an arm around Alex's shoulders. "The second announcement is just as exciting, and it's the reason I wanted Captain Goddard to be here today. Our director of engineering has just informed me our transport ship is ready for use. That means we can double our efforts to prepare Fort Stearns for its eventual residents. In fact, Captain Goddard and Captain Eldred will be leading a joint force of GMT and Resettlement troops down there beginning tomorrow, to make final preparations."

Alex clenched her fists in anger. Another mission tomorrow? And one that had been announced to the whole city? And still, she couldn't object. If she caused a scene now, she'd certainly lose her job. Maybe that was even what Fleming was hoping for. She couldn't let that happen. She still believed there was a chance that she could win Firefly over to her way of thinking. And if that happened, Fleming was done.

"It won't be long now," Fleming proclaimed, as he beamed at the cameras. "Soon, you will be setting foot on the Earth. Soon, your children will be running through the grass and swimming in the waters. And someday, your grandchildren will ask you what it was like, and you'll see the envy in their eyes as they hear your stories. Then, they'll tell you how lucky you were to be alive at that moment and to be part of Resettlement. Stay strong, my friends. It is an exciting time. Victory is in sight."

"We're clear," the cameraman said, and Alex felt all her muscles loosen.

Fleming grabbed her hand and pumped it in a shake. "Thank you, Alex. You did well. Ever consider a future in politics?"

Before she could comprehend, let alone answer that ridiculous question, Fleming's secretary stuck her head through the doorway. "Mr. Fleming, I'm sorry, but you have an urgent call from agriculture."

Fleming sighed. "All right, thank you. Alex, I'm so sorry, but we'll have to postpone our conversation. Duty calls."

Before she knew it, Alex was being ushered out of the office.

It wasn't until she was walking out of the Hub that the anger truly washed over her. She'd just been used to advance Fleming's agenda, and it made her furious.

She wished she could face Fleming on the fighting mat. Then, he'd know how it felt to be as powerless and outmatched as she felt every time he took her on in the political arena.

———

"THERE SHE IS," Jessica said with a smile. "Fleming's best buddy."

Alex grimaced. "Ugh, don't remind me."

Jessica, Brian, Owl, and CB were gathered in the GMT hangar so that Jessica could show them the transport ship. Alex was the last to arrive.

"I should have been in that meeting," CB growled.

"You're right," Alex said immediately. "I apologize."

"We can't keep underestimating Fleming. We have to be smarter than that."

"Give her a break, CB," Jessica said. "He just did to her what he's been doing to all of us for months."

"Enough of that," Owl said. "Can we see the ship now?"

There were three ships in the hangar: the away ship, a new backup away ship that was still being built, and the brand-new transport.

Jessica led them aboard the transport and gave them the grand tour. They started in the large cargo hold that had been outfitted with rows and rows of seats. Then, she showed them the large cockpit. "As you can see, it's simple, but it'll do its job."

"What's the capacity?" CB asked.

"A hundred passengers. Plus three crew."

Owl whistled. "That's incredible."

"I can't believe how fast you put this together," CB said.

Jessica nodded. "Me, neither. But we weren't given the option of more time. Besides, the resources Fleming threw at this thing made it possible. The ventilation systems in the agriculture sector are a little less stable without the parts we stripped, and the coolant towers are missing their redundant electrical fail-safes, but the ship's done. Now Fleming's on us to finish the backup away ship. He says we can't risk Resettlement falling behind schedule if there's a problem with the main ship."

CB shook his head. "It's amazing, isn't it?"

"What's that?" Jessica asked.

"How fickle people are. The entire city is eating out of Fleming's hand. Probably even more so after that little speech this morning." He shot a look at Alex.

"So honestly, between us," Jessica said, "is there any way Resettlement could work? I've seen the layout of the prison, and with all the enhancements we're adding, it seems solid."

CB turned to her, a sad look in his eyes. He put a hand

on her shoulder. "I want to believe it could. I really do. There's nothing I'd like more in the world than to be wrong about Resettlement. But anyone we send down there will not survive the night."

Alex took one last look around the ship. Seeing this vessel made the impending Resettlement even more real.

It was happening. And tomorrow, she'd help it take one more step toward becoming reality.

19

THE AWAY SHIP was quiet as they traveled to the newly dubbed Fort Stearns the following day. It felt strangely empty without Firefly and his handful of overeager recruits. The Resettlers, as they were now calling themselves, were flying in the new transport, so the GMT had their away ship all to themselves.

"I still can't believe we didn't get to ride in the new ship," Patrick grumbled.

"This is the first test of the transport," Alex said. "If that thing breaks down, you'll be glad we have old faithful, here. Besides, don't talk about the other ship like that. Owl gets a little... protective."

She glanced out the window and caught sight of the large transport ship in the distance behind them. As much as she didn't like bringing a group of Firefly's recruits along, she was even more against them flying on their own ship, leaving no time to build a little comradery between the two team before the mission. Besides, every moment with Firefly was another chance to wear him down a little more, to make him more open to her way of thinking. As badly as her dinner had gone with him a couple weeks ago, they'd actually built some rapport during their recent missions together.

She tore her gaze away from the window and moved it to the man sitting next to her. "How you doing?"

"Not bad," Chuck answered. "Actually, I've been working really hard, trying to improve as a GMT member, you know? I've been meaning to ask how you think I'm doing. Where do I need to improve?"

She thought a moment. Chuck's hard work was showing results. In early missions, he'd been one of the weakest, but he was developing fast. In truth, there were a dozen areas he could improve, but now wasn't the time to bring them up. They hadn't been to the prison in a week, and if past experience was any indication, it would almost certainly be crawling with vampires again by now. This wasn't the time to shake his confidence.

"Do you mind if I tell you what you're doing right instead?" she asked.

Chuck nodded.

"There are things I like about every person on the team. Ed and Patrick are ultra-competitive and fearless. Wesley's dependable and always puts his teammates ahead of himself. Owl's a genius when it comes to technical stuff. What I like about you is that you're cautious."

"Huh. That doesn't exactly sound like a compliment."

"It might not sound like, but it is. Look, people think the GMT is all about badass heroics and charging into vampire nests without hesitation. But it's actually much more about being smart. The best GMT members understand that instinctively. CB got it. Simmons got it. You get it, too."

"Damn, Captain, that's quite the compliment."

"I don't give it lightly. Here's an example. About a year

back, we had this mission to retrieve these rare electrical components in the old country of South Africa. Owl set us down, and the building looked perfect. The ceiling had caved in, so the whole place was covered in sunlight. All we had to do was walk in and get the parts. CB took one look at the place and called off the mission."

"What? Why?" Chuck asked.

The others were listening too now, drawn in by her story.

Alex shrugged. "I don't know. He told us it didn't feel right. So, we left. I bitched and moaned about it, of course, because back then I bitched and moaned about everything. But the veterans on the team didn't. They trusted CB so much that they didn't even question the decision. And General Craig trusted CB enough that he backed him up when Councilman Stern threw a fit about the GMT abandoning a mission."

"Heh," Ed laughed. "I would have liked to have seen that."

She looked around at her team. "That's what makes a great GMT team. You've got to trust your instincts and each other enough that you're willing to walk away from a job just because it doesn't feel right."

For the first time in the flight, Wesley spoke. "Then how do you explain Resettlement? It hasn't felt right from the jump."

To that, Alex had no answer.

The ships landed in the prison yard. The large open space felt much smaller with the huge transport ship parked in the middle of it. Firefly's crew ran out the cargo door. He'd brought six engineers with him today. The GMT would be in charge of safety, while Firefly's crew wired up the daylights.

"How's the new ride, Captain Eldred?" Alex asked.

"Smooth as *New Haven*," Firefly answered with a smile. "Where do you want to start?"

Alex gestured toward cellblock one. "I figure that's as good a place as any. Think we'll get more than one building done today?"

"Fleming wants us to shoot for five."

Alex frowned. She didn't give a rat's ass what Fleming wanted. And there was no way she was going to put the safety of her people on the line for his pushy demands. But she wasn't about to say that. "We'll see what we can do."

The engineers hauled a large generator out of the transport ship and set it near the door to Building One. As soon as they turned it on and it rumbled to life, a series of angry howls came from various buildings around them.

"Ah, there it is," Patrick said. "It's good to be back."

The engineers then brought out Brian's latest design—omnidirectional daylights. The lights were mounted on eight-foot stands and shone a thirty-foot circle of light for three hundred and sixty degrees around it. An engineer plugged one of the lights into the generator with a long extension cord and it immediately lit up.

"And we're off," Firefly said.

"Ed," Alex called. "You want to do the honors?"

"Hell yes, I do," he said. He shot his brother a gloating look.

"Lucky," Patrick muttered.

"Chuck, Wesley, stick close to Ed," Alex ordered.

Ed picked up the daylight by the stand and carried it to the door of Building One, Chuck and Wesley at his side with weapons drawn. He lowered the light, angling it through the doorway. As he made his way down the entry corridor and past the first security checkpoint, a vampire shrieked.

"Looks like we're in business, Captain," Ed called from inside. "You should have seen the way this vampire started smoking before it ran off."

Firefly grinned. "What are we waiting for? Plug in another light."

———

"I'M SUDDENLY VERY ATTRACTED to Brian McElroy," Owl said as she set up the second daylight in the central room of cell-block one.

"Same here," Patrick agreed.

Now that they had two daylights set up, most of the common area was bathed in artificial sunlight. They'd seen half a dozen vampires scurry either to the basement or into one of the cells when the daylights were brought in. It was testament to their faith in the lights that the entire GMT was comfortable inside the building with the creatures present. Alex had made the engineers wait outside and told them she'd get them when the building was clear.

Chuck scratched at his chin. "I noticed these daylights don't kill the vampires; they just hurt them."

Owl nodded. "The way I understand it, the light is more diffused. It would kill a vampire if it were dumb enough to stand in the light for a minute or two. But the purpose of these things is to act as a deterrent. They're not meant to be fatal."

Ed held up his rifle and grinned. "Good thing we are."

Wesley and Alex finished setting up the third light, positioning it for maximum coverage. Once that was done, the team began the dangerous work of clearing out the vampires cowering in the shadows.

"They're going to be desperate," Alex reminded them, "and they'll probably be angry."

"No different than usual, then?" Wesley asked.

The team spent the next hour sweeping through Building One. Alex's prediction was right—the vampires behaved even more erratically than usual. Some even moved a few inches into the light to try to nip at the humans.

But the vampires were also cornered, which made them easy targets. Since the walkways outside the cells were safely in the light, the team members could shoot the vampires huddled in the cells without risking being attacked.

In less than an hour they'd cleared out the two above-ground levels. Then they dragged a daylight into the basement and spent fifteen minutes clearing that. All told, they killed fifteen vampires in Building One.

"Yo, Firefly!" Alex called out the doorway. "We're ready for your brainiacs."

He frowned. "It's about time. And I don't like being called that name, remember?"

Alex grimaced. She'd been making an effort to use his real name, but she still slipped up sometimes. It bugged her that he was so ashamed of his old nickname. It was as if he were trying to deny that his time with the GMT had ever happened.

Firefly's six engineers hauled their equipment into Building One and went to work, while the GMT stood guard. By midday, they had a generator tied into the old electrical system, a battery backup, and every inch of the building covered in artificial daylight.

"Hot damn," Firefly said. "I think we have our first livable space."

Alex suppressed the urge to disagree. Instead, she said, "All right, then let's move on to Building Two."

The second building went much like the first, with the GMT setting up omnidirectional daylights in the central area to send the vampires running, then hunting them down and killing them. The difference this time was that Alex hung back a little. Her team was good enough that she didn't need to micromanage the operation. Instead, she observed while her team did their thing.

Ed and Patrick were as gung-ho and over-the-top excited as ever, keeping count of their kills and bragging about the accuracy of their shots. Wesley was his usual laid-back self. Chuck was slower, but more methodical. He also kept a close eye on his teammates. Not for the first time, Alex noticed that he had leadership potential.

Owl spent most of her time adjusting the daylights, preferring the technology to the action.

All in all, Alex was impressed. They were working as a team. They'd fallen into an easy rhythm that reminded her of the way the GMT had operated back in the days when CB was running things and Simmons and Drew were on the team. It made her smile. Maybe she wasn't such a bad captain, after all.

Once the building was vampire-free, the engineers came in and got to work.

Firefly stood next to Alex, the two captains overseeing the mission.

"Your team did a great job today," he told her.

She was a bit surprised at that. Firefly wasn't normally one to pass out compliments. "Thank you, Garrett."

"If we can keep this pace, the whole prison will be ready by the end of the week. Fleming will be ecstatic."

She lowered her voice a little. "Let me ask you something. Do you think this can work? Like, do you really believe it?"

Now Firefly looked surprised. "Resettlement? Of course, I do. Otherwise I wouldn't be here."

"Come on, man. You've seen the vampires at night. You know what they can do. The others, Fleming, they've never seen it with their own eyes, so I get their optimism. But you?"

"I've seen Fleming do the impossible before. His plans always work. I believe in him."

"I did too, once."

"When we come back here tomorrow, you'll see," he said. "These buildings will be free of vampires. This plan is going to work."

She looked up at him and saw the dark circles around his eyes. "Are you doing okay? Have you been sleeping?"

He shrugged. "I've been busy. Between the missions with you and all the other Resettlement stuff, I haven't had a lot of time."

"Garrett, listen to me. Fleming's plans have worked so far, yeah. But maybe sometimes the cost is too great."

He looked away, the unspoken cost hanging in the air. "And sometimes sacrifices are worth it to accomplish something truly historic."

Before she could reply, one of the engineers spoke.

"We're all set here, Captain Eldred. Building Two is good to go. Should we move on to Three?"

Alex glanced at her watch. "No, there's only an hour of daylight left. I'm calling it. Let's go home."

20

THE LABORATORY WAS a bustle of activity. Brian and Sarah worked side by side near the center of the room, with a dozen techs hurrying around them. Most of the techs appeared to be assembling daylights as Brian worked on the individual components.

Alex was a bit taken aback. In her experience, the lab had always been quiet, a peaceful place where Brian could work on his innovative designs away from the hustle and bustle of the rest of the ship. But it appeared that tranquility was a thing of the past.

She walked over to Brian and put a hand on his shoulder. "McElroy, what up?"

He looked up, startled, and Alex smiled. The lab may have changed, but Brian never did.

Although, now that she was looking at him, he looked paler than usual. Thinner, too. It appeared the GMT weren't the only ones Fleming was pushing to the limit.

"Hey, Alex, what's up with you?" he asked.

"I just got back from, um, Fort Stearns." She almost

choked on the name. "I was about to grab a bite to eat. Care to join me?"

He glanced down at the work in front of him. "I don't know. We're way behind, and—"

"Don't be an idiot. Even you can't work all the time. You need a break."

He nodded slowly. "Maybe a short one."

Sarah leaned toward them, a friendly smile on her face. "Great idea. Mind if I tag along?"

Brian shook his head. "This is too important for both of us to leave. You keep at it, and you can go when I get back."

Her smile wavered for a moment. "Come on, boss. We all need to eat."

"Sorry, Sarah," he insisted. "I promise I won't be too long." With that, he turned and walked away. Alex hurried to catch up to him.

Ten minutes later, they were sitting at a table at Tankards, shoveling cheap but delicious bar food into their mouths.

"I tell you, that woman's driving me crazy," Brian said, then took another huge bite. The poor guy was going at the food like he hadn't seen any in a week.

"Sarah's that bad, huh?"

He swallowed his food, then answered. "She's on me like glue. I'm in that lab sixteen hours a day, and I can't get five minutes of it away from her. And she's trying way too hard to impress me."

"You know she's reporting back to Fleming on you, right?"

"I'm not an idiot, Alex. And even if I were, she's being pretty damn obvious in her attempts to win me over. She's constantly touching me, coming up with excuses to be alone with me, stuff like that."

Alex raised an eyebrow. "Wow, Brian, sounds like you could finally get laid."

"Yeah, if I didn't mind sleeping with a two-faced traitor." He paused to take another bite. "Speaking of traitors, how are things coming on the Firefly front?"

She laughed and shook her head. "I don't know, man. He's tough to read. And Fleming... let's just say changing the direction of the city and staging a coup is proving to be more difficult than I expected."

Brian took another bite and she watched him, really looking at his face for the first time since they'd sat down.

"I say this in the kindest possible way, Brian, but you look like absolute shit. You need to take care of yourself, or you're going to end up in the hospital."

He looked back at her. "And I mean this in the least creepy way possible, but you look great. How are you dealing with the stress?"

She thought about that a moment. Although she was tired, she hadn't felt like she was reaching the breaking point, like Brian and Firefly appeared to be. "I think it's because I've been so focused on my team. Seeing them come into their own has been... Well, it's been exhilarating. My focus has been on training and working with them. On making sure they stay alive."

Brian was quiet for a minute. "Honestly, even when I do go to bed, I have trouble sleeping. I can't stop thinking about the friends we've lost."

Alex nodded. To her surprise, tears sprang to her eyes. "Not a day goes by that I don't think of Drew, Simmons, and Hope. Hell, even Stearns, though he was a pain in the ass. They died for something, every one of them. If hundreds of more people die during Resettlement, it'll be like our friends gave their lives for nothing."

Brian stared down at his plate.

"I just wish Fleming could have seen how our friends died," she continued. "There's no way he would be trying to bring more people to the surface if he had seen that firsthand."

Brian's voice was thick with venom. "He'd never set foot down there. He'd rather risk other lives than his own. So, he won't see a vampire until it's too late. And brining one up here isn't exactly an option."

Alex set down her fork, her mouth suddenly wide open.

"What?" he asked. "What did I say?"

"Holy shit, Brian. You're are a genius, and I'm kind of an idiot."

"Wait, what are you talking about?"

She put her hand over his. "I'm sorry, but I have to go." She stood up from her chair. "Finish eating. Then go take a nap. You've earned it."

Brian watched, slack-jawed, as Alex hurried out of the pub.

———

"What's this about?" Fleming asked.

"We only need your patience for a few more minutes," CB said.

Alex, CB, and Fleming walked down a long, sunlit corridor. It hadn't been that long ago that Alex had taken this walk for the first time herself, but it felt like another lifetime.

They reached the door at the end of the corridor and CB typed a five-digit code into the keypad mounted on the wall.

"Why haven't I seen this area before?" Fleming asked.

"I promise, you'll find out in a few moments," Alex assured him.

CB pulled the door open and gestured inside. "After you."

Fleming hesitated, and Alex saw a tiny flicker of fear in his eyes. It suddenly struck her that they were asking a lot of him. They'd asked him to accompany two of his subordinates, whom he knew opposed him, to a mysterious room in an isolated part of the ship.

It also said a lot about Fleming's unshakeable self-confidence that he'd gone along with them.

After a moment, the flicker of fear disappeared, and Fleming walked into the sunlit room.

"What is all this?" Fleming asked, his voice filled with wonder. He stared at the steel box in the corner.

CB gestured to a monitor on the wall. "See for yourself."

Fleming turned to the monitor and froze. For the first time since Alex had met him, Fleming was stunned into silence.

The monitor showed the inside of the steel box and the Feral huddled inside.

"My God," he said finally. "How long has that thing been here? Who the hell brought a vampire aboard my ship?"

"His name's Frank," CB said, "and he's been here from the beginning. He was one of the original crew of *New Haven*. He volunteered to be used, like a canary in the coalmine, from the old days."

"I don't know that reference," Fleming said.

"We meant to use Frank as a gauge of how the vampires on Earth are doing," Alex explained. "When he died, we'd know it might be safe to go back to the surface."

Fleming turned to CB. "Why wasn't I told about it?"

CB frowned. "It's a closely guarded secret, for obvious

reasons. People might not act rationally if they knew a vampire was on board. Only the head of the City Council, the director of security, and the field commander of the GMT are meant to know about it. Since the transfer of power didn't follow the, er, normal procedures when you took over, I guess it sort of slipped through the cracks."

Fleming looked back at the monitor and shuddered. "It really is the stuff of nightmares."

"That's not all we brought you here to show you," CB said. He walked over to the cage.

"You're not going to let it out, are you?" Fleming asked.

CB chuckled. "I'm not a madman, so, no." He reached into his pack and removed a blood pack he'd gotten from the hospital. He pulled out the sliding metal tray in the door and set the blood pack inside.

"How often do we feed it?" Fleming asked.

"Poor Frank here hasn't eaten in one hundred fifty years, but that's about to change." With that, he slid the tray through to Frank's side of the cage.

As Alex watched on the monitor, Frank immediately leapt toward the tray, snatching the blood pack with both hands. He tore into it with his razor-like teeth. Blood splashed across his monstrous face and onto his ashen-gray body as he slurped at the bag.

As soon as the blood entered his mouth, Frank began to change. His skin shifted and moved, like it was suddenly made of liquid. It rippled as it reshaped itself to the changing structure beneath, and its color began to change. Legs straightened. Arms thinned. The face shifted to a completely new shape.

Fleming, CB, and Alex watched in rapt attention, unable to tear their eyes away from the macabre transformation.

Frank's spine straightened and he cried out; whether in

pain or relief it was impossible to tell. He put his hands to his changing face, and his claws seemed to retract into his hands.

But to Alex, the most terrifying and wondrous part of the transformation was the eyes. The animalistic rage left those eyes as the irises shrank and the whites began to show. An intelligence appeared behind the eyes, even as they widened with the shock of what was happening.

Alex wanted nothing more than to look away, but she couldn't bring herself to do so.

Finally, after what couldn't have been more than thirty seconds but felt like much longer, Frank's now-human-looking fingers uncurled, and the empty blood bag fell to the ground at his feet. Then he collapsed to his knees and began to sob.

"My God," Fleming muttered.

"Jaden was telling the truth about the Ferals," Alex said. "This proves it."

Fleming didn't respond. His eyes still fixed on the monitor, he said, "We could kill him. Let him out, and the sun would take care of him, right?"

"It would," CB confirmed.

"Will he regain his humanity? His intelligence?"

"Maybe in time," CB said. "I think we should observe him and find out."

Alex put a hand on Fleming's shoulder. "Now that you've seen one of these monsters up close, you understand more about what we're up against. Don't you think we should slow Resettlement down and try to learn more about them?"

"I... I'm going to need time to process what I've seen today. Thank you for showing me this. Both of you."

————

George woke the same way he did every morning: to a blaring alarm at exactly four-thirty a.m. He hopped out of bed and started his daily routine.

Everything in Agartha was based on a strict schedule. This was mostly because the city leaders were hundreds of years old, and liked things to be done in a certain way, but also because there was only so much you could do inside of the city. In George's case, rising early gave him an opportunity to spend a little time with the vampires before they turned in for the day.

He took a quick shower, threw on some clothes, and headed down to grab a quick bite to eat before the daily briefing with Jaden. As he walked to the mess hall, he tried to enjoy the moment. The city was at its most peaceful at this time of day. The vampires were all finishing up their tasks for the evening, and there were only a handful of humans awake. George treasured these moments. In a confined, crowded city like Agartha, it was rare that you got a moment to feel alone.

George walked by the empty school, and for some reason thought of Jessica. He'd always been focused on his work, but meeting the woman from *New Haven* had made him consider other possibilities. She was a woman that he could envision sharing a life with. It would be a long shot at best for anything to happen on that front, but a guy could dream while he walked alone in the city.

George walked into the mostly empty dining area and observed the tables spread out before him. Across the room, Jaden sat alone at a table. That was uncommon. As rare as it was for George to get a moment alone, he knew it was much worse for Jaden. There was always some human or vampire who wanted a moment of his time. There was always a decision to be made or an approval to be signed off on. George didn't envy the old vampire's heavy load of responsibilities.

George intended to leave Jaden alone, but the vampire spotted him and waved him over.

"Morning, George. Grab some food and join me."

"Of course." George was surprised at the offer. He'd only ever spent time with Jaden in professional settings before, usually in Jaden's office. Though from the papers spread in front of him, Jaden was working. It wasn't like he'd suddenly developed a taste for oatmeal.

George had been looking forward to a quiet breakfast, but he supposed it was time for him to jump into work too. He got his food and sat down across from Jaden. The vampire had his hands folded on the table, and he watched George with a slight smile on his face as he took his first bite.

"Is everything okay?" George asked.

"I've just gotten a little stuck in my routine. I thought I'd mix things up a little this morning."

"By coming to the cafeteria and watching people eat?"

Jaden laughed. "Sure. Why not?"

George took another bite. Having a conversation with Jaden was always a weird experience. The vampire's ten centuries of life had given him an odd perspective. It was almost as if everything were a joke to him. Sometimes, when he looked at the humans of Agartha, he bore the same expression an indulgent parent might have when watching a child do something harmless, but silly.

"Something wrong?" Jaden asked.

George hadn't even realized exactly what was bothering him, until Jaden asked the question. "Yeah, I guess there is." He looked around to make sure no one could overhear him before he asked his question. "I don't understand why you let Mark and Aaron go. Isn't that putting the entire city in danger? I mean, we've got two rogue vampires out there running around, planning who knows what."

"They'll be dead, soon enough." He paused for a moment, as if considering how to explain. "I know it's odd from a human perspective, but what Aaron and Mark did wasn't entirely their own fault. They didn't know any better."

George set down his spoon. "Sorry, they didn't know any better? Turning on the people who took them in. Trying to kill you and take over the city. They didn't realize these things were wrong?"

"Before the infestation, things had a set order in the vampire world. Each master taught his progeny for a hundred years. He taught them how to control their almost uncontrollable urges and how to use their powers to their fullest effect. Mark and Aaron didn't have that. They were like children forced to grow up in the wild, with no parents to guide or protect them. Letting them choose their own fates was the smallest of kindnesses. I felt I owed them that."

George tried to see things from that perspective, but he couldn't quite get there. "I don't know. They were traitors. I still think it would have been better to end their lives nice and cleanly."

Jaden smiled. "Agartha has stood for one hundred fifty years. I don't think two rogue vampires of below-average intelligence will change that. Our bigger problem is *New Haven*."

George raised an eyebrow at the unexpected shift. Jaden had briefed George and a few of the others after his conversation with Alex, but he hadn't brought it up since. "Yeah?"

"Their Resettlement efforts are making me nervous. The time's not right. Their plan could cause the destruction of more than half of the human race. Not only that, but it could endanger Agartha."

George nodded. "If they do get eaten by Ferals, there will be a whole bunch of intelligent vampires running around."

"Exactly. I want to set up a meeting with this Fleming guy."

George scratched his chin. "Jessica said he's pretty ruthless. You sure you want to do that?"

"I don't know if I can change his mind, but I have to try. You think you could set it up for me?"

George nodded. "I'll radio Jessica as soon as *New Haven* comes into range."

Jaden's smile widened and he stood up from the table. "Good. Thank you. It's almost bedtime for me. Good morning, George."

"Good night, Jaden."

George watched the vampire go as he considered that he was about to set up the first official meeting between the leaders of Agartha and *New Haven,* and he wondered what it might mean for both of their futures.

21

THE AWAY SHIP cut through the sky, headed for Fort Stearns.

"Okay, here we go," Owl said. "As you know, ADX Florence, aka Fort Stearns, is situated in Florence County, Colorado. We've covered its population, colorful local history, geography, and recreational activities."

"Yep," Patrick said into his headset. "We can probably just skip the facts at this point."

"BUT!" Owl said. "Did you know Florence County is named for John C. Florence, a nineteenth-century explorer and United States presidential candidate?"

"Or we could just go ahead with the lame facts," Patrick said with a sigh.

Owl continued, "Florence was known as 'The Pathfinder.' Aside from his exploration and his political aspirations, he was also known for his passive-aggressive nature, which was noted by numerous historians."

The team waited for more, but none came.

"Sorry, that's all I've got. If we come down here again, I'm probably going to have to start making stuff up."

Alex laughed, glad for the distraction from the anxiety

she was feeling that morning. Today, she knew, would be the moment of truth. Fleming had been rattled by seeing Frank, but that had been her trump card. Whether or not it worked would largely depend on what happened next, she believed.

If the buildings where they'd set up the daylights were overrun with vampires today, Fleming would almost certainly listen to her and CB's pleas to slow the efforts for Resettlement. But if the buildings remained vampire-free, she believed nothing short of a bullet would stop Fleming from moving full steam ahead.

She looked around at her team. She'd done everything she could to keep them away from the politics of this. They had enough to worry about with staying alive. She coached them to focus on carrying out their orders, and not to think beyond the objectives before them.

But was that really fair? By simply working for CB and Alex, they'd put themselves in Fleming's line of sight. If he decided to make a move against Alex, the team would likely pay the price as much as she would.

Maybe in the beginning, it had made sense to keep them in the dark, but she wasn't sure it still did.

"Hey, Captain," Wesley said from across the aisle. "If you don't mind me saying so, you look a little stressed. I just wanted to say, it's going to be okay. You've got a hell of a team here."

She smiled at that. Ever since coming back from his injury, Wesley had been the perfect model of chill. It seemed nothing could faze him.

"I can't argue with you, there. You seem to be the expert in being laid back and taking everything in stride. Got any advice for me?"

He thought a moment. "I guess, once you survive nearly dying from a bullet tearing through your leg, getting hauled through the snow for a mile to certain doom, and you wake up in a city full of vampires, you almost have to develop a sense of humor. I had a moment there, lying in the bed in Agartha, where I either had to scream or laugh. I chose the latter. Kinda changed my perspective on everything."

Alex respected that attitude, but she couldn't apply it herself. It took too much detachment. Her biggest strength and her biggest weakness were the same thing: her passion. She couldn't give that up without also giving up who she was. And that was assuming that she even had a choice in that matter, that it wasn't hardwired into her DNA.

They were once again traveling in two ships today, with the GMT in the away ship and Firefly, his engineers, and their gear in that ridiculously large transport. Alex supposed it would have made more sense logistically to have the GMT ride in the transport, too, but Firefly hadn't offered. Plus, she probably would have had to physically restrain Owl to get her to ride in the cargo hold of that monstrosity, while her own ship sat idle. So, they traveled separately.

The two ships landed in the yard, the transport setting down first and the away ship squeezing in next to it. As soon as Owl gave the all-clear, Alex jumped out the cargo door and motioned for her team to do the same.

"No need to draw this thing out," Alex said. "Let's see if our daylights held up to the night."

She led the way toward Building One.

Even before she opened the door, she could see that the lights were still on in the building. Still, she readied her weapon and proceeded with caution, ordering her team to do the same.

As soon as she stepped inside, she heard the faint hum of the generator in the basement.

"Lights, check. Generator, check." Ed wore a slight smile on his face.

"Let's not get ahead of ourselves," Alex said. "We can declare victory after we're sure there are no vamps in here."

The team spent twenty minutes sweeping the building, carefully checking every room, every cell. There was not a shadow that they didn't venture into. By the time they'd finished sweeping the basement, the verdict was clear: there were no vampires in the building.

When they regrouped on the main level, Owl said, "Holy shit, Alex. Do you know what this means?"

She knew. She knew all too well.

Alex looked at Owl, sadness in her eyes. "It means that we can keep vampires out of an empty building at night. It also means that three hundred people are going to die."

───────

FIREFLY WAS WAITING in the yard for them, an anxious expression on his face. "How we looking, Captain Goddard?"

"All clear," Alex informed him.

The anxious look dissolved into a gleeful smile. "Oh, hell yeah. We are on our way! Didn't I tell you Fleming's plan would work?"

"You did tell me," Alex said, hands on her hips.

"Alex, seriously, thank you. Without you and your team, this wouldn't have been possible."

She was certain he meant the comment sincerely, but few statements could have hurt more. She knew it was true. As much as she railed against Resettlement, she was also helping to make it happen.

"What are we waiting for?" Firefly asked. "Start clearing Building Three."

As Alex gathered her team for another small offensive, Firefly set his engineers to work installing daylights on the tall towers mounted around the wall. Fleming believed this would be the key to keeping vampires outside the perimeter, and Firefly wanted to return to *New Haven* that night with news of how close they'd come to securing it.

"Okay, Ed and Patrick," Alex said, "each of you take a light and let's clear the next building."

They moved in a tighter formation than they had the day before. Now that they knew for certain that the daylights worked, they could all huddle together under them and attack from the safety of the light.

As soon as they passed the first checkpoint in Building Three, they heard a screech, and a vampire scurried away into the shadows.

"Heh," Ed said. "Looks like we spooked 'em."

As he finished speaking, something slammed into him, knocking him backwards. The light toppled over as he went sprawling on his ass.

"Form up around him," Alex shouted.

"What the hell was that?" Ed groaned.

Alex looked toward where the large projectile had skidded after hitting him. Her eyes widened in surprise.

"Ha!" Patrick pointed at the object, a delighted smile on his face.

"Something funny?" Ed growled.

"Yeah," his brother answered. "It's a mattress. You got bowled over by a damn mattress."

Alex reached down and helped Ed stand. The man was more embarrassed than injured.

"Maximum security," Owl pointed out. "The beds are

concrete. The showers and toilets are steel. All of it built into the floors and walls. If they wanted to throw something, the mattress is just about the only option."

Alex cursed silently. Patrick might have found the idea of mattress-wielding vampires humorous, but she did not. It meant that the vampires were looking for weapons that could take out the lights at a distance. They were learning.

This all reminded her of Texas, where a horde of quickly-learning vampires had taken the situation from bad to deadly in a matter of moments.

"Keep a tight formation," she told the team. "Remember, these guys learn from each other's experiences. My guess is, that won't be the only projectile we see today."

Luckily, the daylight Ed had dropped hadn't broken. He picked it up and they continued into the common area.

As they entered the area, the team froze. Twenty vampires stood lined along the top level, looking down at them. According to Owl's schematics, there had once been bulletproof glass between those corridors and the common area, but the glass was long gone.

"Get the lights in position," Alex ordered.

Ed and Patrick set the lights for maximum coverage of the room. They were safe in the light, but the way those vampires were hunched up there, some swaying gently, but none of them moving more than that, unnerved Alex. She'd never seen Ferals behave in quite that way.

"Take them down," she said.

Chuck started firing, and the battle began.

A few of the vampires ducked back into cells, but most just hissed at them. Five vampires were dead within the first ten seconds.

Another mattress sailed through the air and hit the daylight nearest Alex. The light toppled to the ground but remained lit. Alex made a mental note to compliment Brian on how tough these lights were.

"Heads up!" Chuck shouted.

Alex looked up just in time to see a vampire launching itself over the rail. It glided down toward them on its half wings, but it began screaming as it entered the light. By the time it touched down in front of the team, it was in flames.

Patrick fired a shotgun blast into its chest, and the force of the shot knocked it back out of the light. It hit the ground, then began to stand again. The Feral stumbled toward them, its body engulfed in flames and a large hole in its chest.

Patrick fired again, this time taking its head clean off.

Ed coughed and put a hand over his mouth. Alex couldn't blame him. The smell was horrendous: a stale, rotting meat odor mixed with burning hair.

More mattresses flew toward them, but the team focused their efforts, taking out vampires before they had a chance to hurl the objects over the railing.

Something hit the ground near Owl's feet, and everyone froze. That was no mattress; it was a chunk of concrete.

"Son of bitch," Alex shouted. "They're tearing apart the concrete beds."

Sure enough, another piece of concrete flew through the air, just missing one of the lights.

"We need to finish this quickly," Alex said. There were fewer vampires now, but she'd prefer twenty vampires armed with mattresses to six armed with concrete.

Out of the corner of her eye, she saw a vampire rushing toward the railing. She spun toward it and fired three quick rounds, catching it in the chest. It managed to throw a piece of concrete before she shot it, though.

Wesley cried out in pain and fell to the ground, clutching his leg.

Two more vampires appeared at the railing, and the team filled them with bullets.

They stood in silence, waiting for the next attack, but it never came.

"Wesley, what's your status?" Alex asked.

He gingerly got to his feet, still rubbing at his thigh. "I'm okay. I think a piece of concrete grazed me going by. Stung something fierce, but I'm good."

"Too bad," Ed said with a laugh. "I was hoping we'd be able to call you broken leg boy again."

"Nah, you'd miss me too much if I had to sit out the next mission," Wesley countered. "Who'd take out all the vamps you missed? The captain would start to notice what a terrible shot you are."

"I've noticed," Alex joked. "Glad you're okay, Wesley. Now let's get back to work. We've taken care of the dumb ones. Let's root out the rest of them."

They exited Building Three an hour later, having cleared the place of twenty-six vampires. Every one of them was wired from the stress of it all. The vampires had been ready for them, and that was an unnerving experience.

Firefly stood up from where he'd been sitting near the away ship. "Finally. Sounded like you guys were getting a little sloppy in there."

"Yeah, thanks for rushing in to lend us a hand," Alex said. "There were twice as many vampires in that building as there were yesterday."

Firefly shrugged. "You took care of them, though, right?"

"That's not the point. The lights and the scent of humans working in here day after day are attracting more vampires. And they're getting smarter in the ways they're attacking. Something's happening here."

Firefly brushed off his pants and walked over. "The only

thing that's happening is Resettlement. Once we get the daylights rigged along the wall, it won't matter how many vampires we attract, because they won't be able to get in here. Now, are you going to get started on that next building, or is your team scared to take on vamps during the day while armed with daylights?"

Alex opened her mouth to snap back at him, but before she could, she saw the Barton brothers marching toward him.

"You know so much about fighting vampires, maybe you want to show us your moves," Patrick said, the threat clear in his voice. "Maybe try them out on me, right here."

"Or me," Ed added. "Take your pick. Whichever one of us you want to rumble with. We're eager to learn, Captain."

Firefly looked at them in disbelief, as if shocked that they'd talk to him that way. "Captain Goddard, are you going to reprimand your soldiers for addressing a superior officer in that tone?"

Alex crossed her arms. "Actually, I'm going to commend them on their obvious hunger for knowledge. They have a legendary member of the GMT in front of them, and they don't want to miss the opportunity to learn from him. Well done, boys."

"Thanks, Captain," Patrick said, his intense gaze locked on Firefly.

Alex chuckled. "But that's enough learning for today. Come on. Let's check out Building Four."

She started to turn, but Firefly called to her.

"Alex. Sorry about before. I was just kidding around."

She considered another snide comment, but she knew that wouldn't have been productive. She was supposed to be trying to win him over. "Don't worry about it, Garrett. Sorry my guys got in your face."

He shrugged. "Can we meet for dinner again tonight? There's something we need to discuss."

Alex wanted nothing more than a quiet night in, but she couldn't pass up the opportunity to talk to him alone. "Sounds good. I'll be there. But first, I have to kill some vampires."

22

ALEX ARRIVED at the address Firefly had given her five minutes late. It wasn't like her to be late to appointments, even ones she wasn't especially looking forward to, but the dress she wore didn't lend itself to walking quickly. After being under-dressed the last time, she may have overcompensated.

Looking around, she couldn't imagine a nice restaurant in this neighborhood. She was in the heart of Sparrow's Ridge, near the sanitation building. If there was a fancy restaurant here, it was well hidden.

She was beginning to wonder if she might have gotten the address wrong when Firefly stepped out of the shadow of a doorway. To her relief, he was once again dressed in his new, upscale threads.

He waved to her. "Hey, Alex. Over here."

She walked over to him and followed him inside. "Did you bring me to a restaurant in the sewage station, Garrett? Or did you bring me here to kill me?"

"Neither," he said with a laugh. "Besides, the sewage station is down the street. Follow me. It's right up here."

She followed him up six flights of stairs—her dress really wasn't designed for this—and to the door to the roof. This whole thing seemed too elaborate, especially coming from Firefly. She hoped he wasn't going to start hitting on her. They had important things to discuss. Alex had the feeling that after the daylights had proven effective in the two buildings, her odds of winning Firefly over to her way of thinking were slipping away. Things would move quickly now. This could be her last chance.

He opened the door and gestured for her to walk through. She did so, and suddenly the whole elaborate ruse made sense.

There was a single table set up on the rooftop and it had three chairs around it. Fleming sat on one of them.

She fought hard to keep the anger off her face. Fleming had to know she wouldn't agree to another meeting without CB, especially after what he'd pulled with the surprise press conference the last time. The way Firefly had set her up here showed how deeply he was in Fleming's pocket.

For a moment she considered turning around, marching down those steps, and going home. But she didn't. She was about to have dinner with the two key players in Resettlement. Even though the odds of her convincing them of anything seemed insurmountable, she had to try.

Fleming stood up as she approached. "Alex, you look stunning."

She opened her mouth, but realized she had no idea how she was supposed to respond to that. "Thanks. You look fine. Good, I mean. Well dressed."

He nodded demurely, as if she'd paid him a huge compliment. Then he pulled out her chair and gestured for her to sit.

When they were all seated, Fleming poured from the

chilled bottle of wine on the table. They were situated near the edge of the roof, and they had a perfect view of one of the busiest streets in Sparrow's Ridge. Men and women in nondescript, government-issued clothes filed home after a long day of difficult labor.

Alex felt a twinge of guilt prickling her stomach. Here she was, drinking fancy wine, while they trudged back to their overcrowded quarters. Most of them would never even taste the worst-quality wine, let alone the good stuff she was sipping.

"So," Fleming said, interrupting her thoughts, "I hear congratulations are in order. The daylights worked."

Alex nodded. "They did. However, we've also noticed an increase in vampire activity in the other parts of the prison. The human presence seems to be attracting them. And they're learning. Only yesterday, they—"

Fleming held up a hand, cutting her off. "Let's make a deal, you and me. I know your thoughts on Resettlement, and you know mine. What do you say we table the Resettlement debate for tonight and just enjoy our meal and each other's company?"

Alex pressed her lips together, forming a thin line. If she couldn't talk about Resettlement, what was she even doing here? She'd have to agree for now and find a way to work it into the conversation. "Fine."

"Good. It's a big day for Garrett tomorrow. You'll have to make do without him at Fort Stearns."

Her eyes flicked toward Firefly. "Oh yeah? Why's that?"

"I'm going down to Agartha tomorrow evening to have a chat with our undead buddy Jaden," Firefly said.

"He contacted us and requested a meeting with me," Fleming explained. "I'm sending Firefly in my place."

"Huh," Alex said. Did Jaden just want to introduce

himself to the leader of *New Haven*, or was this something more? "Did he say what he wanted to talk about?"

"No," Fleming said. "Just that it was urgent."

"I hope he's not just hungry," Firefly joked.

"We'll find out soon enough," Fleming said. "Garrett tells me the new GMT is doing very well."

Alex nodded. "They are. It's amazing how quickly they got up to speed."

He raised his glass in salute. "That's a result of good leadership. And it's heartening. We're going to need to expand soon. It'll take multiple Ground Mission Teams to support both *New Haven* and Fort Stearns."

Multiple teams? She didn't like the sound of that. Not if it happened at the same breakneck speed as everything else Fleming did. "I thought we were tabling the Resettlement discussion."

"I said we were tabling the Resettlement *debate*. That doesn't mean we can't talk logistics. Did you know Florence County, the area around Fort Stearns, has sixteen prison facilities? Once our initial settlement is established, we'll want to create other communities."

"Ugh, I'm tired just thinking about it," Firefly said. "Can we get Fort Stearns done before we start talking about expansion?"

Fleming chuckled. "Fine—I'm just saying that more communities will offer more opportunities for promotions." He glanced at Alex. "For both of you."

That gave Alex pause. Was he trying to buy her off the way he had Firefly?

"Colonel Brickman is a great leader," Fleming said, "but he can't do everything. And if I'm being honest, he seems to be struggling with his new role a bit."

Alex frowned. "If you're trying to get me to betray CB—"

"I'm not. I'm simply pointing out that there will be opportunities available. And we need strong leaders. Like you."

A man with a large tray stood next to their table. Alex had been so enthralled in Fleming's conversation and how he might be trying to trap her that she hadn't even noticed the man arrive. He set plates in front of each of them. A beautifully prepared bread with two types of sauces drizzled over it, perfectly cooked asparagus, and some sort of flame-seared dish she couldn't identify. The aroma hit her nose and she felt herself go weak.

She started to pick up her fork, then stopped. This was just another tactic. A mind-bendingly, delicious-smelling tactic, but a tactic nonetheless. He was trying to distract her from the important things.

"Okay," she said, "you want me to be a strong leader? Then I'm going to act like one and tell you what you need to hear. Fort Stearns isn't safe. You need to slow down."

"Alex, we said we wouldn't—"

"No, *you* said. I tend to think the lives of the hundreds of people you plan on sending down there are too important not to discuss. If you want to test Fort Stearns out with a few badges for a night or two, fine. But moving in all these people at once is madness."

"It's necessary," Firefly countered. "If we don't have a large group, we won't be able to defend ourselves properly. We need the entire wall manned."

"You're sending them to their deaths!"

Fleming sighed. "All right, you've had your say. Now let me have mine." He gestured toward the people down in the street. "These people are the reason we have no choice but to Resettle. These are the ones I'm fighting for. They deserve to feel the ground under their feet. They deserve the chance to improve their lots in life."

"I'm not saying they don't," Alex insisted. She'd never looked at the Ridge from this perspective. From above it all. It had always been a part of her life and she'd always been part of it.

Fleming looked down at them and shook his head, a sad expression on his face. "They can be a strong people if we just give them a chance. And we will. They'll spread beyond Fort Stearns and eventually beyond the settlements we set up. They'll cover the Earth, if we help them do it."

Alex allowed herself one bite of the aromatic bread. Her eyes closed for a moment as she savored it. Then she washed it down with a sip of wine and stood up. "This isn't how we eat in the Ridge. Come with me. Both of you."

She walked off without looking to see if they would follow.

Five minutes later, she walked through the door of Tankards, Firefly and Fleming right behind her. She pushed her way through the after-work crowd and made it to a table in the back.

Someone across the bar whistled, then yelled, "The GMT got sexy!"

That was quickly followed by, "You didn't have to get dressed up for us, Alex!"

"I didn't, Travis," she called back. "It's for your mom."

"Sorry, Alex," another guy called. "You don't look good in a dress. Come back to my place and I'll help you out of it."

She shot him a withering look. "Trust me, Gavin, you couldn't handle me."

Fleming sidled up next to her, an uneasy look on his face. Firefly took the spot beside him.

"You been here before?" she asked Fleming.

He nodded slowly. "It's been a while."

"Yeah. I remember when you used to hold your political rallies a few blocks down the street. Times change, huh?"

"That, they do," the politician agreed.

Firefly sat quietly, an unreadable expression on his face. Alex wondered if he was reminiscing about the times they'd spent here with the GMT, or if he was angry that she'd torn him away from his fancy dinner.

The bar was the polar opposite of the restaurant he had taken Alex to the previous week. It was loud, cramped, and it smelled like sweat and stale beer.

Alex raised a hand and shouted to the bartender, "Three slops and three beers, Louie."

They were starting to get strange looks as the men and women began to recognize Fleming. The chatter in the bar went down a couple of decibels.

The bartender came over with three pints of beer and three plates covered with a rather unpleasant-looking stew made of scraps from the agricultural department. Every piece of food grown in *New Haven* had to be used, and much of what wasn't used elsewhere made its way to Sparrow's Ridge.

"Dig in," Alex told them.

Fleming let out a laugh. "It has been a long while since I ate slop. I loved it as a kid. My favorite thing about it was that every bite tastes different. It was like a surprise in each spoonful."

Firefly swallowed his first bite. "Then you're going to love this. It's especially... surprising."

"You want to show me Sparrow's Ridge?" Alex said. "This is how you do it. Not from above, looking down on them. These people *do* deserve better, but you can't just experiment with their lives. They're real people, with names and dreams and families. They're no different than the people in the Hub." She took a big drink of beer, then set the glass down hard on the table. "Here's the real difference between you and me. You think these people can be strong. I think they already are."

Fleming took another bite of food and looked around the bar. He turned back and looked Alex in the eyes for a long moment. "Alex, all people are important, but they are not all the same. Look at you. You may be the most gifted soldier this city has ever seen. You accomplish missions that no one else here could. It is the duty of the exceptional to lead the way to a better life for all."

"Is that what you are? Exceptional?"

"Of course. All three of us are. We started in Sparrow's Ridge, and we made it out. And, yes, that means we have to make the tough decisions. If there needs to be sacrifice for the advancement of the greater good, then that's a pill we have to swallow."

Alex felt the anger growing inside her like an approaching storm. She willed herself not to explode. Not here. Not now. "Fleming, I know there's no damn way you're ever going to listen to me. But do me a favor. Listen to him." She nodded at Firefly.

Firefly's mouth opened in surprise. "Me?"

She looked him in the eye. "Firefly, you know in your heart that Fleming is taking us down a destructive path. Be honest with him. You owe me that much. You owe Fleming that much, too."

She dropped a handful of coins on the table. "This one's on me, Fleming."

With that, she stood up and pushed her way out of the bar.

23

"IS THIS STRICTLY MANDATORY?" Ed asked the next evening. "No offense, Captain. I love what you've done with the place. It's just that with these nonstop missions, I barely have the energy to fall into bed at night, let alone participate in extracurriculars."

"He's got a point," Wesley said. "It's not like the old days of the GMT, when you'd go on a mission, what, every couple weeks? We don't spend our days lounging around like you used to."

Alex laughed. "Um, excuse me, that is not how it was."

Owl nodded. "If we weren't on a mission, we wished we were, with the training CB put us through."

"And yes," Alex added, "this is mandatory."

The Ground Mission Team was gathered in Alex's quarters. She'd rounded them up after the mission that day and told them to come to her place for dinner. Now she was serving up plates of a casserole dish her mom had often made, one of the few recipes Alex knew. Only, when her mom had made it, it hadn't been black on the bottom and tasted vaguely like ash.

Patrick took a bite, slowly chewed it, and swallowed hard. "Are we being punished?"

"Not yet," Alex said. "But keep complaining about my cooking and that could change."

He sullenly took another bite.

Alex took a deep breath. She'd been considering doing this for days, but after Patrick and Ed had stood up for her in the prison yard the previous day, she'd decided it was time. They were protecting her; she needed to give them her trust in return.

"This is sort of a GMT tradition," she began. "Back when CB was captain, we used to do this before every mission. We'd gather for dinner, chat, and be together in an environment where our lives weren't on the line."

"Wait," Chuck said, "are you saying we have to do this every night?"

"No."

"Oh, thank God," Ed muttered.

"But tonight's sort of a special occasion. I wanted to talk to you about something. I haven't been entirely honest with you."

The GMT members exchanged nervous glances, suddenly less interested in complaining about their mediocre food.

"I did it because I wanted to protect you," she continued. "I wanted you one hundred percent focused on the mission. I didn't want your heads clouded with politics. That was wrong of me, and I apologize. But it's time to rectify that situation." She took a deep breath. There was no turning back now. "CB, Owl, Jessica, Brian, and I are all involved in a plot to take Fleming down. And we are working to make sure it happens before Resettlement starts."

She went on to tell them everything. About the bombing

of the Council and her suspicions of Firefly's role in it. About how CB was working behind the scenes with Kurtz to gather evidence and to get the badges on their side. About how they planned to free General Craig and place him temporarily in charge until elections could be held.

Most of all, she explained why they were doing this. How she was absolutely certain that anyone who spent the night on the surface in Fort Stearns would die.

When she finished, there was a long silence. She let it hang there, then she said, "What you do with this information is up to you. If you want off the team, that's your call. But I thought you had to know. Because if Fleming finds out what we're up to, he'll come after me, and that means he'll probably come after you, too."

There was another long silence. Then something peculiar happened: Chuck started eating.

Patrick looked at him like he was crazy. "Did you hear what she just said?"

Chuck shrugged. "I don't know about you guys, but I trust Alex. If Fleming comes after her, he's going to have to get through me first." He took another bite, then said through his food, "Besides, he's always seemed like a massive son of a bitch."

Ed scratched his chin. "I voted for Resettlement, but it was just so I could go down there and fight vampires. I already get to do that, so, yeah, sure."

"You're not overthrowing the government without me," Patrick quickly added.

"I'm a little offended I wasn't in on this plan from the jump," Wesley remarked. "But you know I'm into it. I've seen vampires at night, and I'd rather not see them again."

Alex felt a lump rising in her throat at her team's loyalty. She'd expected at least some of them to protest, maybe argue about the merits of what they were doing. She wouldn't have been surprised if one or two of them had walked.

But instead they'd immediately bought in.

"All right then," she said. "Anyone want a second helping of casserole?"

Patrick's face screwed up in disgust. "Um, no."

———

FOR THE SECOND time in his life, Garrett was on the surface of the Earth when the sun went down. The first time had been a botched mission that he hadn't thought he would live through. This time he was here on purpose, sent here by Fleming, who apparently didn't have the balls to stand toe to toe with a vampire in the middle of the night.

He'd been waiting alone in this little room in Agartha for over an hour, and it was starting to wear on him. After weeks of being on the go almost constantly, he felt antsy sitting still with nothing but his thoughts to occupy his mind. Thoughts of the impending Resettlement and all the work that still had to be done to make it possible. Thoughts of Alex and her tireless efforts to plant doubt in his mind. He hated it. He hated the fact that there was a small kernel of truth to her words.

But his faith in Fleming outweighed her flawed logic. He had his moments of weakness, sure, but didn't everyone? He'd do the right thing for humanity when the time came.

The door opened and Jaden strode in, a smile on his face. "Firefly! Good to see you, my friend."

Garrett paused, caught off guard by the warm welcome. "Thank you. Good to see you too. And it's Captain Eldred now. I got a promotion."

"Congratulations." The vampire slid into the chair across from Garrett. "I'll be honest, I was really hoping to meet Fleming."

"He's a little busy at the moment. I'm here as his representative. You can say anything to me that you were going to say to him."

"Ah, scared of vampires, is he?" Jaden asked, a mischievous twinkle in his eyes.

Garrett pushed down the annoyance building within him. "No. Just busy, like I said the first time. So, what's this important thing you wanted to discuss?"

"The continued existence of the human race. That's fairly important, wouldn't you agree? But maybe a little small talk before we begin. That's how we used to do it back in civilized times." He stared at Garrett for a long moment. "So, you're having a hard time dealing with something you did?"

Garrett frowned. This was not going at all like he'd expected. "First of all, you have a funny definition of small talk. Secondly, I don't know what you're talking about."

"I've seen it a lot. It's a specific combination of terror and remorse that sits up around the eyes. You've killed someone, and you're struggling with it."

Garrett didn't even dare breathe. How the hell could this vampire possibly know about that?

Jaden held up a hand. "I'm not judging. I've killed hundreds. Sometimes with good reason, sometimes not so much. Just an observation."

"I don't know who you've been talking to, but that is bullshit. I didn't kill anyone."

"The only person I needed to talk to figure it out was you. You're fractured by it. Hell, you even changed your name. Did you notice the way you tensed up when I called you Firefly?"

Garrett took a long breath before responding. "The only things I kill are foul-smelling vampires. And I take them out every chance I get. Is this really what you called me down to talk about?"

Jaden shrugged. "Okay, then. On to business." He leaned forward and looked Garrett in the eye. "I called you down here to offer you my help."

Garrett raised an eyebrow. "Help with what?"

"Resettlement."

There were many possible things he'd thought Jaden might say tonight, but that wasn't one of them. He had absolutely no idea how to respond. The vampires of Agartha shouldn't even know about Resettlement. And he wanted to offer help?

Jaden waited him out, that small, knowing smile still glued onto his face.

Finally, Garrett answered. "Look, I don't know what you've heard, but—"

"I've heard that Fleming wants to set up a settlement on the surface, and that you are, in fact, helping him do so. And, honestly, I think it's a great idea."

"You do?" Garrett asked, the skepticism clear in his voice.

"Of course. *New Haven* was never meant to be permanent. We knew it would have to come back to Earth someday. And I'd like to help make that happen. I have knowledge, resources, experience, and I'm willing to provide them all. Free of charge, as we used to say."

"Then why do I sense a 'but' coming?"

"No 'but.' Only this. You have to do it at my pace."

"There it is. I knew this was too good to be true."

"It's not," Jaden said. "It's what you need to hear. To do this right will take many years. Even selecting the site for the settlement is something we should research."

Garrett stopped trying to suppress his anger. This vampire's arrogance had pushed him to the limit. "I'm not saying we *are* resettling, but if we were, we'd have all that covered. We'd have weapons to defend ourselves. An ideal location. A plan. You and your kind were the reason we had to leave Earth's surface in the first place. So, when it comes to your offer of help, thanks, but no, thanks. You can take your help and shove it up your ass."

Jaden laughed, true delight in his eyes. "This is a great conversation. I forgot that phrase even existed. This is why I love talking to foreigners." His face grew a bit more serious. "But I'm not making the offer to you, Firefly. I'm making it to Fleming."

"I'll take your offer to him, but I know his answer will be the same."

Jaden nodded. "Fine. That's all I can ask. I can see you're not having as much fun with this conversation as I am, so I'll just bring up one more point for you to pass along. When a human is turned to a vampire, it must obey its creator. He or she will not be able to disobey their master. It's involuntary. This obedience diminishes over time, but it takes about a hundred years or so before a new vamp has full control over their own actions."

"Why are you telling me this?"

Jaden smiled again. "I thought you might want to consider that every human you send down to the surface could become a slave to a vampire. A slave who knows the layout, defenses, and inner workings of both *New Haven* and your new settlement. If the people you send to Earth fail, it could be much worse than just a loss of life for the settlers. It might create an adversary who could destroy you all."

With that, he stood up from the table.

"I've taken up enough of your time. We have a suite prepared for you, if you'd like to get some rest. I understand a ship will be here to take you back to *New Haven* in the morning."

"Yes," Garrett said, his own voice distant in his ears.

"Good. Thank you for passing along my message to Fleming. It was nice talking with you, Firefly."

24

Three days had passed since Alex's dinner with the team and Firefly's meeting with Jaden. The past few days had been a blur of constant trips back and forth between *New Haven* and Fort Stearns. While their progress had been impressive, it had required them to spend nearly all of their waking hours on the surface.

And now they were headed back there for another day of preparations.

As wonderful as the team had been about her revelations, Alex did need the occasional break from them, so today, she was sitting in the cockpit of the away ship with Owl.

"So how long do we have?" Owl asked. "Before Fleming decides to pull the trigger on Resettlement?"

Alex shook her head. "Not long. A few weeks, maybe. Firefly's encouraging Fleming to extend the testing phase a little. We'll see how that goes."

Owl raised an eyebrow. "That's how far we've fallen? We're trusting that rat Firefly to buy us more time?"

"Looks like. I don't trust him, but he's not a complete

idiot. He sees the danger, and he wants Resettlement to succeed."

"Yeah, he wouldn't want hundreds of people to die," Owl said dryly. "It would be a real black mark on his record."

"Let's just hope CB and Kurtz can pull off a miracle before Fleming pulls the trigger."

After the ship landed, Alex gathered the team in the yard and split them up into teams of two. As was their routine, their first order of business was checking the buildings on the grounds, to make sure the lights were still on and that they were clear of Ferals.

"Barton brothers, you can partner up. Wesley and Chuck. And me and Owl."

Patrick shook his head. "The GMT is a real girls' club. When will the men get equal opportunity for facetime with the boss?"

"Today you'll have to be content admiring me from afar," Alex said. "Everyone, stay sharp out there. Just because the buildings have been clear the last three days doesn't mean we can assume they will be today. Let's move out."

Alex and Owl headed toward Buildings Six, Seven, and Eight. She glanced up at the wall where Firefly's team was working on installing more railguns. The majority of the area outside the wall would be protected by the pole-mounted daylights, but there were still a few blind spots. Hence the railguns. Firefly said he wanted every inch of the exterior within range of both daylights and railguns, but if Fleming kept pushing, it looked like that might not happen before the first group of three hundred Resettlers moved into Fort Stearns.

Firefly didn't always come on these missions; he often stayed on *New Haven* to help with the training of the Reset-tlers. Today, however, he was atop the wall, directing his team. Alex had to admit he'd grown into more of a leader than she would have thought possible back when he'd been a withdrawn loner on the GMT.

Alex checked the exterior lights on Building Six and everything was in working order. Then they went inside.

Owl and Alex moved cautiously through the building. Like every day since the lights had been installed, it was clear. As they reached the basement level, Owl said, "Looks like we're vampire-free."

"Indeed, it does."

Owl glanced at the generator and the backup batteries next to it. "You know, this is actually a pretty horrible redundancy system. If something takes out the generator, the batteries are just a few feet away."

"Why is that a problem?"

"Well, say there was an explosion down here. Both the batteries and the generator would be destroyed, right? Boom, no lights."

Alex nodded. "That's a good point. I'll bring it up to Firefly. Along with the mile-long list of concerns I've already mentioned to him."

Owl glanced toward the steps to make sure they were alone. "Have you talked to CB? Any progress?"

"Some, but he needs more time."

"We might not have it. Fleming's going to move the Resettlers down here soon."

"I'll set something up for tonight. Just the core group."

Owl seemed satisfied with that, and she headed toward the exit.

After searching the other buildings, Owl and Alex rejoined the other groups in the yard and confirmed that their searches had had similar results.

Firefly descended the steps leading down from the wall

and joined them. "How we looking today, Captain Goddard?"

"Clear as a bell, Captain Eldred."

"Excellent. The daylights are working. Brian McElroy really is a genius. We should name a building after him, or something."

Alex had to admit that the results had been impressive. The daylights had been working as a better deterrent than she had expected. Still, she couldn't help but wonder if that would hold true once the buildings were occupied. A vampire might not be willing to risk burning to enter an empty building, but one filled with humans? That, she didn't know.

"Let's just make sure we test everything before we start moving people in," Alex said.

Firefly clapped her on the back. "Don't worry so much, Alex. We'll make sure that everything is working perfectly before anyone stays the night down here."

———

ALEX, Brian, CB, and Owl sat around CB's kitchen table, waiting in silence. Alex felt weary. She'd lost track of the number of missions they'd been on lately. Every day seemed to bleed into the next. And there was still so much work left to do.

Finally, Jessica walked through the front door, a large container under her arm. "Sorry I'm late, but I brought enough slop from Tankards to feed us three times over."

"Hell yes," Owl said. "I'm starved."

CB waited until they all had plates of food in front of them to begin talking. "We're running out of time."

"You're telling me," Owl said, pausing to swallow a bite

of slop. "Fort Stearns is just about ready to go. It won't be more than a couple weeks before the Resettlers go down."

"I wouldn't be so sure," Brian said. "We've only made about half the railguns he ordered, and we're out of parts again."

"Huh," Alex said. "Won't he just strip the parts from somewhere else on *New Haven*?"

Jessica frowned. "Not if he wants to keep this bird in the air. We are down to the bone. I've taken everything that won't cause an immediate shutdown of vital systems. It's wildly irresponsible how many backup systems we've dismantled. If something happens..."

She let the thought hang in the air, unspoken.

"Same in the lab." Brian's voice was a little hoarse. He looked even worse than the last time Alex had seen him. "We've got every tech making lights, but we've burned though most of what the GMT got in Las Vegas."

CB turned to Alex. "Sounds like the defenses of Fort Stearns are coming together."

"Surprisingly, yeah." If there was one group she could be honest with, it was this one. "I thought the vampires would have that place torn apart by now, but that hasn't been the case."

CB nodded. "Okay then. That leaves my report." He paused. Everyone had stopped eating. This was the report they'd been waiting for. "I spoke with Colonel Kurtz today, and he's making great progress with the badges. A core group of their leaders are on board, and he's convinced that the rank and file will follow their lead. Especially when they see the GMT is anti-Fleming."

"Believe me, they are," Alex said.

"However, he said we're not ready to make a move."

Everyone around the table groaned.

CB held up a hand. "We're close. We're just not there yet. Kurtz says he has a witness who saw Sarah in the Council room just before the meeting. He has to convince her to come forward with her story."

"Couldn't he do that later?" Owl asked. "When Fleming's sitting in a cell, we'll have all the time in the world to build a case against him."

"Not really," CB countered. "A military coup of a democratically elected leader isn't something to be taken lightly. The people will want rock-solid proof of why we took action, and we damn well better have it. However, Kurtz says we're talking days, not weeks. He thinks he can convince the witness by the end of the week. If not, we move forward without her."

They all took that in and the clinking of utensils against plates was the only sound.

After a few moments, Jessica said, "Can I throw something out there?"

"Of course," CB said.

"Would it be such a bad thing if we let Resettlement move forward?"

Alex raised an eyebrow. "Um, are you new here?"

"CB said it himself. A military coup is not to be undertaken lightly. Let's say we let everything play out. Best-case scenario, we're wrong and Resettlement succeeds."

"Not going to happen," Alex interjected.

"Okay, then look at the other side. What's the absolute worst thing that happens?"

"Three hundred people die horrible deaths at the hands of vampires," Brian said.

Jessica held up a finger. "Exactly! That's what I'm saying. Three hundred people die. I don't mean to be cruel, but would that really be terrible? It would be tragic, but Fleming would be exposed as a fraud, we'd have even more grounds to remove him, and the question of Resettlement would be, err, settled."

Alex set down her fork and glared at Jessica. "I'm sorry, are you actually suggesting we just let three hundred people die?"

"I don't want anyone to die, but if it gives us our best chance to save everyone—"

"I don't believe this," Alex said, the anger rising in her voice. "That's Fleming's way of thinking. 'If I blow up the Council, it'll save lives in the long run.' That's exactly the mindset we're fighting against here. Once we start calculating how many lives are acceptable losses, *we* become the bad guys."

CB held up his hands. "Alex, calm down. Jessica's just bringing up a question that needs to be asked. We have to consider this from every angle. That said, I agree with you. We can't sacrifice lives."

Jessica glared at Alex for a moment, then broke into a smile. "Me, too. I just wanted to see how you'd respond to the question."

Alex laughed and she felt the tension go out of her. "I sort of hate you right now. So, are we going to come up with a plan that doesn't involve people dying?"

Brian scratched his chin. "I think that once Fleming announces the date he's sending the Resettlers down, that's when we need to move. If I know Fleming, he'll want to make a production out of it. That's when we stop waiting for more evidence and get moving."

"Agreed," CB said. "The announcement will be our last chance to make our move, assuming we haven't already. Jessica, how many people in engineering will be on our side?"

"It won't be difficult to get the key people from most departments. They're pretty pissed about the way he's stripping the ship."

"Good. If things don't go our way, we'll have the ability to shut down systems. That's great leverage."

Owl sighed. "I can't wait for this to be over. I just want to have a stable city again. All this is too much for me."

"Don't worry," Alex said. "It won't be much longer."

The group went back to their meals, and the conversation got lighter. As the meal went on, Alex felt herself relax for the first time in days. She was enjoying a meal among friends. Little moments like these were so important; they represented the very life they were fighting to protect.

Alex's radio beeped, interrupting her thoughts. She sighed. "Duty calls." She pressed the radio and said, "Captain Goddard here."

"Alex, it's Garrett. Fleming needs to see us immediately."

Just as he finished speaking, CB's radio beeped.

Before answering it, he smiled at his guests. "I hope you three don't mind cleaning up. Looks like Alex and I have somewhere to be."

25

"THE WATER SYSTEM?" Alex asked, a hint of panic in her voice. "That seems important."

"It is," Fleming replied. "Thanks for your keen observation."

CB and Alex were in Fleming's office. Unlike most times that they spoke to him, there was no entourage. Firefly, Sarah, reporters; none of them were present. It was only CB, Alex, and Fleming. He'd even shut the door to his office.

That had Alex concerned. It meant this was serious.

And then he'd confirmed her fears by telling them there was a problem with the water system.

"More specifically, a problem with the system that collects moisture from the atmosphere," he explained.

"The one that we use as our only source of drinking water," CB said, flatly.

"And irrigation. Bathing water. Sanitation."

"So, all the water, then?" Alex said.

Fleming nodded. "I'm not going to sugar coat this. It's bad. We have enough water stored up that no one outside the essential teams will know anything is wrong for the next day or so. But after that, all bets are off. Which means we need the parts to fix it, and we need them tomorrow."

"Guess the GMT needs to saddle up," Alex said.

"Very much so." He tapped a quick sequence on his tablet. "I'm sending you the location we've identified for replacement parts. Thankfully, any major city from the pre-infestation days would have what we need in their water-treatment plant. So, we're sending you down to Denver, the old city closest to Fort Stearns. That way your trip won't impact Captain Eldred's work."

Alex grimaced. Even now, he was prioritizing Resettlement.

Fleming looked at CB. "The two of us and Colonel Kurtz will meet with some of the badges tomorrow morning to apprise them of the situation. Just in case word gets out and things go badly."

"You're thinking there could be riots?" CB asked.

"If people don't have access to water, sure, it's possible. Let's hope it doesn't come to that."

CB nodded. "Why doesn't Jessica know about this? We just saw her, and she didn't mention anything about this."

"Water collection technically falls under the umbrella of agriculture."

"Yeah, but isn't her department involved in maintaining the system?"

"Yes. And we'll have to tell her tomorrow. But do me a favor. We don't want this getting out, so don't say anything about it to her or anyone else. I'll handle the communication. Got it?"

CB and Alex both said they understood.

"I want the GMT to leave before dawn, Denver time. That way you'll be ready to land when the sun comes up."

"Yes, sir." Now that there was a real crisis, she felt everything else slipping away. It was almost a relief to have a straightforward, save-the-city mission. No political needs. Yet, something bothered her about all of this and she couldn't resist the urge to bring it up. "Sir, how did the water-collection system *and* the backup system go down at the same time?"

The skin around Fleming's eyes creased as his face scrunched up in annoyance. "I think you know the answer to that, Captain Goddard."

"Because you dismantled the backup and used the parts for Resettlement." She wasn't going to let him off the hook, not without at least saying the words.

"Yes," Fleming admitted. "I shouldn't have done that. Lesson learned. Thankfully, this problem will be resolved within twenty-four hours, assuming you and your team do your job."

"We'll do our job, sir. If the parts are there, we'll get them."

"Good. Remember, this doesn't go beyond this room. I don't even want you briefing the GMT on it until you're in the air. I'm counting on you two to help us avoid a citywide panic."

After he'd dismissed them and they were headed out of the Hub, CB said, "Man, as much as that guy likes to shout about his every success, he also likes to reduce every one of his mistakes to a whisper."

Alex couldn't disagree.

She said goodbye to CB and headed back to her quarters. She then sent a message to the team, telling them to report to the hangar at oh four hundred hours. She didn't include any more details, and they knew better than to ask. She lay down to attempt a few hours of shuteye, and unlike most nights, she drifted right to sleep.

Five hours later, she was in the hangar, prepped and ready for the mission. The team arrived, confused and sleepy-eyed, but they geared up and boarded the away ship.

"No briefing, Captain?" Chuck asked.

"Nope." Alex didn't elaborate. Knowing when to shut up was one of CB's best tricks, and one she was trying to learn.

Just as she was walking over to grab her pack, she saw Firefly approaching. He waved hello and trotted over.

"You're here early," she said.

"Yeah. I hear we have to handle Fort Stearns on our own today. Fleming told me."

Alex frowned. Apparently, she and CB had to keep their secrets, but it was fine for Fleming to blab to his buddies. "Yeah. You'll have to check the buildings yourself."

"Ha. I'm not worried." He stood there awkwardly for a moment, just looking at her. He looked even more haggard than usual. His hair looked like a comb hadn't touched it yet that day, and a razor hadn't found its way to his stubble in a week.

"I should go," she said. "Urgent mission and all that."

"Stay safe out there."

"You too." After a moment, she pointed at the table. "That's my bag."

He looked back, apparently realizing he was blocking it. "Oh sorry! Here."

He handed her the bag, and she took it. "Good luck, Alex."

She grinned. "Luck? Luck is for card players. I'm with the GMT."

With that, she turned on her heel and marched to the away ship.

———

CB ENTERED the Hub an hour after dawn. This time, he wasn't heading to Fleming's office, but to the badge headquarters. He, Fleming, and Colonel Kurtz would be addressing a select group of badges to prepare them for the possibility of rioting if news of the water-collection malfunction got out.

Fleming and Kurtz were both there when CB arrived.

The councilman smiled when he saw CB. "Ah, here's the Colonel. We can get started."

"I'm not late, am I?" CB asked, a bit annoyed at the implication.

"Not at all," Fleming said. "Prompt as ever. Must be that military training."

CB exchanged an annoyed glance with Kurtz. The colonel over the badges looked nervous this morning. Maybe he suspected that his badges wouldn't take the news that they might soon be facing a riot very well.

"We'll be meeting with them in the holding area," Kurtz said. "Aside from General Craig, that area's empty now. We can say it's a training exercise, if anyone asks."

"Excellent," Fleming said. "Let's get to it."

Fleming led the way down a long corridor that led through the administrative section and to the portion of the building that served as the jail. Kurtz held the door for them as they entered the corridor, ushering CB through in front of him.

As they walked, CB considered whether he might be able to get some time alone with Kurtz after this briefing. The previous night's dinner had convinced him that they needed to be ready to move on Fleming. They might not have much warning. CB had to be sure Kurtz and his badges would be prepared when the time came. They should probably work out some sort of signal, so they could quickly—

"Colonel Brickman," Fleming said, interrupting the thought, "do you remember the last time we were down here together?"

That surprised CB. Fleming wasn't usually one to bring up the past. Not unless he was talking about his victories, anyway.

"I do," CB said, his voice grim. "You had me thrown in a jail cell."

"Yes. That's right. Remember our conversation that day? The deal we made?"

CB felt a strange tingling sensation on the back of his neck. Something wasn't right here.

"I agreed to let you go to the surface to rescue your team," Fleming said. "In return, you agreed to help make Resettlement happen."

CB glanced ahead down the hallway. It was empty. His pulse was racing now. Fleming was about to do something, reveal something...but what?

Fleming continued, "I held up my end of the agreement, and because of that you were able to bring most of your team home. So, why is it you've decided to betray me, rather than follow through on your end?"

They had reached the end of the corridor and the threshold to the jail area. CB was almost panicking now, waiting for the other shoe to drop.

Then he saw it.

At the entry to the jail area, there was a mirror mounted near the ceiling, angled down at a forty-five-degree angle. Presumably it was to give badges a full view of the area. CB looked into it now, and what he saw was so unexpected, he almost shouted in surprise.

Colonel Kurtz was pointing a gun at the back of CB's head.

CB lunged to his right just as Kurtz fired. The bullet missed by inches and ricocheted off the metal wall up ahead. Fleming looked back at them and gasped. Then he ducked out of the hallway.

CB was already in motion. Spinning, he grabbed Kurtz's wrist hard, then ducked down and pulled, flipping Kurtz through the air over his back. The badge colonel slammed into the ground and the wind rushed out of him.

Reaching down, CB ripped the gun out of the man's hand and put it to Kurtz's temple. "What the hell's going on?! I trusted you, you son of a bitch!"

Kurtz gasped, trying to catch his breath.

Before he could, two badges appeared, coming through the door Fleming had exited, guns drawn.

CB dove toward the ground, but this time he wasn't fast enough. The taller of the two guards fired, and the bullet clipped CB's arm.

Adrenaline surged in him and he gathered himself. He only had a moment, he knew. If he didn't act quickly, he'd either be dead or in a jail cell very shortly.

With a cry of pain, he leapt to his feet and dove across the hall, opening the door to an office and stumbling inside. He slammed the door shut behind him and turned the lock.

Knowing the lock wouldn't keep them out long, he looked frantically around the room. There wasn't much to help him. A desk. A cabinet. A window. But they were on the fifth floor of a six-story building, so jumping didn't seem feasible.

Wait. This was a corner office. And that meant...

As soon as the thought hit him, he sprang back into action. He grabbed the cabinet with his good arm and pulled with all his might, sending it crashing to the floor in front of the door. Maybe that would buy him a few more precious seconds.

Then he raised the gun and fired at the window, shattering the glass. A moment later, he was through it and on the ladder that served as a fire escape.

Up or down? He needed to decide fast. Getting to the ground would be the path of least resistance, and it would give him more mobility. But they'd expect him to go that way. If he could get to the roof, he could jump from building to building, the way he had when he was a kid. All while they would be searching the streets below.

That settled it. He was going up.

He reached the roof and hauled himself onto it just as he heard a ruckus in the office below. Sounded like they'd gotten past the lock and the cabinet.

"He shot out the window! Get some badges onto the street!"

CB lay flat on his back, breathing hard. His arm throbbed where the bullet had clipped him, but the bleeding was more troubling than the pain. The arm was already slick with blood all the way down his hand. Taking off his shirt, he quickly tied it around the wound, hoping to stop the bleeding.

He needed to get up, get moving. He needed to be as far away from here as possible, as quickly as possible.

He was just starting to rise when he heard Fleming's familiar voice coming through the window below.

"What the hell, Kurtz?! How do you miss from three feet away?"

"I didn't expect him to tense up like that, sir. If you'd have told me you were going to taunt him, maybe I would have—"

"Don't you dare turn this back on me, Kurtz. This is an

important day. A *very* important day. And now, on top of everything else, I have the colonel of the GMT running loose, bleeding all over our streets."

"He won't get far, sir. My men are on it." Kurtz hesitated a moment. "What are you going to do about the GMT, sir? When Alex finds out what happened, she's going to come after you."

CB could almost hear the smile coming back into Fleming's voice when he answered.

"Don't worry about the GMT, Kurtz. They're already as good as dead."

26

ALEX WAS STILL RUBBING the sleep from her eyes when Owl launched into her facts.

"We are nearly to the ancient city of Denver. Also known as the Mile-High City, Queen of the Plains, Wall Street of the West, Cow Town, Broncoville, and Queen City of the West. I hope you like it."

Patrick touched his radio. "Are you kidding me with those facts, Owl? That was literally just a list of nicknames."

"I had no time to research, so I had to use the almanac on my tablet. Cut me some slack."

Patrick shook his head in disgust. "I'm just saying, we've been exclusively going to Fort Stearns for the last three weeks or so. I was craving some fresh facts about a new location."

"By the way, shouldn't *New Haven* be the Mile-High City?" Chuck asked.

"Ah, that one I can answer," Owl replied. "*New Haven's* cruising altitude is twenty-seven thousand feet, which would make us the Five-Mile-High City."

Alex kept her eyes on the window as they approached

Denver. Visiting old cities always made her feel nostalgic for a time she'd never seen, a time when humans had walked the surface.

Places like the Colombian rainforest and Fort Stearns seemed so alien, like areas humans had once visited, leaving behind only some old buildings and tools when they'd gone. She could feel the mark of humanity upon them, but they didn't feel human.

Cities were different. Even after all these years, even though nature had reclaimed whole swaths, swallowing them in seas of greens and browns; even though the cars and buildings were so deteriorated, it was sometimes difficult to imagine what they'd looked like back when they were new, even with all that, Alex could always feel the deep humanity of the places. The cities wore it like a fingerprint cast in concrete. It was like an apartment whose residents had stepped out for the evening.

Being in cities made the pre-infestation past feel real. These had been human beings, no different from her or the people on *New Haven*. They'd had families. Jobs. They worried about mundane, day-to-day stuff the same way she did. And most of them had died horrible deaths. Many of them were still out there experiencing the hellish half-life of a starved Feral.

Seeing all this only built up her resolve. She wouldn't let such a thing happen to her people again. When the time for Resettlement did come, they'd do it right.

Owl set the away ship down in an open lot next to a dilapidated three-story building and the team got out. Chuck and Owl started preparing the rover while the rest of the team disembarked.

The water-treatment facility was in what had once been an industrial area, so there were a lot of open spaces that had once been parking lots. Due to the dry climate, the city was not as overgrown as most Alex had encountered.

They made their way to the front entrance of the building and discovered it was locked.

"You want to find another way inside?" Ed asked, raising his gun. "Or should I use my key?"

Alex considered that. "Time's of the essence. Let's get this over with as quickly as possible and then get back to *New Haven*. Use your key."

"Excellent," Ed said with a grin. He fired, blowing the door open.

Through the doorway, they saw the dim interior. This place had windows, but not many.

"Looks about as bright and cheery as our usual targets," Wesley remarked. "Just once, could we go on a mission to a sunny rooftop or something?"

Alex cracked a smile. "Where's the fun in that? You want sun, you should have stayed airborne."

They were just about to step through the doorway when Owl spoke in their headsets, her voice tense.

"Captain, we've got a problem. The batteries are missing from the rover."

Two minutes later, the team was back in the cargo hold of the ship. Alex frowned as she stared at the rover. "I don't understand. How could this happen?"

Owl shook her head. "Me, neither. Brian's team has a checklist they run through before every mission. They should have made sure that the batteries were fully charged. If they'd done their jobs, they'd have noticed the batteries were completely missing."

"Maybe they were going to replace them and forgot to install the new ones," Chuck guessed.

Something clicked in Alex's brain. "No. That's not it."

Time seemed to slow as everything came into focus. Fleming hadn't told Jessica about the water-collection problem. Last night, Alex had wondered why he'd called the GMT before Jessica, but she hadn't given the question the consideration that it deserved. Maybe it had been her tired mind, or maybe Fleming had just done that good a job of selling it.

She realized now what she should have realized then: there was only one reasonable explanation for why Fleming had called the GMT before the Director of Engineering.

"There's nothing wrong with the water-collection system," she said softly.

"Wait, what?" Wesley asked, confusion clear on his face.

Alex looked at Owl. "We need to radio *New Haven* and tell CB it's time for us to make our move. Fleming is sure as hell making his."

"Is someone going to tell us lowly peons what's going on here?" Patrick asked.

"Hang tight," she said as she followed Owl to the cockpit. "I'll explain soon."

Owl slid into the pilot's seat and punched the radio to turn it on. Nothing happened.

"You gotta be kidding me," she muttered as she pulled the panel off the front of it. "Circuits burned out."

"Seems an odd coincidence," Alex said.

Owl hit another button on the control panel. Then she hit it again. And again.

"Alex, we're in real trouble," she said, her voice quivering.

"Why?"

"Because that button is supposed to start the ship."

"So, we're stuck?" Ed asked. "On the surface? With no way off?"

"That's about the size of it," Alex said. Looking at her team gathered, the shock on their faces, she had to fight the urge to be sick. It was her fault they were here. If she hadn't been outmaneuvered by Fleming, if she hadn't been goaded into hurrying the team out to a mission without doing her due diligence, this wouldn't have happened.

And now they were trapped. In the old state of Colorado.

"Sarah must have been the one to do the pre-flight checks," Owl said. "Damn it all, why didn't we think of that? We should have seen it coming."

"With this many enemies, it's hard to keep an eye on all them," Wesley said.

"Here's what I don't understand," Chuck said. "If Fleming wants us dead, why not just rig the ship so it would crash? Or, hell, blow it up, like he did with the Council?"

"Fleming's an asshole, but he's an asshole who's strapped for resources," Alex explained. "He wouldn't want to lose the ship."

"Holy shit," Patrick muttered. "So, he's going to wait for us to die and then come get the ship? That's cold."

"That, he is. I underestimated just how cold. The good news is, he underestimated us, too. We're not done yet, and we're not going to die tonight."

The team looked at her, surprised.

"What, did you think we were going to give up? The way I see it, we have two possible outs. One, we wait here and try to survive the night. Maybe hide inside the ship. Then, tomorrow, when Fleming's people come to retrieve it, we put the hurt on them and steal their ride back to *New Haven*."

"Huh," Wesley said. "That would mean surviving the night and hoping the Ferals can't find a way into the ship."

"And that Fleming will send the crew down tomorrow," Chuck added. "Could be he'll wait a few days, to make sure we're dead."

"That's exactly why I don't like that option," Alex agreed. "As for the other option... Owl, how far are we from Agartha?"

Owl raised an eyebrow. "Too far to walk, that's for sure." She pulled out her tablet and began tapping at the screen. "Looks like about eighty miles."

"And how fast can the rover move when it's fully functional?"

"Twenty-five miles an hour. Assuming level terrain and clear roads. Which we won't have."

"So, let's assume we can average half that. That means it would take six hours to get to Agartha." Alex looked down at her watch. "It is currently ten a.m. local time, which means we have approximately two hours to figure out a way to get the rover functional. Let's get to work."

The team spent the next hour brainstorming, pulling parts off the ship, and experimenting with any possible way to get the rover going. During this time, Alex ceded control of the team to Owl, and the pilot wasted no time in putting them to work.

The most obvious solution would be to pull some batteries off of the ship and use them for the rover. That presented a number of practical problems. First, the batteries themselves were bigger than the entire rover, by half. But they would fit on the rover's eight-foot trailer.

The team got to work stripping the ship and lining the bottom of the trailer with two sets of batteries, enough to make the trip to Agartha three times, according to Owl.

They weren't taking any chances with one set of batteries. Patrick and Ed took some metal doors from the water-treatment facility and rigged them to lay over the batteries, giving the team a place to sit.

Owl and Chuck wired the batteries together and rigged up a connection to attach them to the rover's motor.

When they'd finished, Owl stood back and put her hands on her hips. "Well, it looks like shit, but it'll get us there."

Alex glanced at her watch. "And with ten minutes to spare. Nice work, team. Let's load up and head out."

Even though Alex knew the truth of their situation, she wasn't about to say it out loud to the team: the odds of them making it to Agartha in the next six hours were low, and if they didn't make it to Agartha in the next six hours, they would die.

27

CB STUMBLED from rooftop to rooftop, trying to make his way out of the Hub. The buildings were close enough together that he was able to easily leap from one to another, but he'd bled through his make-shift bandage and was leaving a trail of blood drips that even the worst badge in the Hub would be able to follow.

How he'd gotten this far without being caught, he did not know. He also knew his luck wouldn't last. The city was bustling below him as badges shouted and ran through the streets. He currently had a couple things going in his favor. The bright sun shone through the ship windows above him, as it always did on *New Haven*; hopefully it would mask him a bit if someone below happened to glance up.

But eventually someone would think of climbing up the ladder at badge headquarters. When they did, they'd find the trail of blood. Then finding him would be easy.

He needed to go to a friend. But who? He would be putting that person in immediate danger. Not that his friends weren't in danger already. If Kurtz had been on Fleming's side from the beginning, that meant Fleming knew that Brian, Jessica, Alex, and Owl were all directly in on the plot against him.

And then there was the most troubling question of all, the one that was gnawing on him like he was a mid-morning snack. Fleming had said the GMT was already as good as dead. That had to mean he'd somehow compromised their mission that morning.

CB was still considering this when the screens mounted around the city lit up, displaying Fleming's image. The camera was in close, and his toothy smile filled the width of the massive screens.

"Hello, my fellow citizens," he began. "Today, I'm coming to you with some truly exciting news."

CB resisted the urge to stop and watch. This was his chance, he knew. Every eye in *New Haven* would be fixed to those screens. If he could make it to the edge of the Hub while Fleming was bloviating, he might be able to climb down to the street without anyone noticing. Then he could make his way to the agricultural district and hide while he figured out his next move.

"We've had a rough go of it lately," Fleming continued. "I've asked for sacrifices from each and every one of you. My engineering crews have dismantled non-essential systems, and we've all felt the impact of that in our lives. The first thing I want to say this morning is, thank you. Thank you for believing in my vision for the future. Thank you for helping to make this day possible."

This day? CB wondered.

"Before we continue, I do have one piece of disturbing news to report. Despite the overwhelming support for our mission, there are still a few people who haven't been able to see our vision. They like their lives the way they are. They enjoy the privileged lifestyle aboard this ship that is the result of the hard work of the majority, and they don't want to give that up. One of those people is Colonel Arnold Brickman."

CB had half expected his name to come up, but it was still jarring to have a face on a giant monitor declare him a traitor.

"Colonel Brickman took action against our city today, storming the badge headquarters in an attempt to free General Craig, presumably so the general could help him stage a military coup. Colonel Brickman failed, and he was injured by a heroic badge, but he remains at large. Please, if you see him or have any information that could help us find him, contact a badge immediately. However, Brickman's dangerous and violent actions will not stop Resettlement. Which brings me to my real reason for speaking with you today."

CB leaped over a gap and landed on the next rooftop, this one at the edge of the Hub. The buildings beyond this point were much shorter, and he'd have to climb down here. For the first time in his life, he was thankful that Fleming was so damn wordy.

"The Resettlement preparations have gone even better than we'd expected," Fleming said, "due in no small part to the heroic efforts of Captain Garrett Eldred and his team of Resettlers. Captain Eldred has overseen both the GMT and his civilian teams in clearing Fort Stearns of vampires and preparing it to be a safe and comfortable home."

"Overseen the GMT," CB muttered as he stumbled across the next rooftop. "Like hell, he has."

"Today is a day of celebration. Even as we speak, a group of one hundred Resettlers are already in Fort Stearns. A second group of one hundred is en route, and the third will be joining them shortly."

CB forced himself to keep running as the news washed over him. This was it. Resettlement was happening. Fleming had beat them.

"Tonight, they will spend their first night on the surface. Captain Eldred has managed to keep Fort Stearns free of vampires for a week now, so I'm confident our Resettlers will be safe and secure. Any vampire who wanders into the perimeter outside Fort Stearns will be in for a nasty surprise."

CB reached the edge of the last building and began descending the ladder.

A thought hit him, a thought that made him push aside his devastation, fight the pain, and keep moving. His GMT was in trouble, and Fleming had purposely put them there.

CB couldn't lie down and die. Not yet. He had to save his team. Or, if he couldn't do that, he'd make sure Fleming paid the ultimate price.

"This is truly..." Fleming paused, as if overcome with emotion. "Ladies and gentlemen, this is truly just the beginning of what we are going to accomplish together. The Resettlers in Fort Stearns are the tip of the spear that we are going to drive into the heart of the vampires. Humanity *will* take back the Earth. Not in ten years. Not sometime soon. Now. The Earth is ours, and we are going to claim it."

The screens went dark just as CB's foot touched the street. He didn't stop to see if anyone had spotted him. He didn't look ahead to see if the way was clear. He just ran.

———

CAPTAIN GARRETT ELDER sat at his desk in the administrative building of Fort Stearns. It was a simple metal desk, barely big enough to get a chair under, but it would do for now. They hadn't been able to bring a lot of furniture down yet; they'd been afraid it would have led Alex and the GMT to guess that Resettlement was going to happen sooner than they were letting on. But Fleming had promised Garrett that he would requisition a desk that was more worthy of his station very soon.

Shirley marched up and stood at attention in front of his desk. The strain was clear around her eyes. He couldn't blame her. She was part of his inner circle, along with Henry and Mario. He'd burdened the three of them with a lot of responsibility very quickly. He just hoped they could handle it.

"How are we looking?" he asked her.

"Good, sir. The first hundred are pretty well settled in, the second hundred have been given their essential supplies and weapons, and the final group is in the process of disembarking from the transport."

"Excellent." He was pleased with the way things had been progressing so far. Granted, to the outside observer, it would have looked like chaos. With the way people were scurrying around, it resembled an anthill that had just been kicked. And yet, there was order within the apparent chaos.

One team was checking the daylights on the walls. Another was checking that all the backup batteries were charged and connected. Some of the former badges were checking the railguns on the walls to ensure that they were ready for use. Still others were unloading food and weapons from the transport. Everyone knew their job, and everyone was doing it.

For all the times Garrett had doubted himself, and even occasionally doubted Fleming, he had to admit that things were going smoothly.

And this was only the beginning. Things weren't going

to slow down anytime soon, Garrett knew. When the people of *New Haven* found out how well things had gone on Fort Stearns, their faith in Fleming would grow even more solid than it already was, and they'd demand that other settlements be launched as quickly as possible. And Fleming would comply.

If everything went according to plan, Garrett Eldred would hold the rank of major in a month's time and general before the year was out. He'd be overseeing not just one settlement, but dozens.

So why did he have this nagging feeling in his gut that made him want to run to the bathroom, close the door, and hide until the world disappeared around him?

He knew the answer, though he didn't want to think it.

While he sat safely behind these walls, his old GMT teammates were out there alone, afraid, and waiting for night to fall.

He told himself it wasn't his fault. He'd given Alex every chance to join the good guys. He'd reasoned with her, coerced her, and practically begged. Yet, she'd insisted on continuing down the dark path, working to undermine Fleming at every turn. And still, he'd given her one last chance at survival, as thin as that chance might be.

Garrett pushed the thoughts of Alex and the GMT out of his mind. Not only did he not deserve to feel guilty, but he didn't have time. There was too much to be done.

He watched through the window as a group of Resettlers filed into the admin building, carrying a crate of weapons. The admin building would serve as the hub and storage facility for the bulk of food and weapons.

Garrett smiled up at Shirley and picked up the microphone sitting on his desk. "What do you say we try out this PA system?"

"Absolutely, sir," she said with a grin.

He took a deep breath and pressed the button on the microphone. "This is Captain Eldred. Tonight, we will make history and give hope to humanity. I know most of you haven't been to the surface before today, so I wanted to take a moment to ease your minds. The lights in this base have kept vamps out for a week, and they'll do the same tonight. They will keep us safe. But you have something even more important than that. Look at the men and women around you. These are our best assets. You are all part of the most important moment for humanity since the final wave. You will be remembered as heroes and legends. Each of you has a legacy that will ring through the generations, and that starts tonight. I need all of you to remain calm and focused. Our lives on the surface have begun. It's time to start living them."

He set the microphone down and looked at Shirley.

"How was that for a first speech?"

She smiled at him, tears standing in her eyes. "It was wonderful, Captain."

28

DRIVING the rover through the streets of Denver was like trying to get to the bar at Tankards on a crowded Friday night: slow going. From abandoned cars to barricades to rubble from decaying buildings, it made for slow travel. The rover could go over almost anything, but with the trailer, it took a little more finesse.

Alex, Owl, Wesley, and Chuck rode up front, with Ed and Patrick sitting over the batteries on the trailer. The rover was loud as it made its way over the obstacles in its way, and they had to keep a constant grip on the roll bars, or risk being bounced from the vehicle.

It was slow going, but it wasn't until they'd been traveling for over an hour that they came to their first truly daunting obstacle.

"Huh," Wesley said when they saw it. "Owl, that twelve-and-a-half--miles-an-hour estimate accounted for giant piles of cars in the road, right?"

"It did not," Owl said hollowly.

The road ahead of them was blocked by a massive pile of vehicles five cars tall and ten cars long. What it was doing there, Alex did not know. Perhaps the cars had been stacked there in an attempt to blockade the vampires. Whenever the original reason, it sure was a pain in the ass now.

"Can we get over it?" Alex asked.

"Yeah," Owl said, the forced confidence clear in her voice. "We can get over it."

The rover slowly began to roll up the pile, and the passengers held on for dear life. It was bad up front, but Alex could only imagine how bumpy the ride was for Patrick and Ed on the trailer.

The rover was almost to the top of the pile, crunching its way over car after car, when they heard a howl from directly beneath them. Then another and third.

"Holy shit," Chuck whispered. "This is a nest."

Alex's pulse quickened as she realized he was right. "Owl, get us off this pile."

Owl's voice was strained when she answered. "Doing my best, Captain. But unless you want me to flip this thing, we have to take it slow."

Everyone held their weapons at the ready as Owl kept them moving forward. No one spoke.

Alex heard a strange creaking noise coming from a car to her left. "Nine o'clock," she shouted to the team.

A vampire burst up through a gap between cars, its teeth bared.

Before anyone could fire, the creature burst into flames. It started wriggling back down between the cars, screaming in pain, but Alex put a bullet through its head before it could.

The cries of the burning vampire were answered by howls from beneath their feet. The stack of cars shifted as the vampires moved around below them.

"Hang on!" Owl called. She turned hard to the left,

setting the front wheels on a more stable car. The trailer twisted behind them and almost tipped, but Patrick and Ed quickly moved their weight to the right, steadying it.

The rover continued rolling forward, on the downward angle now, and soon they were back on solid ground.

"Let's not do that again, ever," Ed called from the trailer.

The howls continued coming from the pile. Alex looked back and saw eyes staring out from the darkness underneath the cars.

"You know what?" Patrick said. "Screw them."

With that, he tossed a grenade onto the stack.

"What are you doing?" Alex shouted.

The grenade exploded, send the husks of several ruined cars jumping into the air. The howls of hunger turned to howls of rage and pain.

Ed laughed and high-fived his brother.

"You morons!" Alex yelled. "We can't afford to waste grenades like that."

The howls were coming from the buildings all around them now. Every vampire in that part of the city knew they were there.

They drove on in silence for a while. The roads were becoming clearer as they went further from the center of the city, but they still had to work their way through, around, or over the occasional obstacle. And they were way behind Owl's original estimated schedule.

"What should we do to Fleming when we get back to *New Haven*?" Patrick asked.

His brother was the first to answer. "I hear boiling in oil is painful."

"That could work," Owl said. "What about throwing him out the hangar door? That way he'd have some time to think about what he'd done on the way down."

"Nah," Patrick said. "I say we make him spar with the captain. She can put the hurt on him more effectively than any of that other stuff. I speak from personal experience."

They all laughed at that.

"Everyone, I'd like to apologize," Alex said, her voice serious. "It's my fault we're in this mess. Fleming wanted revenge on me for going against him. I'm sorry you got caught up in this."

"Are you kidding?" Wesley said. "I'm not mad that your actions got us stranded on the surface. I just wish you'd brought us in on it sooner."

"Agreed," Chuck added. "You're our captain. You've kept us alive and taught us how to survive on the surface. You showed us what the brotherhood of the GMT is all about. I think that I speak for everyone here when I say that we will back you over any politician. Right, team?"

"Hell, yeah," the rest of them agreed.

As the rover continued down the street, the howls in the buildings around them started to be less frequent. Soon, they would be out of Denver and hopefully, they'd be able to keep moving at a faster clip.

"How we doing on time?" Alex asked.

Owl checked the monitor in front of her. "Not great. But if things are clear up ahead, we should still be able to make it to Agartha by sunset. It'll be tight, but we can make it."

"Okay," Alex said. "Let's make it happen."

29

THE GMT REACHED the edge of the city. There were a few more buildings cutting vertical lines in the horizon up ahead, but beyond that there was nothing but mountains and sky. The road beneath them was cracked and potted, and there were occasional gaps that Owl had to slow to traverse.

The team sat in silence, taking in the beauty of the world around them.

"You ever wished you'd lived down here back in the pre-infestation days?" Ed asked.

"Sure," Chuck said. "All the time. Imagine being able to stretch out. Down here you could walk for miles and not see another human. Even back in the pre-infestation days, once you got out of the cities."

"That would make it much easier to avoid my ex-girl-friend," Wesley said.

"We still can live down here," Patrick told them. "All we have to do is kill a couple hundred million vampires each, and we're golden."

"I could probably handle five million myself," Ed

announced, "but one hundred million might be pushing it. Patrick would probably kill about eight vampires. That leaves the rest for you guys."

Alex chuckled. "Let's worry about getting through the day before we worry about ridding the world of vampires."

Though the trip so far had gone more slowly than they would have liked, everyone seemed to be in good spirits. Everyone except Owl. In fact, she looked like she was on the verge of vomiting all over the rover.

"You okay?" Alex asked her.

She answered in a quiet voice that still managed to carry to the whole team. "We're not going to make it, Alex."

There was a long silence.

"How close will we be by nightfall?" Alex asked.

"Close, but not there. Five miles from Agartha, maybe. Less if we're lucky."

Ed slammed his hand down on the metal door he was sitting on, and it clanged loudly. "So that's it? We die on this stupid mountain? Fleming wins? This is total bullshit!"

Alex turned back to look at him, steel in her eyes. "Of course, that's not it. Get a hold of yourself." She looked each team member in the eye so that they could see her resolve. Her gaze settled on Ed. "I don't know about you, but I'm still drawing breath, and until I'm not, this isn't over. We can do five miles in the dark. Hell, we could do twenty if we had to. We're the fiercest badasses on the ground or in the sky, and any vampire who tests us will learn a hard lesson about squaring off against the GMT."

Her team stared back at her, probably aware that she was filled with false bravado. Five miles in the dark was insanity. They wouldn't make it a quarter mile once the sun fell. But she also saw in their eyes that they'd follow her to the end. They'd keep fighting until the last drop of blood had drained from their bodies.

"Owl, push the rover to the max," she continued. "The rest of you, look through your packs and make sure you've got your weapons in order. Sundown is in an hour, and I want us ready."

A chorus of "Yes, Captain" split the air.

As the team began to dig through their packs, Alex did the same. She prepared her spare clips and made sure her grenades were easily accessible. Then she saw something that shouldn't have been there.

"What the hell?" She pulled the object out of her pack. It was a radio.

She hadn't put that in there. They traveled with their headset radios for communication between the team and the long-range radio on the away ship, but not these types of handheld units.

"Let me see that," Owl said.

"Can we reach *New Haven* with this?" Alex asked.

Owl shook her head. "Not unless they're really close. This thing's got, I don't know, maybe a twenty-mile range."

"Huh." As she considered how the radio had gotten there, she remembered something—Firefly standing awkwardly next to her pack for too long, then handing it to her.

Firefly had known they were being set up. He'd planted the radio to give them a chance at survival.

"We don't need to reach *New Haven*," Alex said. She played with the dial, selecting a channel she knew was monitored. "Agartha, this is the Ground Mission Team. We are headed to you, and we need assistance. Do you copy?"

There was no response.

She kept trying for the next thirty minutes, repeating the

same message every few minutes on a number of different channels. Until sunset, the radio was the only weapon that had any chance of keeping her team alive, and she was going to use it.

When the team was five miles out and shadows around them were growing too long for the team's comfort, they got their first response. "Who is this? No one is authorized to be outside this close to sunset."

Alex's eyes lit up. "Listen up, I need you to get George on this radio, and I need you to do it now."

There was a long pause. "George?"

"The director of engineering! Get him on the radio. Tell him it's Captain Alex Goddard."

There was a long silence on the other end.

"Man, Captain," Patrick said, "you even bark at strangers over the radio. You were born to be an officer."

A full two minutes passed, then George's voice came through the radio. "Alex, what are you doing flying in so close to dark? We could have used a little warning. Where you landing?"

"George, we are not flying. We're on a rover and we're headed straight for you."

Another pause. "Uh, what?"

Alex glanced west and saw the sun was touching the mountaintops. It wouldn't be long before it disappeared. "There's no time to explain. We are headed your way, but we're not going to make it in time. We need some help from your end."

"Our end? How far out are you?"

Alex looked at Owl.

"A little more than three miles," Owl said.

"Three miles, George," Alex repeated. "Listen, I need

you to wake Jaden. Tell him if he really wants to save humanity, he can start with us."

"Okay, Alex, keep heading our way as fast as you can. I'm on it."

She let out a breath. "Thank you. Now quit talking to me and get us some help!"

30

GARETT STOOD IN THE YARD, his hands behind his back, staring at his three top lieutenants. "Are we ready?"

Henry nodded. "Yes, sir. Every light has been checked and switched on. The generators and batteries are all functional and ready. The railguns have been activated, and each gunner has a supply of six thousand rounds. Snipers and lookouts are in place atop each guard tower. Our patrol teams are already in motion in the yard, and everyone else is in their designated building, armed and ready to be called into action, if needed."

"Excellent. Time?"

Mario checked his watch. "Sundown in five minutes, sir."

"Then let's get to our stations."

Garrett climbed the stairs leading to the tower on top of the administration building, Shirley following close behind him. From this centralized location, he'd have a three-hundred-sixty-degree view over every external wall.

He took his station and surveyed Fort Stearns. The

daylights lit an area sixty feet beyond the walls. Anything the lights didn't kill, the railguns would.

He looked west and saw the faint glow of red sky over the mountains. That, too, would soon disappear.

Night had fallen on Fort Stearns.

Garrett drew a deep breath and felt a calm wash over him. All the hard work of the past month had led to this. Humanity was back on the surface, finally home.

Shirley pointed beyond the eastern wall. "We've got movement, sir."

A vampire was rushing forward. Garrett raised his binoculars for a closer look and saw dozens of vampires sprinting from the same area, popping out of the ground like they were being propelled. He frowned. For the vampires he'd seen awake during the day, simply pulling themselves from the dirt had been an arduous process.

He focused in on one as it sprang from the soil, landed in a crouch, and sniffed the air. It immediately spun toward the prison and let out a terrible howl. It sounded different, more powerful than the howls he'd heard during the day. More feral. Answering cries came from outside every wall.

"Jesus," Shirley whispered. "They're everywhere."

Garrett put a hand on her shoulder. "It's all right. We knew the first couple nights would be rough. A lot of them are going to die tonight."

A rush of vampires raced toward the prison, as if the howls had unleashed them. As the light touched them, smoke rose from their skin. They screamed, but the yells seemed to hold more fury than fear. Some turned back, but others kept pressing forward, until they eventually burst into flames.

"Dumb animals," Garrett muttered.

The snipers in the guard tower opened fire. The vamps

standing just outside of the ring of light went down, one after another, as large-caliber rounds went through head after head.

Garrett put his radio to his lips. "Snipers, hold your fire for now. Let's see how they react to the light."

The line of vampires standing just outside the light was growing denser as more and more undead creatures on every side of Fort Stearns reached it. Some howled in rage. Others just glared up at the wall, teeth bared. More and more of them were coming out of the darkness.

How was it possible so many vampires were gathered outside? This place had been a small town. Maybe there was something to Alex's theory that the scent of humans working here over the past few weeks had drawn them.

It didn't matter. They could line up there all night for all Garrett cared. Or he could have the rail gunners take them out, and that would be that.

A vampire on the south side disappeared back into the darkness, then reappeared a moment later, sprinting toward the light. Just before it reached it, the vampire leapt, springing into the air with unbelievable force. It rose two hundred feet into the air, easily out of the range of the lights and well above the wall. As it fell, it stretched out its arms and its webbed wings caught the air. It glided swiftly toward the yard.

Shirley gripped Garrett's arm as several more vampires followed the first's example and leaped over the wall.

"Snipers, open fire!" Garrett called into the radio.

One by one, they picked off the airborne vampires. A few managed to land unscathed, but as soon as they entered the yard, they began to smoke and quickly burst into flames.

Garrett watched, his eyes widening as a vampire rushed toward the nearest Resettler, either unaware, or not caring that it was on fire. The flesh was melting off its bones, but still it tried to feed. The nearest patrol officer fired on the burning vampire, dropping it before it could reach any of them.

When all the vampires inside the wall were dead, Garrett looked around. The vampires were no longer leaping the wall. Maybe it was that psychic link Alex had talked about. Maybe they knew they would die if they went past the wall.

For a moment, Fort Stearns was quiet.

Then a howl broke the silence.

This howl wasn't the desperate, piecing cry Garrett was used to hearing. This was a low, rumbling sound that seemed to vibrate through the very tower where he stood and into his bones. It began outside the north wall, but quickly spread, growing louder, becoming a full-throated roar.

Garrett looked around and saw that most of his people had their hands to their ears now. He fought the urge for a moment, but then did the same. It didn't matter; the sound still rumbled into his brain.

More and more vampires emerged from the darkness, joining the roaring horde. There was a sea of them that stretched into the darkness and continued who knew how far. He wondered how many more were back there in the dark, summoned by the smell, or the roaring, or their mysterious mental link.

Looking out at the sea of vampires, he felt like his flesh had turned to ice. Even from this distance, he could smell them, an earthy, rancid odor, like decaying meat and rotting mushrooms. All the while, that horrible roar shook the tower around him.

And through it all, he heard Alex's voice. as if she were standing beside him. "Resettlement is suicide."

He raised the radio to his lips. "Rail gunners. Light. Them. Up."

The gunners opened fire, tearing through the front lines of vampires.

The roar became more disjointed and broken as the creatures responded to the attack. Ten of them outside the western wall formed a wedge and leaped in unison toward one of the daylights. The rail gunners on that side were ready, sending a barrage of ammunition tearing through the group. Pieces of vampire flesh flew as they were all shredded by the gunfire.

All but two of them. The two in the back of the wedge.

The final two landed on the daylight. They instantly caught fire, but they punched at the light, breaking through the protective outer glass.

A rail gunner fired on them, killing them both, but destroying the light in the process.

Garrett's mind raced as he thought about how much ammunition had just been used to take out ten vampires. Two hundred rounds? More? Whatever the answer, at this pace they would run out of ammunition much sooner than they ran out of vampires.

He wasn't about to give up yet. That wasn't how CB had taught him. If they could just survive this initial onslaught, he was sure they'd have a chance. He raised the radio to his mouth.

"Rail gunners, hold your stations. Everyone else, fall back to the administrative building."

He watched from the guard tower as his Resettlers hurried to carry out his order. He could see even from there that most of them were in full panic mode. Some screamed as they ran. Others pushed, shoving their fellow Resettlers out of the way.

Looking down at them was almost as terrifying as looking out at the horde of vampires. As hard as he'd worked to prepare them, it hadn't been enough. But could you really prepare someone for this type of horror? He only knew a handful of people who wouldn't crack in this situation, and every one of them worked for the GMT.

A loud crash came from the south wall, and Garrett spun toward it. As his watched, a rock the size of a fist flew over the wall and slammed into one of the buildings below, exploding into dust.

"Holy shit, sir!" Shirley cried. "What do we—"

Garrett whirled on her. "Get in the administrative building with the others."

Another rock flew, and this one slammed into one of the daylights. The reinforced glass held, but how many more hits like that could it take?

More rocks flew, hitting the lights and the railguns.

Most of the people were inside the administrative building now, and the rest would be, soon. That would buy them a little time.

He swallowed hard, driving down the lump of fear and sorrow that seemed lodged in his throat. He'd do his best to keep them fighting. They'd take out as many vampires as they could before this was over.

But Garrett Eldred could already see how this was going to end.

31

THE ROVER HUMMED up the mountain toward Agartha, its motors smoking from the strain of the trip.

"Um, is that bad?" Chuck asked, nodding toward the motor.

"It's not great," Owl answered through clenched teeth.

The sun was a thin line at the horizon now. The team was close to Agartha, but Owl's calculations had proven correct: they were still two miles out and the sun would be gone at any moment.

"Okay, everybody, prepare for incoming," Alex told the team. "They're going to be coming fast, much faster than we're used to. Remember the fundamentals and focus on things you can control. Pick a target. Eliminate that target. Repeat. Watch your buddies' backs." She paused. "We're about to face vampires at night. You want to put yourself to the ultimate test? This is it. Whatever happens, we go down fighting."

"Is it strange that I'm both petrified and absolutely thrilled right now?" Chuck asked.

Patrick grinned. "Nah, just means you're as much of a weirdo as the rest of us."

In the distance, a howl came from the shadows. Then, something else: the roar of an engine.

"If that's George, I am going to kiss that man on the mouth," Owl shouted.

"Me too," Ed added.

A large armored vehicle sped around a bend up ahead and careened into view.

The radio in Alex's hand sprang to life and George's voice came through. "I see you! Keep moving. Let's get to Agartha."

Alex quickly answered. "George, don't you want us to get in the armored transport?"

"No time. This thing is not tough enough to survive a full-on vampire assault. What I have inside is, but that doesn't mean that we're safe. Just keep heading to the entrance like your life depends on it, because it does."

The large vehicle raced past them, then turned a surprisingly sharp one hundred eighty degrees and pulled up alongside the rover.

"Can't that thing go any faster?" George called.

"It can barely go the speed it's going now," Alex shot back.

She looked to her left and saw glowing eyes in the growing shadows. The last sliver of light shone on them, keeping the Ferals at bay as they raced along the road.

Owl looked at Alex. "I hope that there is a miracle inside of that truck, because we're about to have some hungry visitors."

"Get ready, team," Alex called. "This is it."

All at once, the sun disappeared behind the mountains and night was upon them.

Alex gripped her pistols hard as day turned to night.

The Ferals sprang from their hiding places, leaping at the rover.

As the team picked their targets and fired, an animalistic roar came from the armored vehicle next to them. Jaden rocketed out of the back of the truck, followed by ten vampires. They moved at an incredible speed, landing in the midst of the Ferals and tearing through them.

"Focus up, team! We still have incoming." A wonderful and terrible battle lust coursed through Alex's veins. She fired, hitting a Feral that was racing toward them square in the forehead. The Ferals on either side of it fell too, taken out by Chuck and Wesley. She turned just in time to see a Feral's head explode a moment before it landed on the rover, taken out by Patrick's shotgun.

The Ferals were coming at them with such speed and with such numbers that it seemed impossible even to fire fast enough to hit them all. The rover wouldn't last much longer if something didn't change fast.

Then Jaden charged from where he'd landed, entering the fray. Watching him was mesmerizing. He moved so quickly, her eyes could barely track him, but that was only the beginning. To watch him fight was like watching water flow. He carried two long, curved swords, and he wielded them as if they were extensions of his very soul. Each movement melted into the next in a dance of righteous carnage. His blades whirred through the air, creating a humming sound that added a kind of music to his dance.

Alex thought that it was the most beautiful thing she had ever seen.

He moved along the line of attacking Ferals, slicing through them. Heads parted from necks under his blade. He cut one of them clean in half, cleaving its heart in two along with the rest of its torso.

The Ferals were so focused on the humans that they barely seemed to notice Jaden carving through their companions, much to their detriment. In the time that it had taken Alex to shoot two Ferals, Jaden had dispatched ten with his twin swords.

Alex tore her gaze away from Jaden and appraised their situation. Owl was still focused intently on the road ahead, as it there wasn't a battle raging all around her. The vampires of Agartha were moving closer, forming a protective circle around the rover. They ran alongside it, easily keeping up with its speed even as they fought. The members of Jaden's team were almost as lethal as he was. Within a minute, all of the Agartha vampires were covered in blood and the remaining Ferals fell back.

Alex knew better than to think it was over. No. It was just getting started.

32

GARRETT MARCHED through the administration building, shouting orders into his radio. "Teams, I want every gun trained on the entrance. The daylights will burn any vampire that gets in here, but we better make damn sure none of them makes if far enough to destroy a light."

People moved quickly to follow his orders, but in such a chaotic fashion that someone was likely to get trampled in this crowded area. He looked around and saw panic in the eyes of the Resettlers as they shuffled for space.

"Sir," Shirley said, "people aren't listening. They're running around like they have no idea what they're doing."

He couldn't argue. In retrospect, this was probably not the best mission on which to work out the kinks with a new team.

His radio beeped and Mario's voice came through. "Captain, everyone's inside. We've got two rail guns set up in the hall like you said. We'll blast anything that tries to come through."

"Nice work," he said. "Weld the doors shut."

"Yes, sir."

Mario's team immediately got to work.

Most people seemed to be calming down a little, now that they'd found their places and there seemed to be a plan. Garrett looked around, not displeased at what he saw. Maybe they could salvage this thing, yet.

The plan had always been to use this building as a last stand in a worst-case scenario. He just hadn't thought that it would happen in less than ten minutes after sunset on their first night.

He made his way to the bank of monitors set up in the main room. On them, he could see vampires raining down on the yard. Some of the lights were still functional, and many of the vampires were on fire. Still, others managed to find the gaps and slip through unharmed.

On another screen, Ferals were bashing away at the lights with rocks even as they burned.

The building reverberated with an unending stream of thuds as vampires and rocks landed on the exterior. It would just be a matter of time until they made it into this building.

He knew that this was the end for the three hundred Resettlers, but he wanted to be damn sure that they took three thousand vampires out with them.

"Are we going to make it, Captain Eldred?" Shirley asked.

"I don't know," he said, "but do me a favor. Just for tonight. Call me Firefly."

He hit a button on the control panel in front of him, activating the PA system. Then he spoke into the microphone. "All of you brave men and women have proven your courage here tonight. I need you to hold your ground one more time. Everything that makes humans great—"

At that moment, the lights went out.

He stood frozen, unable to believe this was happening. A

few scattered shouts of fear came from the gathered Resettlers. A few managed to turn on their headlamps.

Someone fired, and someone else screamed, but it was impossible to identify either the shooter or the target.

Somehow, impossibly, they'd been compromised without the rail guns firing a single shot.

He turned on his headlamp and shone it around the room. Everyone stood frozen. He didn't see any Ferals, but—

His light caught a blur of movement on the other side of the room. He heard someone nearby shout. People were screaming, but he couldn't see any vamps. He turned his light to another part of the room and was shocked to see four people lying on the ground and covered in blood, their necks ripped open.

Screams and isolated gunfire rang out from various parts of the room, but Firefly kept his eyes on the four dead Resettlers. It was as if he was frozen; he couldn't make himself look away. These were four brave individuals who'd risked everything because they'd believed in the cause. They'd believed in Fleming. They'd believed in Captain Garrett Eldred. And they'd paid the ultimate price.

As he stared at them, something impossible happened. They opened their eyes and stood up.

Seemingly unaware of their massive wounds, they got to their feet and stood perfectly still. It was as if they were waiting for something.

Firefly turned, casting his light around the room in a slow circle. Everywhere he looked, he saw the same thing. Resettlers with gashes in their necks and blood-drenched clothes standing at attention.

And then something grabbed him.

He fought hard, flailing against the strong arms that held him, but he may as well have been trying to bend steel.

His hand went for the weapon at his belt, but before he could raise it, something sharp and cold sank into his neck and icy pain surged through his body.

As if from a distance, he felt himself sink to the ground, and then everything went black.

And then he opened his eyes again. He felt different. Changed. Cold, but strong.

Within two minutes of the administration building losing power, every one of the three hundred Resettlers were dead. Two minutes after that, there were three hundred new vampires on Earth.

From the darkness a voice called out, "Who was the leader of this settlement?"

Firefly felt no shock at the sudden appearance of an intelligent vampire. It seemed right.

At first, he thought no one would respond to the question. After all, wasn't everyone dead? Then he heard a voice answer. It wasn't until he was already speaking that he realized the voice was his own.

"I'm the commander in charge of this operation."

A moment later, two vampires stood in front of Firefly. From outside, he could still hear lights smashing and vampires howling.

The taller vampire wore a big smile. "I can't believe this all worked so well. We figured this building would have the most humans in it, but you served yourselves up to us before the Ferals could even get to you."

Firefly felt a surge of anger at the vampire's words. He willed his arm to raise his gun and put a bullet through this asshole, but it refused to do so.

The shorter vampire glared at Firefly. "I can see that you want to use that gun on us. You can give that idea up right now. We are your creators. You will not be able to hurt us or disobey us."

The taller one chuckled. "Honestly, you should really be thanking us. If we hadn't turned you, the Ferals would have torn through your defenses in the next few minutes and drained each and every one of you dry. You would be gone, but we saved you. All we ask in return is that you obey each and every one of our commands without question for the next hundred years or so." He laughed again. "And since you will have no choice, it looks like we are going to get along just fine. My name's Aaron, and this is Mark. But you can call both of us Master."

Firefly looked around the room. Somehow, he could see in the darkness as clearly as if the lights had been on. Every soldier stood in silence. Some had tears streaming down their cheeks, but none moved. He reached up and touched his neck. His fingers came away sticky, but not wet. His wounds were already healing.

"How?" he asked in a weak voice. "How did this happen?"

Aaron stared at him a moment. "I don't really have to answer your questions, but you'll find I'm a kind master. I'll answer this one. Then I have a few questions for you." He took a step back and scratched his chin, as if deciding where to begin. "Mark and I recently spent some time in a city called Agartha. We didn't, let's say, assimilate well. But we knew there was another human city, so we've been hunting for it. Vampires have a mental connection. It's kind of awful, actually, constantly having Feral instincts shouting in your head. You'll see what I mean, soon enough. But we could tell the Ferals in this area were all kinds of agitated, so we came down to check it out. I'm pretty glad we did."

"From there, we made it inside before you had all those

damn lights installed," Mark said, "and we buried ourselves next to a wall in the sub-level. Then we waited for moving day. Once the action started up top, we cut the power lines. Honestly, I never thought it would be so easy to get an army."

Aaron nodded. "You should be embarrassed, commander. Anyway, as you might imagine, we have big plans for settling the score in Agartha, but we're also dying to hear all about your city. Why don't you go ahead and tell us? Now."

Firefly felt himself begin to speak.

33

BOTH VEHICLES ROLLED FORWARD, making progress toward Agartha, but Alex feared they wouldn't get there quickly enough. The smell of blood and the sounds of battle had certainly alerted every Feral in the area by now. It wouldn't be long before the second wave of Ferals hit them hard.

Two Ferals slammed into the side of the Agartha transport and sank their claws into the armored vehicle.

"George!" Alex called. "Heads up!" She cursed, realizing he couldn't hear her. "GMT! Protect George's transport, and make sure you don't hit any friendly vamps. Got it?"

"First time I've ever heard her say *don't* shoot the vampires," Patrick laughed.

The team unloaded, knocking the Ferals off the transport.

This time, the Ferals seemed aware of the vampire protectors—perhaps because of their mental link— and they went straight for them.

The Agartha vampires kept a tight circle around the rover, even as the humans inside circled up as well, focusing on taking out the Ferals before they got to Jaden and his team.

Those that did slip through were quickly dispatched. All the vamps fought masterfully, but Jaden was the most ruthless creature that Alex had ever seen. Three Ferals lunged at him together, and he dodged a slash from one of their claws at the perfect angle so that the claws sank into another Feral's neck. He spun, slicing off the heads of both entangled Ferals as he drove his other sword through the third Feral's heart. As he fought, he continued to keep pace with the rover, never failing a single step behind.

Alex saw a blur of movement in her peripheral vision and looked up to see a Feral swooping down from above. She fired a round into its head and shouted to her team, "Watch the skies. Make sure that they don't get to the ground."

More Ferals attempted that tactic, leaping at the rover and soaring down at them. The team picked them off one by one, not letting any of them touch the ground alive. Corpses of the monsters rained down around them, and the rover bounced over the dead in the road.

One of the Agartha vampires broke away from the group and shifted over to defend George's transport. He lunged at a Feral climbing the transport, but didn't see the other two on the roof of the vehicle. They jumped down onto the vampire's back.

Alex fired, putting a round into each of the Ferals' heads. She dropped the empty clips and reloaded without taking her eyes off the battle. Her hands and body worked on muscle memory fueled by a lifetime of training, leaving her mind free to concentrate on the danger all around them.

She knew they were only a few minutes away from Agartha, but lasting even that long could prove impossible.

Waves of Ferals were coming at them hot and heavy, attracted by the battle and crazed with blood hunger.

Alex glanced ahead to the vampires fighting in front of the rover and saw a horde of Ferals charging down the mountain. There were at least one hundred Ferals, all of them racing at full speed. This would be too much for even the Agartha vampires, she knew. The would wash over them like an avalanche.

"Munitions fifty yards to our twelve o'clock!" she yelled.

Ed, Patrick, Chuck, and Wesley launched grenades into the oncoming wave of Ferals. The Ferals ignored the tiny flying object and kept running. Four grenades exploded moments apart, tearing into the horde. Feral appendages flew like shrapnel all around the road and surrounding forest. The concussion wave hit the team hard enough to blow Alex's hair back.

The Ferals attacking the Agartha vampires were distracted for a moment by the light and the noise from the explosion. The vamps didn't let that mistake slip by without extracting maximum damage. They sliced through the Ferals one after another, their blades performing a deadly dance.

For a moment Alex thought that they had made it. After everything they'd been through and the impossible odds, she thought this was it. She looked past the smoke of the explosions and saw the entrance to Agartha in the distance. Aside from a few straggler Ferals and lots of Feral corpses, the path looked clear.

The moment passed quickly as she spotted a boulder the size of her torso flying at the rover.

"Look out!" Alex yelled. She grabbed Owl and jumped, pulling them both off the rover.

Chuck, Wesley, and Patrick moved fast, following their captain's lead and leaping from the vehicle.

Ed was firing at a Feral behind them and didn't see what was happening until it was too late.

The boulder slammed into the rover, nearly ripping it in two. The trailer careened onto its side, and Ed went flying into the snow beyond the Agartha vampires.

In an instant, Jaden was in motion. He leapt to Ed and scooped him up with one arm, holding a sword in the other. "Get them in the transport!"

His team responded just as fast. In a moment, every member of the GMT was being tossed into the back of the transport. Another wave of Ferals hit the group, and the Agartha vampires only had seconds to see to the GMT before rejoining the fight.

Through the back of the truck, Alex saw Jaden tearing through more hostiles. He looked different now. The graceful but brutal calm he'd displayed at the beginning had been replaced with something more animalistic.

He threw one of his swords, and it slammed into an approaching Feral, burying itself to the hilt. With his freed hand he plucked a flying rock from the air. He spun as he caught the rock and used the momentum to send it rocketing toward the oncoming wave. The speed and force of the object was so great that it tore the head off one Feral and buried itself in the chest of the one behind it. Jaden's momentum carried him forward, and he sliced through a Feral as he grabbed his sword from the chest of his fallen enemy.

The Ferals all moved as fast as Jaden, Alex realized, but they were mindless brawlers with no strategy. Jaden dodged their attacks and cut them down, predicting their every move.

Alex looked past Jaden and saw one of his team, a short female, bringing up the rear of their defense. She carried a great sword covered in blood, and she sliced through Ferals as she ran.

As she attacked another Feral, a rock flew at her from behind, smashing into her upper back. There was a loud *crack*, and she tumbled forward.

"No!" Alex shouted.

Four Ferals were on her in an instant. They tore at her ferociously, claws ripping flesh. In seconds, they'd separated her arms from her body. Then one of them sank its claws deep into her neck, not to drink, but to destroy. With a mighty pull, it ripped her head off her body.

Alex stared in disbelief at how fast the Ferals had dismembered the poor woman.

"We're here!" George yelled.

Alex spun, looking out the front of the transport. The blast door slowly opened as they raced toward it.

Alex's eyes widened with delight as she saw what waited for them just beyond the door. Agartha's other ninety vampires stood at the ready, lined along the edges with a space in the center for the transport.

The truck did not slow, even though the door wasn't all the way up. Alex ducked instinctively as they sped through, their roof just clearing the door.

Jaden and his eight remaining vampires dashed inside behind the transport, but they were followed by two dozen Ferals.

The vampires of Agartha made quick work of the Ferals.

"Get the door!" Jaden called. "And turn the guns back on!"

The door slid downward, and the vampires removed the

head of any Feral who attempted to duck inside through the ever-shrinking opening.

As the door was almost shut, Alex heard the rail guns ramp up. The Ferals screeched as the automated weapons activated and riddled the horde with bullets.

She fell back on the floor of the transport and allowed herself a moment just to breathe.

There was so much work left to do and so many questions left to answer, but for now, they were safe. They were alive.

And then the moment was over. It was time to once again be a leader. She got up and looked her team over.

Ed was clutching a nasty gash in his leg, but other than that, everyone appeared uninjured. Battered, blood-splattered, and dazed, yes. But they were alive. She was alive.

"All right, team," she said. "Welcome to Agartha."

They climbed out of the transport and stood, unsure of what to do next.

The GMT of *New Haven* and the vampires of Agartha regarded each other.

Then Jaden looked at George. "Get them inside. Once this area is secured, we have a lot to discuss."

EPILOGUE

JESSICA KNEW they were coming for her, she just didn't know when.

She'd known she was in trouble from the moment Fleming had given his address the previous morning, so she'd immediately dropped off the grid. She had a bag with a few essential items at the office, and she'd grabbed that, told no one she was leaving, and disappeared.

One nice thing about having spent the majority of her adult life in the Engineering department was that she knew the inner workings of *New Haven* better than almost anyone. There were networks of passageways that no one but the people who worked on them even knew existed. The badges would never find her down there, and even the people in engineering could spend days searching these tunnels and never stumble across her.

It wasn't a permanent solution, she knew. Eventually, she'd have to come up with a plan. CB was on the run. Alex, Owl, and Brian? She didn't know, but she had to assume they were probably in a jail cell by now.

She was alone.

So, she was rather surprised when she heard footsteps rushing down the tunnel toward her. She looked around, searching for somewhere to hide, but the tunnel was narrow. The only option was to fight.

She steeled herself, promising to get a few licks in before they brought her down.

A man rounded the corner, and her mouth dropped open in surprise.

It was Brian.

A wide smile appeared on his haggard face when he saw her. "Thank heavens you're alive."

She blinked hard. "I don't understand. How'd you find me?"

He held up a small device in his hand. "It's an echolocation device I was working on for the GMT before Fleming put me on full-time daylight and railgun duty. It's just a prototype, but apparently it works. I figured you'd be in the tunnels somewhere."

She grabbed him and pulled him in for a quick hug. "What about the others?"

The smile faded. "The GMT was sent on a mission this morning and they never came back. We think it was a setup."

Jessica's stomach dropped at the news. If night had fallen with her friends on the surface, they were surely dead. And if Fleming had succeeded in taking out the GMT, they had truly lost.

As if reading her thoughts, Brian spoke again. "It's not over yet. CB's alive."

Her eyes widened. "Is he okay?"

"He's pissed as hell, but he's alive."

"You can take me to him?"

Brian nodded. "Beyond the three of us, I'm not sure who we can trust."

"No one," Jessica said quickly. "We can't put anyone else at risk. It's just us."

"That's what CB said, too. But he thinks it will be enough."

"Enough for what?"

"Come with me. I'll let CB explain. He has a plan."

———

ALEX SAT across from Jaden at a narrow table in a small room. "So, what happens next?"

Jaden smiled his usual knowing smile, but there was a sadness in his eyes. "What would you like to happen?"

She considered that for a moment. Rather than answering the question, she said, "Thank you for saving us. And I'm sorry about what happened. With the woman on your team."

"Her name was Joyce." Jaden bowed his head. "I've known her a very long time. Losing her is... difficult. And you're welcome."

She didn't know what to say.

"Your team is doing well," he told her. "Ed's leg is cut pretty badly, but we stitched it up. His brother instantly started making fun of him about it, which seemed an odd reaction."

"Not if you know them."

"The rest of them are helping my team with some duties around the city. They said they were too wired to sleep."

"They're just happy to be alive."

"I'm glad they are. Alive, I mean." He paused. "Agartha is a nice place to live. The first hundred years or so were a little rocky, but we have a pretty good system, now. I think you'll like it. And I've considered the possibility of a daytime mission team. You seem like a very qualified candidate to head up that initiative."

Alex smiled. "Thank you. I'm honored. But I'm not interested."

"I suspected as much. But you never answered my question from before. What do you want to happen next?"

She let that hang in the air a moment before answering. "You know Fleming, right? Guy who runs *New Haven*?"

"I know of him, yes."

"Well, he's the reason my team got stranded down here. I tried to make a move against him, and this is how he smacked me down."

"Ouch," Jaden said.

"Yeah. I've been losing a lot to him lately. Every time I think I have him, he outmaneuvers me. But I figured something out. I've been going about it all wrong. Politics? He's going to beat me there, every time. I need to go after him my way."

Jaden cocked his head. "You want to go after Fleming? That's what you want to happen next?"

"Not just that. I'm done losing. I'm going to go after Fleming, and I'm going to win. If you are really interested in protecting humanity, you're going to help me. It's time to save *New Haven*."

DEAR READER

The stage is set. The players are in place. Mark and Aaron have a vampire army. Fleming has *New Haven*. Alex has her team, her new friends, and her resolve.

It's going to be one hell of a battle.

THE SAVAGE DAWN is out now. Visit myBook.to/The-SavageDawn to get your copy.

Thank you so much for reading THE SAVAGE NIGHT. We truly appreciate it, and we can't wait for you to find out what happens next.

Happy reading,

PT and Jonathan

ABOUT THE AUTHORS

P.T. Hylton is the author of the Deadlock Trilogy, the Zane Halloway series, the Storms of Magic series, and the Vampire World Saga. He podcasts about movies and guitars, and he makes YouTube videos about books. Yeah, he's a major nerd. He lives with his family in eastern Tennessee. Visit him at www.pthylton.com   .

Jonathan Benecke is the author of the Vampire World Saga. An avid movie watcher, he co-hosts the Movie Fixers podcast. He lives in Colorado with his wife and two amazing children. Hiking in the mountains and enjoying the beauty of the natural world is his favorite pastime.

BOOKS BY P.T. HYLTON & JONATHAN BENECKE:

The Vampire World Saga (Post-Apocalyptic Horror/Adventure)

BOOKS BY P.T. HYLTON:

The Deadlock Trilogy (Supernatural Suspense):

- Regulation 19

- A Place Without Shadows

- The Broken Clock

Zane Halloway: Assassin for Hire (Sword and Sorcery Fantasy)

Storms of Magic series (Pulp Fantasy w/Michael Anderle)

- Storm Raiders

- Storm Callers

- Storm Breakers

- Storm Warrior

Valerie's Elites (Pulp Space Opera w/Justin Sloan & Michael Anderle)

- Valerie's Elites

- Death Defied

- The Prime Enforcer